THE LAST ORPHAN

JEFFREY LOWDER

This book is dedicated my grandmother
Lily Watkins Searle
youngest of 32 pioneer children
And to her mother, Maryann Sawyer Watkins

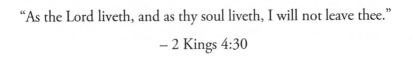

"As the Lord liveth, and as thy soul liveth, I will not leave thee."

– 2 Kings 4:30

~1~

East Parowan, Utah Territory - August 12, 1859

Numerous cracks webbed the weather-darkened logs, allowing the outside air to slip into the cabin's single room. Inside, the wood was still the hue of fresh clover honey, and this summer day the drafty walls were a blessing to twenty-five-year-old Millie Gale. Sitting in near darkness, she settled into a heavy rocking chair, humming softly, the lap of her aproned dress cradling a shirt and some socks that needed mending. "How I miss you, Sean," she whispered to the empty room. "How my heart aches with wishing you'd remained with Clara and me. You'd be prouder than proud that your young daughter's growing up so smart and kind and—"

Someone burst through the cabin's only door, screaming, "They're coming for him!" Millie looked up to see a petite woman with coal-dark hair. "You have to help, us, Mil!" her best friend Evie Dunning yelled in a voice as gravelly as the nearby streambed.

Millie jumped up from the old rocker, spilling needle, thread and half-mended clothing to the rough pine floor. A jagged half-breath caught in her throat, but she managed, "Evie, what, who—"

Blowing breaths so hard and rapid Millie feared her friend might at any moment collapse, Evie paced the floor, fingertips pressed hard against her sweat-slick forehead. "Men are coming to steal my Thomas away!

~2~

Oblivious to the panic inside the nearby house, Tommy Dunning swung a leg over and slid down the old mare's side to the dust in front of Aunt Millie's house. The five-year-old dropped to one knee and looked directly into the dark eyes of his black and brown best friend. Woobydog was about half as tall as Tommy, three-legged, with a thick, curly coat that collected lots of burrs. He leaned in, and his cheek caught a few strings of drool that dripped from the dog's lolling tongue. "This is a happy day, Woobydog. A day to play with Clara." Tommy used the back of his hand to wipe away the dog spit. He didn't really care, but Clara sure would.

"Hi, Tommy." A skinny girl stepped from around the corner of the little cabin. Clara Gale was two years older than him, with pretty hair tightly braided into two tails the color of the silky strings that grow on an ear of corn. And she was his best friend.

Tommy broke into a wide grin. "Clara!"

She took a good look at Tommy, then burst into laughter. "What's that, then?"

"What's what?"

"Your hair, silly Billy." She leaned in for a closer look. "Grow weary of being red-haired?"

"Huh?" Tommy touched the back of his head. He looked at his darkened fingertips and remembered his mother funning him back home, quickly rubbing in a handful of ashes from the hearth. "Mama said it'd give you a grin."

Clara turned up her hands and gave a little shrug of her bony shoulders.

Maybe it wasn't as funny as Mama thought, but no matter.

"Children!" The hurry-up in Aunt Millie's voice caused Tommy to jump. "Come! Now!"

He looked up to see Clara's ma just inside the open door and his own mama hurrying out to his side. She soon knelt next to him on the brown-orange ground. "This is utmost urgent, Thomas."

Her voice made his heart go too fast. Mama sounded all scared, and it made him scared, too. He thought hard but couldn't remember a single time she'd been so troubled. *Are there Indians about, or maybe . . .*

"You do all that Aunt Millie tells you," Mama said. "I'll be back for you soon as I can." She opened her arms and he stepped into a shivery hug. "Each and every bit you're told, Thomas," she said, giving him a gentle push toward Aunt Millie.

"Y . . . yes, ma'am." He didn't do it, but Tommy wanted to bawl like a baby when his mama stood, grabbed Ginger's mane then swung onto her back. She reined the horse away from the log house, and the old mare loped down a dusty track that split a small field of yellow wheat. Deep in his belly, the little boy felt a hollow kind of ache. *Why's she leaving me? Got to be something real bad.*

Aunt Millie clapped hands on Clara's shoulders. She looked into her daughter's eyes real strong and said, "You and Thomas are going to hide in the root cellar."

"Hide?" Now Clara sounded scared.

"You make sure he stays there till I come and fetch the two of you . . . no matter what."

"Injuns, Ma?"

"No." Aunt Millie shook her head. "Americans."

He had heard it spoken in anger many times before, but that word—*Americans*—always confused Tommy. Or maybe he was just too scared to remember what it meant.

⇨◦⇦

Aunt Millie hurried out the door pulling Clara along by one hand. She grabbed Tommy's wrist and walked them both behind the house, where he blurted, "What're we—"

"We're to play in the root cellar," Clara said. "Away from the terrible heat."

Tommy's chest pained him, and his chin began to quiver. "But, I . . . I'm scared in the dark."

"I'll be with you. It'll be pleasant fun." Clara was real smart, but his chest still pinched. He was pretty sure she was wrong about the second part.

"There." Aunt Millie pointed to a spot behind the cabin where the ground went uphill. Partway up, hard to see among the tall sage bushes, an old wood door lay flat in the dirt.

Clara's vegetable garden was growing great, filled up with potato vines, yellow and green squash and fat red tomatoes, but Tommy walked by hardly looking. His eyes were on a nearby corral, mostly round, made of peeling posts tied to gray branches from a dead cottonwood tree. When they reached the pen, the big brown and white sow was asleep in her own mess. Tommy tried to cover his face. He hated that pig stink worse than anything, now it was trying to get inside his nose and his eyes to make them burn. Tommy looked about—no Woobydog. She had been following close behind but was now nowhere to be found. Not a surprise, she hated pigs as bad as he did.

"Scramble over the fence and tread through the sty," Aunt Millie said. "You first, Clara."

She planted a fist on each hip. "That's sheer folly, Ma!"

"There'll be no arguing with me!" Tommy'd never heard Aunt Millie's angry voice before. *Or maybe it was her scared voice.* The sound made his tummy feel like that one day in the spring when he ate four green apples.

"Fine!" Clara clenched her jaw, hiked up her prairie dress and climbed over the low fence. When she stepped off the last rail, her nice deerskin moccasins went into the stinky wet. "But I don't understand."

"Hurry, Tom. Get on with it." Clara's ma made Tommy feel like when a mean dog barked at him.

He struggled, and Aunt Millie helped him across, then she walked to the other side and beckoned them with impatient hands. "Make haste!"

Tommy knew if he threw up, it would make this terrible time even worse for Clara, so he forced down the gags and kept walking through the smelly slime.

Finally, finally, he and Clara climbed over the fence and out. Tommy looked down at his slop-covered boots and started to cry. Papa would be so angry, he got them special from the Bishop's Storehouse. They weren't new, of course, and Tommy sometimes wondered about the boy who wore them first. He shook those thoughts from his head and stomped the ground a few times. Most of the mess was still there.

Aunt Millie grabbed their hands and hurried the children through the bushy yarrow and pepper-smell sages to the old piece of wood on the ground. The door was heavy or stuck or something. She had to bend her knees and pull real hard on the rusty ring, all the time scolding herself to hurry. She finally pulled it open, and Tommy looked in—it was mostly dark and smelled like onions, too-ripe fruit and weeding Mama's garden after it rained.

In the dusky light, Aunt Millie walked to the back of the low cave like a duck. She lifted her apron to make a basket, then filled it with apples from a rough burlap bag. When she got closer, Tommy thought the yellow fruit looked as wrinkly as some men at church, the old ones that were fixing to die.

"Come in, Clara." Aunt Millie took her daughter's hand and they walked together, stopping where the floor flattened out. She moved wooden boxes off two stumps and pointed for Clara to sit.

"Now you, Thomas." He hesitated, tears burning his cheeks. He didn't want Clara to think he was a bawl baby, but the dark cellar scared him ever so bad.

Aunt Millie nodded at the apples in her saggy apron. "The both of you do as I say and there'll be warm apple pie later." The pie promise didn't make it one bit better.

"I can't hardly see . . ." Tommy heard his own voice, thin and scared. Then Woobydog ambled in on her three legs and nuzzled so close she might have heard his pounding heart.

"Stay quiet a minute or so," Aunt Millie said. "Your eyes will soon accustom to the dark. I'm so sorry, Thomas. I'll need Woobydog with me."

Tommy tried hard to be brave, but he just couldn't stop whimpering. "But when you leave and close the door—"

"There's nothing in here can hurt you," Aunt Millie said. But the dark seemed to grow denser. Would it suffocate him? She made a kissing sound to get Woobydog's attention. "Come, girl," and just like that, his best dog friend did his little three-legged trot to her side. Then Aunt Millie turned to Clara, something different in her eyes. "Your task is to keep the boy calm," she whispered. "Can you do it?"

"I . . . I think so." But Clara's voice sounded only a tiny bit braver than his own.

❧

Her heart still beating like the wings of a flushed grouse, Eva Dunning urged Ginger to move as fast as the old mare could.

Almost back to her farm, the aging horse was nearly spent, *'wheezing like a grampus,'* as Granny Eadie likes to say. *Guess I better ease up a smidgeon—even a nag like this's a rare thing out here in the Iron Mission.* She slowed the horse to a trot, each bounce sending a solid judder up her spine. Between jolts, she attempted to calm her high emotions, slow her breathing. *God alone knows what I'll find when I get home. I have to think on something other than the danger, lest the fear betray me.* She filled her thoughts with cherished moments. The day Thomas first called her Mama. The little boy nearly bursting with pride when he finally mastered the laces of his boots. Contented hours watching him in peaceful slumber. "For two years," she whispered to the breeze, "I've loved Thomas, kept him safe from all the world. The danger is now upon us, but with the help of God who gave him to me, my son and I will weather this awful storm."

They reached the wide path that snaked through their apple orchard. From there, the tired animal turned toward home without signal or command. Water and rest were near.

"Whoa, girl." Despite the day's heat, Eva felt a cold lump of fear fill her throat—in front of the two-story adobe brick house stood a familiar buckboard, its horse tied to the rough-hewn hitching rail. The rig belonged to her father-in-law, Bishop Warren Dunning. Eva secured Ginger near the water trough and hurried to the house, every ounce of her being dreading what was certain to come. She prayed aloud for courage, then stepped inside where her husband and his father waited.

"Where's the child?" Bishop Dunning demanded. He was head of the Parowan Ward, the local Mormon congregation. With long, kempt hair and neatly trimmed white beard, Warren Dunning looked like the man he was: one who followed his betters without question and expected the same obedience from his ward, a flock of perhaps 200 souls. "Tell us his location, Sister Eva."

She drew herself up to full height but felt the two men towering over her by several inches. She made a vain attempt to sound strong, but the roiling deep in her gut sapped her courage, reminded her the situation might swerve out of control at any second.

"He's safe," she whispered.

"Speak up, Evie." A taller, thinner version of the older man, her husband Bennet stood in solemn solidarity beside his father.

She managed to force a mite more volume from a throat constricted with distress. "Our son is safe."

Bishop Dunning harrumphed. "That's scarcely an answer to my question."

It feels as if my soul is being torn from me. I love and respect Father Dunning, but I'll not betray my son. "Forgive me, Bishop. It's the only answer I have till the Americans have left the mission."

Bennet gave his wife a stern look. "Eva! Take mind of who you're talking to."

"I'm sorry." she said, eyes cast downward. "I mean no disrespect to either of you. It's the wellbeing of my young son I—"

The bishop held up a silencing palm, and she obeyed. "We find ourselves in perilous times, Sister. President Young promised the army all the children would be returned. To do otherwise would surely—"

"Returned? To whom?" Her voice was just above a whisper. "Not a mother nor father survived that day." She tried with a pleading glance to say, *Help me, Bennet, please,* but her husband quickly averted his gaze.

"To aunts and uncles, grandparents," the bishop said. "Their blood relations, Sister Eva,"

"How're they going to round them up? The army doesn't know so much as how many yet live."

Father Dunning's face furled into a frown, and his tone went low with obvious exasperation. "Brother Jacob Hamblin gathered the Cedar City and Fort Harmony children to his ranch. Turned sixteen of them over to Mr. Forney yesterday.

"Forney?" The name was unfamiliar to Eva.

"Government's Indian Agent. Jacob told him there's one or two more endured the Indian attack on the wagon train."

They know of more children? Eva felt her very soul sag.

"Now the army's involved . . . a Major Carleton. And the man's none too happy 'bout going door to door looking for the last of them."

She thought she saw a welling in his eyes as Bennet laid laborer's hands on her shoulders. "I care about him too, Eva. But if the army snares us in a lie . . ." He paused and solemnly shook his head. "And we're not the boy's blood kin."

Eva's weeping became helpless sobs, through which she said, "To this day . . . the poor child suffers nightmares of being torn from . . . his first mother's arms. You and I are all he has. Please, Bennet. Please don't let our son be reared in a loveless orphans' home."

A single tear escaped her husband's eye, and Eva's heart leapt with hope he would stand up for the boy they had raised. "As your husband and priesthood head, I now command you to tell me where the boy is." She felt the fragile hope shatter like a crystal goblet cast upon granite. *God forgive me.* She remained silent.

After a few seconds, Bishop Dunning tried a softer tone. "Sister Eva, do you recall Father Abraham?"

Abraham? From the Old Testament?

"It surely broke his heart when the Lord commanded he give up his only son. But he was full willing to take young Isaac's life if God required it."

Eva found herself unable to meet her father-in-law's eyes. "Abraham," she murmured, "was never a mother." *I've now stepped over a line. God help me.*

The bishop turned to his son with a look of increasing vexation. Bennet responded with a shoulder hike and, "Might have took the boy over to the Gale place. I'll try fetching him there."

"You'll not find him at Millie's!" Eva blurted. But she knew the fright in her voice had betrayed her.

Her husband was on his way out. Eva caught up in a few quick steps, but when Bennet threw open the door, he stopped suddenly, and she slammed into his back. Over her husband's shoulder, Eva saw what had frozen him mid-stride. She stifled a gasp.

ॐ

The cellar's cold as winter, Tommy thought. He tried hard not to sniffle. "I'm near frozen. Can we go now, Clara?"

"Soon. I know you can be brave, Tommy." He felt Clara's hand on his arm, but her voice came out of thick darkness. "We both can."

"M . . . maybe tell me a story," he said. "Nothing scary, a course."

"How 'bout Helaman and his 2,000 stripling warriors?"

"I 'member Helaman, but what's 'stripling?'"

Clara gave a tiny chuckle. "I'm thinking it means they were young."

"Like us?"

"Or older a smidge."

Clara told him a Book of Mormon story about brave teenagers who fought for the righteous Hebrews that sailed to America before Columbus. Tommy didn't understand some parts, but hearing Clara helped him forget the cold and the dark . . . almost. Still, he couldn't stop fretting, *Where's my mama? Is Aunt Millie safe? Why did the Americans come here?*

~3~

On the Dunning's porch, Eva stared in horror at the three men in dark blue uniforms blocking their exit—they seemed as startled as the Dunnings at the sudden encounter. Ten yards behind them, a fourth man perched in a boxy wagon hitched to a pair of sand-brown army horses.

"Afternoon, folks. Everything alright?" At about thirty-five, the speaker looked to be ten years older than the men who flanked him. He was tall and narrow-waisted, with mutton chop sideburns tapering to a neatly trimmed mustache.

"Um, good afternoon," was all Bennet managed.

Eva gulped down enough of the vinegary fear to speak. "Bennet and Eva Dunning."

"Ma'am." The soldier nodded toward her and doffed a cowboy-styled hat that bore the gold braid of a U.S. Cavalry officer. "I'm Major James Carleton."

Major Carleton! The rising ferment in her throat kept Eva silent for a moment. She finally managed, "Why are you—"

Before she could finish, a pitiful wail issued from the nearby wagon. "Mama! Where my mama!" The driver struggled to contain a squirming three-year-old dressed in a rough woolen nightgown. Rosie? *Why would Charles and Lottie Hopkins's child be?*— Then it struck her like a falling pine: *She's another secret orphan child, rounded up like some kind of animal to be herded off to Arkansas.*

"It's all right," Eva called, then ran to the wagon. "Come here, Rosie." She reached for the little girl to hold and comfort

11

her, but the soldier grabbed the child's deformed right arm and snatched her back, the poor babe screaming in pain.

Eva wheeled to the major, tears of pity burning her eyes. "What's the meaning of this?"

Carleton spoke with no apparent emotion. "We depart tomorrow to return the orphans to their people in Arkansas."

"Rosie's no such orphan. She's Charles and Lottie Hopkins's child."

"They've been raising her, yes, ma'am. And the family was loath to give her up. But the . . . what's he called? *The bishop* allowed she's not their blood kin."

Father Dunning betrayed the Hopkinses? Take heed to what you say, Eva—he may already have told the Americans about Thomas.

"So, Rosie's the . . . last one?"

"The seventeenth, ma'am."

"Then what is it that's brought you to our door?"

"Family back in Arkansas's cocksure their grandson's still alive. Boy'd be number eighteen."

The words staggered Eva like a physical blow. She stared into her husband's eyes, wordlessly warning him not to expose their invention.

"How's someone back there to know if their child is among the living?" Bennet asked, a hint of challenge in his voice.

God bless you, my love.

"Woman says she's his grandmother." The major paused. "Claims she visioned him in a dream."

Eva felt a pinch of hope. *So they don't know to a certainty about my Thomas!*

Bennet shook his head. "A dream? She sounds plumb mad."

Carleton made no attempt to hide a sneer. "Mad as your Joseph Smith seeing the Lord Jesus Christ?"

Bennet ground his teeth in apparent anger—but proffered no reply.

The major continued, "Woman sent word he's a red-header, near five years old. An extra toe, of all things."

Eva swallowed hard. "If ever there was such a child, he . . . he was one of those perished in the Indian attack, God rest their souls."

"That so? Killed by the *Injuns?*" The major emphasized the word in such a way it sounded like a kind of indictment. "Anyway, Arkansas senator's a friend of the family . . . or something. And mad or not, I got my orders." Carleton's thumb traced the brim of his hat. "My men are out looking now. Likely won't find the dream boy. But if we do, I'll round up every Mormon lied to me and convey them to Fort Leavenworth in shackles."

Fear and fury warmed Eva's face. "Out of pure Christian love the good folk of this community took those little ones in, fed them, clothed them—"

"Regarded them no better than household slaves."

Eva ignored Carleton's accusation. "It's been full two years since the Indians massacred that wagon train, Major." Anger now ruled fear, and she spat, "In all that time, no one's so much as asked after the waifs. Now you come 'round treating the folks who saved their very lives like outlaws?"

"Injuns? Again?" the major huffed. He paused for a long breath. "Now, what about that redheaded boy?"

All color left Bennet's face, and he nervously cleared his throat.

No, Bennet. Do not speak the words!

But he did. "In truth, Major Carleton—"

Eva cut him short. "In truth, we're well acquainted with every family in the southern part of the Utah territory. There's no such child as you've described." Her heart prayed the lie would somehow convey more confidence than she at that moment possessed.

Carleton glanced about. "You have young'uns, Mrs. Dunning?"

"To my shame and sadness, the Lord has left me barren."

Apparently unable to draw a proper breath, Bennet simply gaped at his wife.

☙◦❧

Millie Gale's pulse throbbed in her temples while troubled thoughts bounced and bobbed like a frightened jackrabbit. "Got to busy myself, think of something other than those poor children hiding in the cellar," she said to the empty cabin walls. The cast-iron oven glowed with heat, and she used a thick cloth to pull the heavy door open to check her creation. The pie's crust was acorn brown that darkened toward the edges, thick filling bubbling from spoke-like slits. "'Tis your ambrosia, well and truly, Sean." She took the cloth from the door handle and used it to move the steaming pastry to a pine sideboard.

Millie had turned just halfway back when an angry bark from outside stopped her. "Woobydog's growling? Must be the—" An aggressive rap on the front door startled her, and she dropped the cloth, overwhelming dread freezing her in place. *Just keep up breathing, Millicent Gale. You can do this—you have to do this.*

She opened the front door, its creaks not quite masking her rapid breathing. The dog was crouched on the covered wooden porch, menacing two men in blue uniforms.

"Best call that bitch off," one soldier threatened. He was overweight with a patchy beard and a faded uniform that had caught many a dribble and crumb since its last wash.

"Woobydog! Leave it!" The animal whimpered a bit then jumped off the porch and disappeared around the cabin's corner.

The younger, clean-shaven man touched the brim of his short-billed kepi cap, and both men inclined their heads upward to meet the eyes of the taller woman. "Afternoon, ma'am. I'm Corporal Ledger." He pointed a thumb in the direction of his unkempt counterpart. "That there's Private Daniel Deetz."

Americans. "Uh, hello," was all Millie could manage.

"What's your name, ma'am?"

"Gale, Millicent Gale."

"Sorry about the interruption, Mrs. Gale," Ledger said. "We're seeking a boy—five years old, red hair."

Millie felt her heart might escape from her chest. "There . . . there's a few orange-haired in the mission. All girls, as I recollect."

Ledger gave her a shallow nod. "You got children, Mrs. Gale?"

Millie sneaked a calming breath, then, "Uh, yes, a seven-year-old daughter." She forced a chuckle. "But Clara's blond, not rusty."

"Just the one, then?"

"My husband has sons—all older. Come around some-times to help out."

"Your husband's? Not your sons?" Deetz blurted.

"I'm the younger of two wives," she said through gritted teeth. *Stay strong, gal.*

"Two wives? We ought to arrest all three of you and drag you back to—"

"That's not our orders, Private," Corporal Ledger barked. He turned back to Millie and asked, "Any of the children about just now?"

Millie exhaled the breath she'd not realized she was holding. "Clara. Only just sent her out back to muck out the pig sty."

"We'll have a bit of a look around," Ledger said.

Millie's blood ran cold as a creek, and her vision blurred. "I'm not so certain I want you—"

"That weren't no purty please," Deetz sneered.

അൎ

The two soldiers began by searching the small cabin. Millie noted they lingered in the cooking area, drawing deep breaths while staring at the cooling pie.

"I trust you'll have time for a slice before you leave," Millie said.

"Goddamn right we'll have time," Deetz said.

"Watch your language around the lady," Ledger ordered. He turned and walked to the door. The slovenly soldier—and Millie— followed him outside.

When they reached the pig's stall, the corporal propped a black boot on the lowest rail, his comrade at his side. The look on the men's faces said they were unhappy at trading the smell of fresh-baked pie for sour pig dung.

Ledger turned to her. "Don't appear anybody's cleaned this out. Where's your girl?"

Willing herself to at least appear calm, Millie made a show of scanning the area. "Can't imagine where she's got to."

Ledger seemed to take in most of the Gale property with a single glance. "I'm not seeing—" He stopped. Woobydog was whimpering and digging at a spot on the nearby hillside.

"What's there, Mrs. Gale?" Ledger pointed to the object of Woobydog's attention, a door lying in the dirt

Millie's mind raced ahead like a train, but she couldn't think of a way to distract the man without raising his suspicions. "Just an old root cellar," she mumbled.

"We'd best take a look."

"Be careful," Millie said. "Dog probably scents a snake. Rattlers sometimes seek the shade in there." She followed the two soldiers up the little hill to the door.

"Open 'er up, Danny," Ledger said.

"But what about—"

"Open the door!"

Private Deetz lifted the slab off the dirt, and Woobydog streaked past him into the little cavern. Deetz cautiously peered in after the animal, then jumped back. "Somethin's in there!"

"The cur, you dolt," Ledger said.

"Nah, somethin' else." The fat soldier sounded genuinely fearful.

Millie stepped around him and squinted in. "Clara Alice Gale, come out here this minute!"

Clara ducked out the opening, but Woobydog remained inside.

Much as it grieved her, Millie gave her daughter a swat on the bottom. "Hiding out in the cool instead of mucking out the pig pen?"

"But Ma—"

"Don't you 'but Ma' me." *Father in Heaven, please . . . please help my Clara understand what's happening.* She gave her girl another whack.

"I'm sorry, Mama," Clara said. She looked down at her filth-crusted moccasins. "We, uh, got started, but the day's so hot."

Millie blanched at the word 'we.'

"This your daughter, ma'am?" Ledger asked.

"Yes. Clara."

A look of sick anticipation filled the other soldier's face. "We just supposed to take your word for it this here's a girl?" He took a step and reached toward sweet Clara.

Fueled by devotion and instinct, Millie leapt between Deetz and her daughter. She leaned into the man's disgusting face stubble and growled, "What're you—"

"Could be a girl, could be a boy," the man sneered. "Sayin' we best check."

Of an instant, fear became fierce loathing, and Millie slapped the repulsive beast hard enough to jerk his head to the side. "I'd sooner die than let you put your filthy hands on my daughter," she hissed.

Deetz growled and cocked a fist. Millie glared into his eyes without moving.

"Stand down, Private!" Ledger yelled. "Now!" He turned and addressed the trembling little girl. "I'm very sorry about that, Miss Clara. You said 'we.' Is someone else—"

He was interrupted by a weak voice out of the darkness. "It's me, Aunt Millie. Come over to play." Millie breathed a tiny sigh of gratitude. While she was not the boy's blood aunt, the endearing term surely fit the immediate circumstance.

Woobydog and Thomas emerged, and the boy collected his spank. Millie thought the smack probably hurt his feelings more than his behind. The scene that she and Clara were acting out for the soldiers had to be confusing.

"But, Aunt Millie, you said—"

"There'll be no sassing me, Thomas Gale! And no pie for either one of you."

Thomas Gale. Millie offered a silent prayer that the boy would not correct her mistake, that the fire in her eyes would overawe him into silence.

Corporal Ledger looked the child over. "Who's the boy?"

"Thomas, Clara's brother."

"Brother? But you said—"

"Half-brother. Belongs to Jezzie. That's why he calls me aunt." *Oh, God, make the man forget I said the brothers were all older.*

"Jezzie?"

"Quincy's first wife."

Millie's body tensed when Ledger turned to Thomas and said, "How old are you, boy?"

Before he could speak, Clara blurted, "He's seven, same as me. Undersized for his age."

"I'll hear it from him." Ledger turned and laid a friendly-like hand on Thomas's shoulder. "Now, what's your age, son?"

Millie held her breath. *Lying's not always a sin, Thomas.*

"Barely seven," he tilted his chin as if putting truth to the words. "Same as she said."

Ledger looked Thomas over, from his dusky hair to the disgusting shoes. "Probably not the one we're looking for."

"Maybe. But oughtn't we to check his toes?" the dirty one asked.

"Toes?" Millie blurted. Panic struck her like sudden thunder. *Heavenly Father*, she prayed silently, *please let the pig dung stink to the highest heaven. If they take off the child's shoes, they'll know to a certainty.* "That's just absurd."

Ledger ignored her and looked down at Tommy's muck-covered boots. "You do it, Private."

Deetz did not look happy. "Take off them boots, boy."

"Can't, sir."

"Whaddya mean you can't?"

"Don't know how to tie them."

"You're not tyin' them, you're untyin'."

The boy shrugged. "Same thing to me, sir."

Millie allowed herself the tiniest smile. *Good boy, Thomas.*

"Sit your arse down and I'll get the dashed things off," he growled.

Thomas sat in the dirt. Deetz knelt next to him, but when he reached for the first mucky boot he started to retch.

Thank you, Lord, Millie thought.

Corporal Ledger shook his head. "For God's sake, Deetz," he said.

The private stood and took a step back from the boy. "You like to give it a try?" he snarled to his superior.

Ledger looked the boy over from head to filthy feet. "We're wasting our time," he said. "Child's too old, not even a redhead."

Ever so softly, Millie finally exhaled.

Without further comment, both men started walking back to their horses.

"Got time for that slice of pie?" Millie called out. The second the words were out of her mouth, she scolded herself. *I had a chance—could have just hushed up and watched them leave.*

"We'll sure as hell make time," Deetz replied.

Millie turned back to Clara and Thomas with a forced frown. "Children who don't finish their chores get no sweeties."

The soldiers tracked their dusty boots into the house. Millie served the pie, then worried as she watched them tuck in. *What if they'd sensed my deceit and threatened Clara's life? The truth of it all would have poured from my lips like a creek in spring. Had God not intervened to save us, Tommy and I would surely be taken in chains, me to prison, the poor boy to a place and people not remembered.*

They finished off the entire pie, then licked their plates clean. When the two finally stepped outside, Ledger carefully brushed crumbs from his uniform. Deetz went to no such bother.

The Americans were soon gone, but Millie felt no relief from the terror. "I'd wager that's not the end of it," she muttered.

~4~

The sun was low over the mountains west of Parowan, casting an orange glow on the Dunning's wooden porch where Eva and Woobydog kept a close eye on Thomas. Carleton was said to be on his way north. They'd been safely home for an hour or so, and now Thomas sat neck-deep in an old tin tub, a helmet of white suds making his squarish head look bigger than usual. "I don't understand, Mama. What were the bad men looking for?"

Eva ignored the question and said, "Shut your peepers." She dipped a crockery pitcher into the lukewarm water and poured it over her son's soapy head.

"Were they—"

"Two more times, Thomas." After filling and rinsing twice more, Eva handed her son a thin towel and he wiped the wet from his face and eyes with considerable energy. When he stepped from the tub, she wrapped him in a thick blanket. Eva took a deep breath, then began, "The Americans just—"

"Aren't we Americans, Mama?"

"I guess so . . . in a manner of speaking. But I mean the soldiers . . . and the government. We've learned by sad experience they're not to be trusted."

"'Bout what?"

"It was naught but their blunder showing up at Aunt Millie's," she said. "They were seeking orphans, children without mamas and papas."

"But I'm a orphan, aren't I?"

21

Eva felt a little stab. She put her hand under her son's chin and looked him in the eyes. "You are the one and only Thomas Dunning," she said. "You have a mother and father who love you and reared you from a babe. Now you remember that, and never tell anyone differently."

Thomas smiled. "But I had another mama. I sort of 'member."

Eva paused for a moment to consider her reply. "Yes," she said. "And you can talk to me about her, but no one else. You're not to forget that promise."

"Of course," Thomas nodded. "Did you ever know her?"

"Sadly, no. Tell me again what you recall," she said, aware of a thread-fine line between paying respect to his birth mother and harrowing up more of the poor child's night terrors.

"I was little then. I only 'member smidgens, like she was warm and she smelled good." He paused for a few seconds. "Puts me in mind of when you make fresh biscuits on a cold morning."

"Those sound to be fond memories."

"I also 'member her dress."

"Her dress?" Eva said. "What color, Thomas?"

"Blue. She hided me behind it when the bad men came."

"The Indians, right?"

"Don't like to 'member that part." Tears filled her son's eyes, and soon his little shoulders heaved with sobs. "I don't want anybody to take me away from you, Mama. Please don't let them."

Empathy for her poor little boy was a physical ache deep in Eva's bones. She drew him to her bosom, surrounding him and the blanket with sheltering arms. "Nothing can keep us apart, my son. Not anyone or anything on this earth."

They held the embrace, and Eva's mind wandered back to the day two years before when Warren Dunning had delivered Thomas into her care. A dog came with the newly orphaned boy, and it was three full days before the child finally unclenched his little fists and for a moment let go of the three-legged animal he called "Woobydog."

Over some weeks, she'd gently quizzed him about name and age. At one point, he held up three fingers and said quite clearly, "Levi fwee year old." There was, of course, no way to determine the precise day of little Levi's birth, so September 12, 1857, the day he arrived in the Dunning household, became the boy's third birthday.

When Bennet performed the Mormon naming ritual, he surprised Eva. "Thomas Warren Dunning is the name by which he shall be known upon the records of the Church and during his sojourn here upon the earth." Bennet had refused to discuss why Levi had of a sudden become Thomas.

"I can't hardly breathe, Mama."

Eva released the embrace and returned to the present. "I'll never let bad happen to you, Thomas. That's my pledge." She bussed the top of his still-damp head. It had a faintly bitter taste of fireplace ash.

෯෯

Clara sat on the bed in her slant-ceilinged sleeping area, a loft that extended about halfway over the little cabin's single room. She smiled at the creaking of the wooden ladder, her favorite sound in the whole world. It meant Ma was coming up to share a story and give her a nighttime hug. Winter bedtime was better, of course. That's when the light from the fireplace reflected off the logs, bathing her little space in a honey glow, when her nest was the warmest, coziest place in the tiny home. But this was August, and thick heat filled the windowless spot, making it hard to fall asleep.

Ma was so tall she had to hunch over a bit to make sure her pretty wheat-colored hair cleared the sloped roof. She took the few steps to where Clara sat propped up on her bed, a wooden frame with crisscrossed ropes in the place of springs or ticking. Resting on a low wooden stool next to the bed, a sputtering candle provided the only light. She nodded to the family's copy of the Book of Mormon Clara held close to her chest. "So, where are you?"

"In my reading?"

"Of course, your reading."

"Book of Alma."

"Alma?" Ma looked surprised. "That's a ways in, isn't it? Sounds like Aunt Evie's schooling's working pretty good."

"Pretty *well*, you mean," Clara said. It made Ma laugh a lot.

"Yup. Even weller than I thought." This time they laughed together. "And I'm well proud of you."

Clara smiled at the compliment. "'Course I know she's not really my aunt."

"No. Just your ma's best friend. Now, where were we?"

Clara gave a little cough and cleared her throat. She opened the book and began. "'Now they had never fought, yet they did not fear death; and they did think more upon the...' What's that, Ma? *Library*?"

Ma leaned over and Clara pointed to the word she was stuck on. "Liberty . . . it means freedom, Ducky."

Clara continued, ". . . 'the *liberty* of their fathers than they did upon their own lives; yea, they had been taught by their mothers, that if they did not doubt, God would deliver them.'"

"Your reading's top shelf, Clara Alice."

"I told Tommy the story of the stripling warriors while we sat in the dark." Clara felt her eyes get teary. "I wish you didn't spank me today."

Ma embraced her. "It frets me too, darlin'. But the soldiers—"

"They were going to take Tommy away, I know. But why?"

Ma nodded. "His parents were ruthlessly murdered when Injuns raided a wagon train not far from here. 'Bout two years back."

Tommy's parents are dead? Sad confusion clouded her seven-year-old mind. "But he has a ma and pa," Clara protested, "and they're fine."

"God smiled on Tommy the day Eva and Bennet took him in. They couldn't love him more if he was their own. That you know."

"'Course, but—"

"The Americans don't like us. They want to remove the wagon train children so's they can't be reared by the teachings of the Prophet."

"Take them away? Where?"

"Back to great aunts and second cousins and such who probably got no use for them."

"But Tommy never spoke a single word about—"

"And don't you be talking to him—nor anyone else—about it."

Clara looked down into her lap, her mind still a bit jumbled. "If you say so, Ma."

Ma gently rubbed her daughter's back and said, "And do not share with a single soul what we witnessed today. Ever."

❧

Eva bustled around the Dunnings' cook area. She was making Brigham tea, a mild stimulant created by steeping twigs of a desert shrub in boiling water. The summer night was sultry, but the hot, licorice-like infusion was a year-round ritual. She used a rag to grasp the handle of a blackened saucepan, then caught the bushy bits in a small cloth strainer, pouring steaming yellow-green liquid from the pan into two china cups.

"Thanks," Bennet muttered. He spooned in honey and gave the concoction a listless stir. Eva watched him in silence, distressed about what was likely to come.

"The boy abed?" Bennet asked, staring at the steam rising from his cup.

"Thomas. Your son's name is Thomas."

"I know his name," Bennet said, sadness seeming to overtake him. "But he's not my son, Eva. And not the fruit of your womb."

She struggled not to sound angry nor perverse. "He's ours—God Himself entrusted him to us."

"Eva, please," he sighed, shoulders sagging. "This is not about you and me. You're placing our community in grave danger. You heard the major, the Americans are seeking any excuse to put us Mormons out of the way."

"Bennet." She rested a hand on her husband's. "I beg you. Don't ever compel me to choose between my son and the Saints."

"You oughtn't to even be saying that, Eva." Bennet's eyes looked suddenly sad. "You know what happens to apostates."

Eva twisted her apron till her fingers went white and the smock had become a tightly wound cotton cord. "I made a solemn vow that my son would never again be seized from his mother's arms. Not so long as I draw breath."

~5~

Carroll County, Arkansas - August 16, 1859

With fifty-four slaves tending more than a hundred acres of cotton, Mary and John Baker were wealthy. And the jewel of their holdings was the white-columned mansion John's father had dubbed River House for its location on a long bluff overlooking King's River.

Mary's ruined hip made stairs impossible, so she sat in a white wooden rocker, fanning herself and watching. The perch on the raised veranda gave her a view of about a hundred family, friends and neighbors. All were gathered in the shade of two ancient oaks, a gentle breeze rippling the gray-green moss that tinseled the lowest branches. A half-dozen old colored men in white jackets and black bowties balanced trays of apple cider, the servants and the cool drinks sweating in late summer heat. Refreshments notwithstanding, the gathering was not a party. Most of the guests were visibly unsettled, their collective conversations rising to Mary as a low murmur.

She gave a nod and smiled to the Seddons, local dirt farmers who stood near the edge of the raised portico. Weathered by hard work and with few creature comforts, Ruby Seddon looked older than her sixty years. She was tall and sturdy, with a mannish jaw and dark eyes that darted about in nervous anticipation. Her hair, the color of sky before rain, was pulled back in a tight bun. Next to Ruby stood her husband,

Harold. Five years her senior, he was a large man, his bald head, face, and thick hands mottled by the fierce southern sun.

Without warning, melancholy once more gripped Mary's grandmotherly heart like an eagle's talon. She ached for her grandchildren and prayed somehow—*somehow*—she might see them again. Two years prior, she and husband John had been feeling the effects of advanced age, looking forward to a day when their son, George Washington Baker, would take on management of the sprawling plantation. That plan evaporated like night fog in the southern sun the day George announced he was departing, taking his family to carve his own notch in California.

It was sad enough that G.W. was leaving his father without help, but knowing she might never again see her grandchildren, Mary Lavinia, Martha Elizabeth, Sarah Francis and baby Billy, had weighed like a bale on her heart. Painful though that had been, it was a wound she might have survived. But the devastating news she and John received three months after their loved ones left was a blow both feared—and sometimes hoped—would prove fatal.

The murmuring stopped suddenly, and Mary turned to see an approaching single-seat surrey, the coach gleaming black, wood-spoked wheels painted red.

"Whoa, now. Whoa." A stout colored man with close-cropped white hair reined back the two-horse team. When the animals were at full stop, the coachman laid the leather straps across the footboard and climbed down from his seat.

With the driver's helping hand, a single passenger stepped onto the lawn, then reached back into the carriage for a carved wooden cane. He was over six feet tall and still trim for sixty-plus years. His hair was hidden by a black top hat, but his beard was thick and full, more silver than white. *It quietens my heart to see William again. He's been like a port in the storm these past few years.*

The lanky man was immediately surrounded by people, their voices a loud jumble of "Any news of . . ." "Why are you . . ." and "Where's our . . ."

"People, please. Give the senator a bit of breathin' room," John said. The thick crowd parted a bit, and Mary's husband stepped forward and gave the newly arrived guest a firm handshake. "Welcome to River House, William," he said, just loud enough for Mary to hear.

"Good to see you again, John. How's your Mary?"

"Time's been far from kind. The hip, and . . . well . . ."

The visitor replied with a gentle nod. "So sorry for her pain—for all our pain."

"Get on over here, William Mitchell," Mary called out. "Rather have you talking *with* this old woman than *about* me."

John led him up the wide stairway and across the veranda to where Mary sat. William removed his hat to reveal a full head of hair that matched the luster of his beard. Wincing in apparent pain, he knelt next to Mary and laid a wizened hand on hers. "Mary, how wonderful to see you again."

She smiled. "Your presence is always a comfort, William. I do hope you'll pardon my not getting up. 'Fraid these old hips . . ."

"'Tis nothing, Mary." He used the cane to raise himself back to a stand, then shared a knowing nod. "A thing I understand completely."

"Please don't keep us waiting," Ruby Seddon called.

Mary wished to visit further with her dear friend, but John said, "Guess we should begin, Senator." Both men stepped to the rail overlooking a small sea of faces, each twisted with a level of disquiet.

∼✷∼

At the front of the crowd, Ruby Seddon gazed up at the important-looking man, then turned to Harold and asked, "Who's that feller again?"

"That there's your William Mitchell, United States Senator."

A woman to Ruby's right interrupted, "Don't hesitate to call himself Senator, but the man's too high for his nut. Never seen the inside of the U.S. capitol, so far as I know. Mitchell's in the Arkansas State legislature, nothing more. 'Fore that, he's a preacher down to Little Rock."

Ruby stood a little straighter. "The man I sent the letter to," she said to no one in particular. "I'll be pleased and proud to make his acquaintance."

"Welcome," John Baker hollered. "Without further ado, I present Senator William C. Mitchell."

The neighbor shook her head and nudged Ruby. "Shouldn't be calling himself no senator."

Ruby spoke without taking her eyes off the stately presence. "If the man brings my grandson home, I'll call him God Almighty if he likes it."

Senator Mitchell held up both hands as if to quiet applause, but there was no ovation, just rapt attention. "Fellow citizens of the great state of Arkansas," he began, his preacher's voice deep as the nearby river and smooth as just-skimmed cream. "I come bearing news of your loved ones." At the mention of 'loved ones,' hot tears filled Ruby's eyes, spilling down her cheeks. "Less than two years ago, I stood before you to deliver the tragic news that the Baker-Fancher wagon train had been attacked in the Utah Territory."

Man pronounced the name Fan-sheer like us locals do.

"And many of your loved ones—men, women and children— brutally murdered, God rest their souls."

Scattered *amens* rippled through the audience behind. More folks commencing crying.

"Y'all know me," the senator went on. "You know on that day, September 11, 1857, my two sons, a daughter-in-law . . ." Tears traced down his cheeks, but his voice remained steady. ". . . and my own precious daughter, Nancy, were murdered in the most foul and evil infamy ever inflicted on this great country. Like you, I shall never cease to mourn their deaths."

More *amens* from the crowd, and Ruby wept silent bitter tears for the senseless loss of her daughter.

"And I've worked tirelessly," the senator continued, "pressing the United States government—"

"Burn in Hell, James Buchanan," some man hollered.

Mitchell scanned the crowd and cleared his throat. "As I was saying, I've been working to obtain more details so's you might have justice and maybe a portion of peace. Today I bring news." He paused, like a man trained to give his words the time to sink in.

"News?" Ruby gasped. *Dear God, let it be my little boy.*

He continued, "Back then, all we knew was that there may have been survivors—all young children. Like you, I been praying night and day to know if my three grandbabes still drew breath—but those damnable Mormons weren't talking." Murmurs of wrath rippled through the assemblage. "The United States army finally sent a contingent of cavalry to investigate the godless atrocity."

Her hope took voice, and Ruby called out, "Did you get the letter? One about my Levi?"

With no indication that he'd heard the outburst, the senator continued, "The army has now established to a certainty that some of the young'uns were spared."

"Praise God," Ruby gloried, her spirit swelling to overflow. The information was not completely new, of course, but it finally wiped away the web of rumors.

"As I speak, Major James Henry Carleton is on his way back, transporting the orphans direct to Fort Leavenworth up in Kansas. I'll meet the party there and bring those children home to their grandmas and grandpas and aunts and uncles—where they surely belong."

"How many?" Ruby called out.

Mitchell drew a sad, deep breath. "I'm afraid there are but seventeen surviving children."

"Seventeen? They set out with more'n fifty!" Ruby's head slumped to her chest, and heaving sobs racked her limp body. *Don't give in to the fear, Ruby gal. Remember what God revealed in the dream.*

"Fifty-four," Mitchell said.

Some woman hollered, "Names. Tell us their names!"

Senator Mitchell's shoulders drooped. "A rider brought news of the orphans, but the letter bore no names. Haven't yet been able to reach them via telegraph nor train." Mitchell paused as breath seemed to catch in his throat. He finally choked out, "We're mired . . . stuck waiting and praying . . . not knowing if my three innocents . . . and your grandchildren are returning home . . . or naught but bones bleaching somewhere in the desert sun." He took out a white linen handkerchief and wiped his eyes and cheeks, then rolled wide shoulders back with a sigh. "Truth be told, some of those yet living may be too young to remember their own names."

Ruby yelled up again, "So where them seventeen been these past two years?"

This time she was heard. He fixed his eyes on hers and said, "As I understand it, they been staying with families in the southern part of the Utah Territory."

"Mormon families, right?" she called out.

From the raised veranda, Mitchell looked Ruby in the eyes. "Yes, it pains me to relate. Mormons."

She turned to address the crowd, squinting into the sun. "Trying to turn the hearts of our children from the Lord Jesus," Ruby yelled.

Anger grumbled through the group like a gathering storm

~6~

Carrollton, Arkansas - September 16, 1859

One month to the day after the senator's announcement at River House, Ruby scanned a new scene. With six hotels, three livery stables and a couple mercantiles, Carrollton was one of the larger communities in northwest Arkansas. *Over the years, I've seen some celebrations here, but nothing the likes of this.* The day was clear and bright, the summer heat made less by approaching autumn. Under yards of red, white, and blue bunting, Ruby, along with the rest of the town's 1,200 residents, filled the covered wooden sidewalks that bounded Main Street. In contrast to the festive decorations, the crowd's mood seemed somber. Ruby felt she could read their minds: *Just seventeen of fifty-four. Will my grandson be among them? Is my precious little niece one of those blessed to have survived?*

But no such battle raged in her own soul. *My grandson Levi surely lives, as God in Heaven revealed it.* The certain knowledge that she and Harold were but moments from the glorious reunion sent her spirits soaring, as if into the bright blue sky.

"They're coming!" someone yelled. Others in the crowd took up the cry. A minute or so later, approaching clouds of dust gave up eleven carriages, each decorated with its own colorful streamers and bearing the thirty-three-star flag of the United States of America. The buggies held the young survivors of the Utah Territory atrocity, all staring out at the strange surroundings in evident confusion. Ruby's heart felt near to

33

leaping from her breast as she strained to see their faces, catch a glimpse of dear Levi now two years older. But they were as yet not near enough.

A military escort was part of what folks were calling "The Buggy Parade." Ruby smiled up at her Harold, one of two dozen mounted members of Arkansas's Spavinaw Volunteer Rifle Company flanking the wagons. *He may be the oldest, but my man's setting high and proud as any in them tan uniforms— and with a heart near as big as those hands.*

All creation waved hard and high—a few smiling, more weeping as the buggies paused at the top of Main Street where some men had built a wide wooden stand. Seated on it were Senator Mitchell, Governor Conway, Mayor Baker and David C. Patton, captain of Harold's Spavinaw regiment. When the drivers had worked the carriages into a half-circle between the stage and the townsfolk, Ruby and the others converged, elbowing, jostling, desperate to find and reunite with loved ones. *My boy, my sweet boy. Your gramma's right here, soon to take you into her arms and never again—*

"Y'all step on back," Mitchell called out. "Let's give them a bit of room to breathe." The people retreated a couple paces as Mitchell stepped from the parade stand down to the street.

A woman called out, "Afore you said seventeen children, Senator. I count but fourteen."

"Fourteen, yes," he said, "One poor babe failed to survive the journey home, and the government kept two older boys behind to bear witness against the killers."

The pain Ruby felt for the child who died along the journey was overwhelmed by keenness to rejoin with Levi. "I'll present each of the fourteen, one at a time," the senator said, "so y'all can be sure which is yours." Ruby's heart verged on bursting.

The senator's process was orderly, but more frustrating than Ruby expected. For two long years, the Mormon captors had called every child by some made-up name. The older children were quickly matched, they remembered their true Christian names and recognized extended family. However, seven of the children had been less than two years old when their parents were killed. They had no clear memories of life back home, and, in most cases, had grown to look quite different from loved ones' recollections. It took nearly thirty minutes for Mitchell to sort it out, but in the end, everyone was confident each child had been returned to blood kin.

Ruby sagged into desperate sobbing. "Oh God," she muttered, "why has thou forsaken me?"

∾∾

The families were heading home, a few rejoicing over rescued children in their arms, more, like Ruby, awash in loss and wrath. Through eyes tender with tears, she watched the senator relax a mite, even break into a little smile. *Man has to be relieved his talking's over. No doubt looking forward to some fried chicken and re-acquainting time with his two granddaughters.* She knew he also carried a deep sorrow—his baby grandson was not among the living.

Before he could get away, Ruby hurried to his side. "Senator, I'm Ruby Seddon," she said. "You remember—"

"Of course. You wrote me of your grandson, Mrs. Seddon."

"What about those boys you said were left behind? One perchance red-haired, with a extra toe?"

"One eight-year-old, one six—John Miller and Emberson Tackitt. Neither was redheaded."

The flicker quickly died. *Not my grandson.* "Please don't dismiss me, Senator. But I got just the strongest feeling my daughter's boy is still alive. Levi Cantrell is his name, son of Frederick and Samantha Seddon Cantrell—would have been just three at the time, the time of the—" Her voice choked out in tears.

The senator took her hand and said, "For two years I've held that same hope. But they murdered more children than they spared. My own grandbaby . . ." The poor man's voice cracked. ". . . was no more than a babe in arms. He—" Mitchell pulled out a white handkerchief and wiped his wet cheeks. "I'm sorry, so sorry, Mrs. Seddon."

Despite the senator's emotion, Ruby persisted. "The whole thing must have been mighty confusing. Can you offer a poor grandma even a bit of hope?"

Mitchell just regarded her with sorrow in his eyes.

Ruby's will was nearly broken, but she forged on. "Senator, please."

"Major Carleton passed along a rumor about possibly one more orphan, the eighteenth. Two of the older children thought they may have remembered the child. But there's no name, no real evidence of—"

"They saying girl or boy?"

"A boy. But it's just an unfounded—"

Ruby felt her very being flood with faith. "That boy is Levi Cantrell, Senator Mitchell, the son of my murdered daughter! I just know it—I even dreamed about him."

The senator nodded. "Of course. You mentioned the dream in your letter."

"Senator Mitchell, I swore an oath afore God in heaven that I'd return Levi to his kith and kin no matter what the cost nor how long the effort."

Mitchell sighed. "May the Good Lord give you peace, Mrs. Seddon

~7~

Parowan, Utah Territory - September 26, 1859

Not long after the sun set, Eva opened the firebox door and fanned the stove coals. Then she sat, elbows on the table and chin on the backs of her hands, staring into the ever-changing orange flames, hoping to somehow find comfort in the familiar pop and crackle of the pine pitch. *What's next? By now the other orphans are back with their Arkansas kin. That should be the end, should it not? But what if Carleton told others about the rumor, the persistent whispering that there's one child yet to be discovered?*

A sudden twinge of something set her heart to racing like a bird's—Doubt? Guilt? *Thomas's—Levi's—mother surely perished, but is someone somewhere on her knees this very moment, praying to know if her nephew . . . or grandson . . . is still alive? But God gave Thomas to be my son as surely as if the boy had come from my own womb.* She interlaced her fingers and bowed her head in prayer. "Lord, I know he's not my blood. But his poor mother's back in your arms, and you delivered Thomas to me—not to some distant uncle he's never met nor a grandmother about to die and leave him alone. You gave my son to me. Help me keep him sheltered, keep him here where he—"

Her prayer was interrupted by the deep creaking of the front door. Bennet called, "Who you jawing with, Eva? Boy still up?"

"Just talking to my own self." Her husband closed the door behind him, walked over and joined her at the table. "Awfully late tonight," she said. "Militia drill?"

He responded with an unintelligible grunt, as if she deserved no more.

"Supper's still warm. Dug the carrots and potatoes for stew today. And there's freshly churned butter for the bread."

Neither spoke as Eva served, and Bennet set to the dish. He finished within a few minutes, mopping up the last of the venison grease with a slice of dense brown bread.

"Supper to your liking?" Eva asked.

"It was." He drew another breath as if to continue.

"Anything else?" she asked.

"No. Uh . . . yes." Bennet stared into his empty bowl. "Tonight, we'll try again to make a child." It sounded like anything but an invitation to a lovers' tryst.

"Don't you call it that," Eva said, shaking her head.

"But we're—"

"I know what it is you want to do. But let's not deceive ourselves that this time a child will result."

Bennet's face flushed. "The Lord works in mysterious ways."

A smile warmed Eva's visage. "True enough. He brought us Thomas."

"But the boy's not—"

The boy? Again? Her smile fled and she sighed. "Just go to the bedroom and get yourself undressed."

When her husband was through the door and out of earshot, Eva muttered, "May as well get it over with."

A minute later she entered the bedroom. It was small, eight by ten feet, with a sagging bed and a narrow dresser. The chamber pot next to the breakfront was a convenience in the warmer months, an essential item when winter's cold and snow made a late-night trip to the privy miserable. The bowl gave off a faint whiff of piss, which tonight she found particularly repellant. The dull light of a single candle revealed Bennet on the edge of the bed, clothed in nothing but his temple garment, mandatory underwear resembling an ankle length union suit. The cotton vestment was held together at the front by strings tied carefully into the double bowknot that God required.

Eva unclothed slowly. She saw how he leered, perhaps assuming her intention was to tease him to arousal—it was not. Either way, just above Bennet's crotch, the unbleached fabric revealed a growing bulge.

When Eva's outer clothing was shed, Bennet looked her up and down. Her underclothing was identical to his, but she felt the heavy fabric sag on her small frame and knew it could not completely hide the shape of a twenty-five-year-old woman. She allowed him one last look, then blew out the candle and lay across the rough cotton ticking. There was no kissing, no prelude of any kind. As prescribed, the coupling took place through gaps in the front of their undergarments. He was rougher than usual, but she did not complain—like so many times before, it was over quickly. *Is this the lot of every wife, to lie still, eyes closed, and pray for an early ending?*

❧

Some twenty minutes after the brief union, contented snoring leaked through the closed bedroom door. Eva sat at the table, both hands wrapped around a cup of tea. She stared into the rising steam, lost in thought. *If God wrought a miracle, would I even want another child? I've never had to care for a wee one— Thomas was already three when he came to us. Do I have sufficient love for two? Would Thomas resent being the odd child, the one not carried in my womb?*

Her heart answered, *Indeed I would welcome a baby. And Thomas would be well pleased with a tiny brother or sister.*

But somehow, even deeper in her soul, she knew such a day would never come.

The door opened, and Bennet yawned and stretched his way to the eating area, clothed in nothing but his undergarment. "Fetch me a cup," he said, sagging onto a chair and resting browned wrists on the tabletop. Water still simmered on the stove, and shortly, Eva set a mug in front of him along with a spoon and the small dish of precious honey.

He muttered something—*thanks*, perhaps—then stirred the sweet into his tea and blew on the cup. After a cautious sip, he leaned back, balancing the old chair on its hind legs, and exhaled deeply. "I think it's time, Eva."

She was genuinely perplexed. "For what, then?"

"Old Brother Shand's been dead some three months now."

In an instant, Eva went from confused to so certain she knew where the conversation was going that she added the next bits for him. "And the pitiable Widow Shand has none to care for her. It's time a good man took her for his wife," she mocked. "Your father put you up to this?"

He ignored the question. "Indeed, she does need a priesthood bearer to stand as head of the household."

"A priesthood bearer—like you, perhaps?"

"Something wrong with me?" Her husband seemed genuinely hurt.

Eva's vision blurred and reddened with fury. "There is something sorely wrong with you," she fumed. "You're married to another!"

Seven years prior, when she and Bennet had wed, she'd made it clear she would not share him with another woman— *or women*. Both spouses agreed they could be faithful Saints without living *The Principle*. At the time, it didn't seem a problem, they were still in the Great Salt Lake City, and a number of men there, especially those not in the church's upper ranks, had just one wife. But the Iron Mission was failing, hemorrhaging population, and the local brethren were expected to do their part.

Panic fluttered through her like a thousand moths. *Sister Shand's the biggest gossip in the mission. And her children seem naught but cruel. Such an arrangement would surely put our secret—and my son—in peril.*

"Are you asking my consent?" she said.

"The bishop called me to this union, Eva."

"The bishop?" Her voice rose. "You mean *your father?*"

"Calm yourself, you'll wake the boy."

But they were too far down the path for her to settle down. "And this is your way of asking for my blessing?"

"I hoped you'd stand with me," he mumbled. "But I don't require your—"

"And just what do you think this would mean for my son?"

"*Your* son?" Bennet's face was an expression that Eva had seen too often, a look of condescension that bordered on disdain.

But this time, she would not endure in wifely silence. She grabbed a nearby book and slammed it onto the table, sloshing tea from both cups. The lettering on the worn leather cover identified the heavy tome as *Doctrine and Covenants of the Church of the Latter Day Saints: Carefully Selected from the Revelations of God.* Eva riffled through the Mormon holy book, then found the certain page she sought, dog-eared and yellowed. The section recited a revelation given by God to Joseph Smith, recorded July 12, 1843 in Nauvoo, Illinois.

"What's this, then?" Bennet demanded.

"The Prophet Joseph's revelation on marriage."

"I don't think you need to—"

She held him in a merciless gaze. "And yet I do."

After flipping a couple more pages, she ran her finger down the paper and read out loud:

"And again, as pertaining to the law of the priesthood—if any man espouse a virgin, and desire to espouse another, and the first give her consent, and if he espouse the second, and they are virgins, and have vowed to no other man, then is he justified; he cannot commit adultery for they are given unto him; for he cannot commit adultery with that that belonged unto him and to no one else."

She angrily poked the page three times with an index finger. "'. . . and first give her consent!' Such a union requires my sanction. It's the word of God—right here."

"Don't be so—"

"And furthermore," she interrupted, "Naomi Shand has three children. It's some years since that woman was a virgin."

"Eva, please," Bennet said. "Just assent to—"

She glared back at him, wishing the fire she felt could somehow issue from her eyes and sear its way into his. "Never," she said.

࿊

Eva and Thomas were off for a visit to the Gale cabin. Near the end of the ride, Ginger picked up speed a bit, rousing Eva from dark thoughts of Bennet's pronouncement the previous night. Woobydog trotted alongside as best she could, matching the old horse pant for pant in spite of a missing leg. Eva was relieved to spot the Gale cabin. As always, her sitting bones were tender after twenty minutes straddling the old horse's bony back, but mostly she needed to talk to her best friend. She held the reins in both hands, arms wrapped loosely around her son to steady him. Thomas usually secured himself by holding onto the horse's mane, but today he used both hands to carry the surprise: a pie baked with honeyed peaches fresh from the Dunning orchard. The boy leaned over till the treasure sat just under his nose and he inhaled deeply.

"Smell good?" Eva asked.

"Smells like home."

Eva wasn't sure if the sweet and fruit reminded him of her own kitchen or perhaps the mama more than half-a-life before.

"Tommy!" Clara ran out from her hiding place among the tall stalks of wheat.

Thomas's back straightened. "Clara!" he called down from horseback. "We brought you a special sweetie."

Minutes later, Thomas and Clara sat on the raised wooden porch, dangling their legs over the side. Eva smiled at them kicking up and down. *It's an energy only the young possess.*

"Gonna have a pie party!" Thomas said.

Millie and Eva fetched chairs from inside. When they'd put them face-to-face in the porch's shade, Millie said, "Come with me, Clara." She followed her mother inside, and they soon came back with four china plates, each bearing a thick slice of pie. Millie delivered a piece to Eva, and Clara handed Thomas the biggest one.

"Thanks for the scrumptious pie, Aunt Evie," Clara said.

"My thanks for what you did for Thomas." Eva smiled at Clara. "A shame you didn't get so much as a sliver of your ma's pie back then." A short, nervous titter followed.

Woobydog gave a little whimper. Thomas shared a bit of crust with the dog, then finished the rest in two big bites. "Can we have another, Mama?" Eva cocked an eyebrow, a silent signal for Thomas to use his best words.

"I mean, *may* we have another?"

"In a bit, perhaps," she said. "You kids go off and play now."

"Soon as Clara's done."

Thomas was, as Eva had come to call it, little-boy wiggly. Clara took her time finishing the rest of her treat, then the boy took both their plates and forks inside without being asked.

He came back, and the two set out, Clara calling back over her shoulder, "See ya later."

They found a willow fishing pole leaned up against the back of the cabin and skipped off. When the trio passed the smelly pigpen, they picked up the pace. Woobydog gave a little bark as if to say, "I'm right behind."

"Watch out for snakes, Duckies!" Millie hollered after them. Neither child seemed to hear the caution.

Eva gazed into the distance where an endless silver carpet of sage stretched to the horizon. It was a sight she had once found haunting, even beautiful. Today it was naught but desolation, a wretched reminder of her isolation. *Thank the Lord I still have Thomas—and Millie.* The two fast friends were finally alone. She could unburden herself, commune with another woman who understood what it was like to live amongst "peculiar people" who eked out their existence beyond the edge of civilization.

She looked at Millie and smiled. Her friend was as stately and fair as Swedish royalty. "He up and did it," Eva said. "Guess I shouldn't have been surprised."

"Who did what, precisely?"

"Bennet's set on taking a second wife."

"Ohh, nooo," Millie moaned. "Who's he got his lecherous eyes on?"

"Remember Edward Shand?"

"Killed in a mine cave-in few years back?"

Eva nodded. "The same. Bennet's after Shand's widow, Naomi."

"That old cow?" Millie said, wrinkling her nose.

"She's not that old—still in her thirties."

"Barely, I'd say."

"And," Eva said, "she's got at least two things Bennet wants, of a certainty."

Millie pulled her shoulders back, thrusting out her own breasts and giggling like a girl. "Odds are he can't hardly wait to get into that apple dumplin' shop."

"They might find the poor gent smothered in his own marriage bed," Eva said, and both laughed until tears ran down their faces. She stood and gave her dearest friend a hug. "Love you, Mil," she said. "Thanks for keeping me from going mad."

"He ask for your blessing, Evie dear?"

She rolled her eyes to the sky. "He did . . . but I dug my heels in."

"That's the end of it, then."

Eva shook her head in disgust. "Bishop Dunning's behind the whole intention—wants Bennet to have a blood son to carry forward his name."

Millie reached over and patted her friend on the knee. "And Bennet's in full agreement, of course?"

Eva replied with a nod.

Millie continued. "I'll wager he's stiff as a stick at the mere idea of giving it to a new brood mare." They shared a laugh. "And designing to take over that elegant house, all that land, a nice herd of cattle—"

"That had not yet occurred to me," Eva said. "Small wonder the bishop wants her in the family." She stared at folded hands in her lap. "Mil, he—" She began sobbing. "I told him *no* in the clearest way a person could. But I've surely not heard the last of it."

Millie spoke through clenched teeth. "Hellfire, Evie, what makes most menfolk so wretched?"

Eva sat without speaking for half a minute. "How it must peeve you, Mil, your husband portioned 'twixt two women."

Millie's expression hardened. "Being truthful with you, I'd have left some years ago if I could of. Hell, I'd leave with you this moment. Head out for San Diego." She broke eye contact, staring off at who-knew-what. "Always wanted to soak my toes in the sea."

It was a fantasy Eva dared not entertain. "How could we turn our backs to the gospel? And beyond that, where's a woman like you or me to go? We'd surely starve to death, if the militia didn't find us first."

"Seems so." Millie sighed and stepped inside the cabin, returning with cups brimful with water. She handed one to Eva and said, "First thing they say is you'll come around to loving his other wife like your own dear sister—that's a heap of road apples. Two of us fight like bobcats over everything: food, how to rear the children. Everything. Then there's the problem of the calendar."

"Calendar?"

"Who he joins giblets with and when. It's disgusting— making a plan for such doin's."

Eva felt her stomach roil. "Does he ever, uh, you know, both wives in the selfsame night?"

"Just once he darkened my door with his bun already buttered. Best believe I sent the old man scampering."

Eva responded with a nervous little laugh. "Not sure I know how old Quincy is."

"He don't like talking about it, but the man's near sixty. With a little luck, he'll keel over and die one day soon." She put her hand to her mouth and whispered between spread fingers, "Shouldn't be speaking ill of the dead."

Eva couldn't keep herself from sniggering. "Quincy's not dead, nor even ill."

"Just yet," Millie winked. They shared a guilty laugh, then Millie said, "But while the man draws breath—between you, me and that fencepost out there—'bout half the time his old Nebuchadnezzar's not up to the task." Millie flashed her blushing confidante a conspiratorial wink. "If you grasp my implication."

Suddenly saddened, Eva cast her eyes downward. "That'd be the only good part."

"Meaning what?"

A solitary tear rolled down Eva's cheek. "My husband's distant and always in such a hurry."

"I'm sorry, Sweeting. But at times the liaising's most agreeable, huh?"

"Not in such a . . ." Eva's voice trailed off and her eyes wandered into a vacant stare, ". . . a very long, long time."

Millie changed the subject. "The sister Shand's got three children, am I right?

"Two boys and a girl. All older than Thomas."

"Seen them around. Unbroke, far's I can tell."

"Of course, Thomas and I'd be at my place," Eva said. "Naomi and her children would remain in the big Shand house. But they're bullies, even the girl. Left to their own devices, I'm afraid they'd make my son's existence a nightmare."

"I do loathe it when Jezzie's boys come 'round," Millie said. "Think they'd throw Clara down the nearest well, given half a chance."

"Should it come down to it, I'll protect Thomas the best I can."

"'Course you will," Millie said. "But Naomi's not gonna take kindly to you swinging a switch on any of her litter."

"I don't suppose she would," Eva said.

"So, beyond this marriage poppycock, you think Thomas is safe?"

"Safe?"

"Rumor has it the army feller's coming back after delivering the orphans."

"To what possible end?"

"Investigating into the attack on the train those two years back," Millie said. "But his coming is no more'n a rumor."

"We got Thomas the same day we arrived in The Mission. The bishop thought it'd be best if no one knew he wasn't ours by birth." Eva stroked the cleft of her chin with a thumb, lost in thought. "And even if he was found out by locals, seems no reason any of the saints would betray us."

~8~

Santa Clara, Utah Territory - October 5, 1859

Tommy sat next to his father while Mama and Woobydog rode in the back of the wagon. He was holding Ginger's reins, proud as peach punch. "We there yet, Papa?" he asked.

"Hold your horses, well, your horse. You'll see it soon enough."

Papa went quiet until the wagon traveled around one more bend in the Santa Clara River. "We're here," he said with a big arm wave. "Brother Hamblin's spread. What you think, my boy?"

"Looks like a bunch got here before us."

Papa nodded. "And more yet to arrive."

"How come it feels like summer?"

"Elevation here's a lot lower than back home," Papa said. "October in the Santa Clara means warm days and clement nights."

"What's evelation?"

Papa chuckled. "*Elevation* means how high a place is. Like the mountains are mostly colder than the desert."

Tommy nodded and took in the wonderful view. Heavy canvas tents, covered wagons and wool bedrolls freckled the two-acre meadow. It already smelled good—like the grass was maybe scythed this morning. It was a gathering of friends and family the likes of which he'd never seen. He was so glad his papa was finally smiling. "I like that you're happy today. You are, aren't you, Papa?"

"Seems I am," his father answered. "Harvests were bountiful this year, so everyone's coming together for a three-day thankfulness celebration."

The Dunnings, Gales and other Parowan families had traveled two days to join with the Saints at the big farm by the Santa Clara River. Papa said the spread belonged to Jacob Hamblin. Brother Hamblin was president of the Santa Clara Injun Mission, but Tommy didn't really know what that meant.

Near the Hamblin house, half-a-dozen sweaty men peeled off jackets and rolled up their sleeves to tend to a fire where the carcasses of two huge cattle roasted. Fat dripped and sizzled into a bed of glowing coals, the gentle breeze blowing around a smoke that made Tommy's mouth water. He soon found Clara and they set off to explore the farm.

There was a broad field between the cooking and camping areas, blessed by the shade of three big cottonwood trees. Papa had said this was the nicest spot on Hamblin's farm, left open for families to come for meals, dances and just plain talking. There were dining tables made out of long half-logs laid flat side up on feet that looked like big Xs. The chairs were just short stumps. *Somebody'll probably use them as firewood later—if it ever gets cold at this evelation.*

Tommy and Clara found a shady patch of grass and kneeled down to tickle Woobydog's pink belly. It was the best day ever—till three teenage boys trotted by. Ammon, the youngest, called out, "Hey, Copperhead. I come across your ugly cur's fourth leg."

"Not unless you just got here from—" Tommy stopped himself before he spoke the word he promised Mama he'd never say. *Arkansas.*

The reply seemed to confuse Ammon, who wasn't very smart to begin with. "Oh yeah?" he said. "Well, I seen it back yonder, roastin' with the steers."

"She's still got one more'n you," Tommy called. But the boys were already too far away to hear how clever he was.

The lads that had passed were Clara's half-brothers. Ammon was about twelve years. The older ones were Nephi, age fourteen, and Sam, fifteen. Tommy didn't have any brothers or sisters, but from what he'd seen, most older brothers came in two kinds: protectors and pesterers. The Gale boys fit into their own corral: downright mean.

Clara must have been thinking about them, too. She said, "They're older, but I'm the one who's most mature. Ma even said so."

Tommy wasn't sure what 'mature' meant, but he smiled anyway. It was Clara, it was surely something good.

❧⚜❧

While stretched shadows of late afternoon gave way to the full shade of early evening, Eva watched Bennet and some other menfolk emerge from the Hamblin home, finishing up earnest conversations—likely about weather, church and the rumored return of Johnston's army. The last man out was Brother Jacob himself. He clattered a metal bar around the inside of a triangle dinner bell, and the children came running. Families soon found each other and sat together at the long tables.

When everyone was seated and quiet, Bishop Dunning's superior, William H. Dame, President of the church's Parowan Stake of Zion, local mayor and commander of both Southern Utah militia regiments, stood. He was just forty years old, but the past few years had left the leader thirty pounds lighter and an apparent decade older. Sunken cheeks and permanent frown wrinkles now dominated his visage. His height was average, and wispy gray hair stuck out almost comically on both sides. Despite all that, the man's unvaryingly stern expression and piercing blue eyes still communicated strength and natural leadership. And he had the voice of a bellowing bull.

ঔৎ

Tommy felt the Holy Spirit when President Dame held his hands in front of himself and bowed his head. He followed his leader's example, lowering his own head and squinting his eyes closed.

"Elohim, our most Eternal Father, the God whom we seek," the president began, his voice kind of like thunder. He went on and on and on, giving thanks for everything from the spring rains to "the steers that gave up their ghosts that all may feast. We implore thy forgiveness for every man, woman and child here assembled. Send thy richest blessings upon our lands and flocks." The prayer that felt to Tommy like a Sunday sermon finally ended with a part he didn't understand: "We beseech thee, Almighty God, to deliver us from our enemies, stop the mouths of those who speak ill of thine anointed and to avenge the blood of the prophets upon this nation unto the third and fourth generation. In the sacred name of Him who died to save us, even Jesus the Christ. Amen."

"Amen," the congregation roared in one enthusiastic voice.

"Time to eat?" Tommy asked, a mite too soon and maybe too loud.

Older girls, the prettiest in The Mission, began serving the finest supper Tommy had eaten since, well, forever: juicy slices of beef, endless smashed potatoes, and cobs of corn with butter!

When everyone was stuffed from dinner, the music began. The band was two fiddles, a guitar, a trumpet, a drum and a giant horn called a tuba. They played real loud, "with sheer enthusiasm," Mama said. And soon everyone was dancing jigs, square dances and something called the Virginia Reel. But Tommy's favorite was the cakewalk. He pranced around the circle at least twenty times before finally winning the most beautiful dried-cherry pie he'd ever even imagined. He and Clara sat down to share it, but her brothers showed up and stole most away. The theft made Tommy angry, but mostly embarrassed that he couldn't fight the bigger boys and make them give the sweetie back to Clara.

꘡꘡

Next morning, Mama left him to sleep later than other days. He finally peeked out from between dew-wet blankets to bright sunshine and emerged to greet the day with a smile. Woobydog nuzzled her way past him, then stretched over her front paws and flapped loose ears.

Squatted by the cook fire, Mama called out, "Morning, Sleepyhead. Ready for some breakfast?"

"Sure. Where's Papa?"

"Had a cup of tea, then headed out to find Brother Jacob. Something about birthing calves. Want a slapjack? Got fresh milk and a little sugar."

"For certain." Thomas grinned. "Be right back." He pulled on his britches, then headed to the dense brush along the edge of the field, the men's and boys' necessaries. Woobydog normally trotted along and looked after her boy wherever he went, but this morning she was hard at work mining marrow out of a bone from the night before.

Walking back, Tommy found himself face to face with the mean Gale brothers. He looked around—nowhere to run, and no Woobydog to help. *I'm not a fraidy-cat, but it's three against one. This is bad.*

Nephi approached him first. He was the middle son, named after the greatest prophet in the Book of Mormon. As far as Tommy could tell, the bully had nothing in common with real Nephi.

"Hi there, Tommy-boy." Nephi surprised him with an almost friendly smile. The two brothers beside him seemed nice, too.

Tommy tried hard to keep his voice from sounding scared. "You gonna fight me?"

Nephi shrugged. "Nah. How 'bout let's be friends."

Friends? The word made Tommy confused. They robbed his pie just the night before.

"Why not friends?" fifteen-year-old Sam asked. "We're ridin' up to Red Cliffs. Gonna tarry a while, swimmin' and catchin' frogs."

Tommy perked up a little. Sam had just described his perfect day.

"Clara's comin'," the older boy added. "You should ride along. Whaddya say?"

"Well . . ." Tommy stalled. He was not about to promise till he knew for sure that Clara was going. "I'll ask Mama if I can—"

"Gotta ask his mommy," Ammon teased.

Sam punched his younger brother hard on the shoulder. "Shut up, skunkbutt. Told you we're supposed to act nice."

ॐॐ

When he got back, Tommy found his friend eating sugary slapjacks with Mama. "Where you been?" Clara asked.

"Talking to your brothers."

"Half-brothers," she said. "And not even that."

Mama looked worried. "You all right, Thomas?"

"Sure. They want me and Clara to go with them swimming and frogging."

Clara shook her head. "We should just stay here and play."

Tommy was confused. "But they told me you already said you'd go."

"First I've heard of it," Clara said without looking up from her breakfast.

"Let's go with, Clara. Mama fries up frog legs real good."

"Really *well*," Mama said.

The girl shook her head, pigtails slapping like Woobydog's ears. "It's my brothers, remember?"

"They were fair nice to me today. Can we go, Mama?"

His mother paused for a moment. "Only if Aunt Millie allows it for Clara."

He ignored the doubt in her voice. "Come on, Clara," Tommy said. "Go ask your ma."

"It does sound kind of fun. But—"

"Then we'll go!"

"Only if Aunt Mil says yes, and you're back before sundown," Mama reminded. "And you can't go wading around in a frog swamp in those boots. I'll work out something else for you to wear."

Clara finished the last couple of bites and brushed sugar from her chin and the front of her dress.

"Meet you at your camp, Clara," he said. "Bet we're in for an adventure."

❧

Eva knelt in the wagon bed, rummaging through a pile of assorted clothing. "Aha." She held up a pair of clogs. "Let's see if these might work."

Years back, she made the shoes for herself by fashioning soles out of yellow pine, then tacking on leather loops to hold her feet. The carving on the wooden foot beds was a bit uneven, making the shoes unpleasant to wear for more than an hour or two, but they were fine for quick trips to the privy and the like—the thick soles helped keep feet up out of the mud or even a little snow and they always dried without damage.

"Sit down, Thomas," she said, climbing down from the wagon. "Take your boots off and we'll try these."

He sat in the still-damp grass, untied his boots and slipped out of them. Eva knelt in front of him with the clogs. "Now the socks."

"Good morning, Sister Dunning."

Eva startled. She'd been focused on the shoes, and Lottie Hopkins's voice took her by full surprise. "Oh, uh, hello."

She stood to greet a short, yellow-haired woman, even thinner than when Eva had seen her last. Sister Hopkins surprised Eva by pulling her into a hug, then she said, "Bennet told Charles you tried to comfort Rosie when the soldiers stole her. Thank you." Tears filled Lottie's eyes, then escaped down sallow cheeks.

This time Eva initiated the hug. "I'm so sorry, Sister. I didn't even know the child was—"

"One of the orphans?"

Eva nodded.

Lottie sniffled, tears now flowing freely. "For two years we lived with the dread someone might take her away. But after so much time, it felt like it was going to be . . ." Her voice trailed off.

"Mama, Clara's waiting for me." Of course, Thomas was getting impatient.

Lottie looked down at the seated boy. "You're a handsome child, lucky to have such a wonderful—" Her gasp told Eva the woman had likely glimpsed that the redheaded boy had one too many toes.

"I . . . I have to be going," Lottie stammered. Then she bustled off without another word.

❧❦

Easy, now. Don't spill. The rusting bucket was full, and Eva set it on the ground with some care. She squatted next to the cook fire and used a stick to arrange the embers into a flat spot, relocated the pail onto glowing coals, then stood.

"They took my Rosie away from me."

Eva looked up to see Lottie was back, her eyes red and swollen, hair in disarray. "I know. I'm so sorry, Sister."

"The bishop, your father-in-law, commanded me to give up my only child . . . and I obeyed."

"Lottie, I know how you must feel."

"No, you've not a clue as to my feelings!" Without warning, Lottie soared to screaming. "Not one God-damned idea!"

Eva glanced left and right. "Be wary, Sister Hopkins," she admonished. "Someone might—"

"Hear me curse—or learn your secret?" Lottie sobbed.

"Listen to me, Sister. You mustn't—"

"My baby!" The hysterical woman fell to her knees and wailed, "My baby, my poor, crippled baby."

Shock and pity washed over Eva like a river as she stared at Lottie rocking back and forth, sobbing. *Lord, I beg you,* Eva prayed, *stop the woman's mouth before—*

"I suspicioned your boy might be the last of them," she whimpered. "Now I know it to a certainty."

A terrible, unbidden memory crowded Eva's reeling mind: a filthy soldier in a boxy wagon, grabbing tiny Rosie's deformed limb and snatching her back from Eva's arms. Then, in a blink, the imagined scene transformed. The heart-rending screams of an infant continued, but the vision of the child had changed— it was now her Thomas.

Eva cleared her head with a hard shake that did nothing for her pounding heart. "Lottie, please. Look at me."

The grieving mother did not look up. "Why, Eva?" she moaned. "My Rosie's gone forever and your little boy's still here. Because your husband's father is the bishop? He lied for you, didn't he? Bishop Dunning lied to the soldiers." Lottie stood and glared at Eva for what felt like forever. "It's gonna come," she finally mumbled.

Eva turned her palms up and shrugged in true confusion. "What do you—"

"Your time to mourn is still to come."

In Eva's ear, it rang more like threat than prophecy.

~9~

Tommy shared a dappled gray mare with Sam and Clara. Nephi and Ammon, the younger Gales, followed on a big roan. They rode north for about two miles, following willows that marked the bank of the Santa Clara River, then made a sudden right. Tommy reckoned they were now headed west. *Makes no sense to leave the river.* "We're going the wrong way, Sam."

"Not so," the fifteen-year-old replied.

"But you told me it's a swimming spot. So, it's got to be on the river."

"This'll be lots more fun," the older boy said. "Just trust me."

He did not trust Sam. Instead, Tommy thought he and Clara were maybe in some kind of trouble. "Let's go back," he said. They were far from camp, and Tommy had no idea what to do about it.

"First we have to see *the site*." Sam said the last words real slow.

"What site?" Clara asked.

Sam's brothers snickered. "It's a mystery," Nephi said. "All the adults know somethin', but they never talk about it when we're around. Somethin' bad must have happened out in the desert, somethin' *real* bad. Probably ghosts there."

"Like the Holy Ghost?" Tommy asked. All three brothers laughed out loud.

In spite of Tommy's complaints and Clara's demands, the children rode two more hours, mostly with the horses at a walk, mostly uphill, mostly in silence. As they went higher in *evelation*, the air got cooler—and no one had a coat. A few times, Tommy heard Ammon or Nephi laugh. But he couldn't understand what the boys thought was funny.

"Piss break," Sam finally called out.

The Gale boys hopped down from their horses. Clara and Tommy remained mounted. She leaned back and whispered over her shoulder, "Hold tight. We're going home."

Tommy grabbed Clara, Clara grabbed a fistful of mane and kicked the gray's ribs. "Gee up!"

The mare did not run fast like Tommy expected. Instead, the horse turned its head as if to see whose little feet were doing the kicking.

The boys returned to find Clara still heeling the horse to no avail. But they did not seem angry, it was worse. They were laughing again.

"Don't think you two babies want to strike out on your own," Nephi said with a sneer.

"Yep," Sam added. "Not long till dark." He paused a second. "Lots of wolves and such 'round here."

"Let us go back. Please," Tommy pled, hating the whine in his voice.

"Sam," Clara said, "take us back this minute or I'll make sure Pa Quincy flays your hide." Tom heard real anger in her voice.

Sam shook his head. "We're close now. Don't you want to see it? Heard tell it might be an ancient Lamanite city."

Tommy's chin quivered—Lamanites were Indians, the bad people in the Book of Mormon. "No. Go back." But they just acted like they couldn't hear him. "What now?" Tommy whispered into Clara's ear.

"Pay close attention," she said. "We may yet have to find our own way home."

For a while, the horses picked their way along a rocky streambed that bottomed a skinny ravine. They came around a bend and stopped to see the canyon opened into a valley that still had some sunshine on it. There were low hills all around and a dozen tiny creeks that watered big patches of bunchgrass. At a certain place, they came together and made a baby river.

"Injuns call this Magotsu Crick," Sam said.

A dozen little groves of scrub oak dotted the area. The setting sun made their leaves glow yellow-orange, and Tommy remembered that they had traveled from summer back to autumn.

"That it?" Ammon pointed at a big pile of rocks some ways out.

"Think so. Let's go see," Sam said. "And best watch out for them ghosts." This time no one laughed.

When they were a little closer, Sam said real loud, "The hell is that?"

Somebody had piled up a lot of light brown stones on purpose. And there was a big "T" sticking up from the top part.

They rode closer to the stony hill, and Sam said, "Who'd put a big old cross way out here?"

A cross? Like what they nailed Jesus to? It was made of rough wood, the sideways board tied onto the sticking up part by pieces of dark leather. On the rocks at the bottom of the cross was a big log. It was scraped flat on the front side and had some words carved into it. Clara read them out loud: "*VENGEANCE IS MINE: I WILL REPAY SAITH THE LORD.*" Beneath the word log was a piece of orange sandstone like they had in Parowan. Somebody had scratched more writing on the big rock. Clara read: "*HERE 120 MEN, WOMEN AND CHILDREN WERE MASSACRED IN COLD BLOOD, IN SEPT, 1857. THEY WERE FROM ARKANSAS*"

"Clara," Tommy whispered. "What does massa—"

"Means killed."

1857? Arkansas? Could this be where Indians killed my first mama and papa? He wanted so bad to tell Clara. But a promise is a promise, so he closed his mouth tight and tried real hard not to look sad.

Everyone else was quiet, too.

Twelve-year-old Ammon finally talked in a kind of whisper. "We should go now. The dark's near upon us." The sun had dipped below the western hills, and the cold was getting colder.

"Whatcha afraid of?" older brother Sam said. "Let's have a peep around."

"How you doing?" Clara whispered to Tommy.

"Not too bad." He wanted to be brave for his friend, but he was shivering from being cold and afraid—and trying harder than hard not to cry.

"Good boy. You stay right here. I'll be back directly."

"No! Don't leave me by myself with—"

"I got to go, you know, the necessary. I'll be quick back." Tommy felt like crying for being alone, but he didn't try to follow her. Instead he watched the Gale boys set off to explore.

Nephi and Ammon tried to climb up the hill of loose rocks, while Sam wandered around the bottom. After a minute or two, the oldest brother hollered, "Come here, boys. You got to see this!"

Clara had told him to stay put, but curiosity got the best of Tommy, and he walked over to see what the fuss was about.

Sam Gale held a human skull in his hand. The bone was brown and yellow with cracks and scrapes Tommy guessed were from the teeth of coyotes or maybe even wolves. His eyes got scared big and he felt sick in his stomach. The skull was tiny—a baby's—with a hole through both sides. Tommy ran from the sight, then dropped to the ground. He hugged his knees and prayed to think of something else. *Please, Heavenly Father. Anything. Anything but a baby got shot in the head.*

After a minute or two, Tommy was still shivering, only partly from the cold. He stood with the idea to walk a little bit to get warm. He also hoped maybe he'd see something to help him not think about that poor baby. He walked around the big rock pile a couple times. On the third time, something stuck on a spiny greasewood caught his eye, a bit of blue against the dark green leaves. He went to investigate.

❧❧

Tommy sat in the dirt, sobbing over a handful of bad memories.

"What's wrong?" Clara asked. He looked up, then opened his fist to show her a six-inch length of blue gingham. He expected her to ask about the scrap, but they were both startled by a yell, a sort of mix between scared and angry.

"Where in the hell did he come from?" Sam bellowed.

Horse and rider seemed almost to appear from nothing. The stranger's mount made barely a sound as it approached on the soft ground. There was green grass all about, but the pinto pony looked like it was starving to death, patches of white and tobacco-spit brown stretched tight over sharp bones. The rider was a scrawny Indian, Paiute, Tommy guessed. He wore dirty buckskin and looked more ancient than the oldest man Tommy'd ever seen. The Indian's skin was thin as paper, wrinkled and brown like a fresh-shelled walnut.

"What do you want?" Sam sounded like he was trying extra hard to be brave.

"You go now," the old man said.

"We'll vamoose when we're cussed good and ready," Sam sneered.

"Very bad place, many unhappy spirits."

Nephi spoke up. "You can't scare us, old man."

"Many die here." The ailing brave sucked a breath. "Leave this place." The pony seemed to understand, it took up walking again, slow and quiet.

"Godforsaken Lamanite," Sam called after him. "'Twas your people killed that little child."

Not much later, Tommy felt a smidgeon of relief. After the worst time in his whole life, they were finally headed back to camp. The edge of the moon just barely peeked over the hills, and for now, everything was dark. The horses smelled their way back down the gloomy trail, moving slow like maybe they were as scared as he was.

~10~

E va's favorite part of the harvest celebration was the final
night, a wondrous music fest. She and Millie had planned
to enjoy it together, but Eva waited alone. She wondered,
worried even, why Millie hadn't shown up. But she soon
relaxed, enjoying instrumental solos, mostly violin, trumpet,
and even a banjo piece. They were followed by a pretty good
string quartet that played three Beethoven numbers. But
everyone's favorite was the grand finale, an extended singalong
of the church's most beloved song, *"The Spirit of God Like a
Fire is Burning."* No matter the occasion, the powerful hymn
was always saved for last.

The congregation stood and launched into the final chorus
with a joyful sound that seemed to swell and fill the whole
outdoors.

> *We'll sing and we'll shout with the armies of heaven,*
> *Hosanna, hosanna to God and the Lamb!*

Eva sensed someone come up behind her. It was Millie
who cupped hands and yelled into her ear, "We can't find the
children, Evie." Then they waited while the assembled poured
their hearts into the final two lines:

> *Let glory to them in the highest be given,*
> *Henceforth and forever, Amen and Amen!*

"I thought Quincy hied after them," Eva said.

"He just keeps saying Jezzie's boys can look after themselves. You talk to Bennet?"

She shook her head angrily. "Started drinking elderberry wine with some other men about midday. Man's of no use to anyone in a liquor drowse."

After a long breath, Millie said, "So it's you and me, Evie."

"And Ginger. Best get a move on." Eva took Millie by the hand and the two mothers hurried to the Dunning camp where they tied a tin drinking cup into a cloth, then climbed onto the mare and started out. Just over the rock ridge to the east, the moon was nearly full. Their eyes adapted quickly, and they made good progress, keeping the river willows close on their left. Every minute or so one or the other hollered her child's name into the darkness, then they waited silently. No response.

After about half-an-hour, Eva said, "Whoa, Ginger." The aging horse seemed happy to oblige.

"Why're we stopping?" Millie asked.

"Looks like trails diverge here. How far do you think we've come?"

"Well over a mile. Maybe two."

"Did Clara tell you how far away this place was?"

Millie thought about it for a moment. "Not sure either of the children knew."

"But it was somewhere on the river, right?"

"Thought so," Millie said.

"Then it must still be up ahead." Eva signaled Ginger, and the mare continued her unhurried walk up the river trail.

Millie resumed calling. "Clara, Thomas, can you hear me? Thomas, Clara!"

Eva stopped the horse again.

"What are you—"

Eva shushed her friend and whispered, "Thought I heard something."

Both women instinctively closed their eyes and focused everything on listening.

"Maaaa!" The child's voice was faint, and oddly, came from somewhere behind them. "Ma!" It was definitely Clara.

Eva turned Ginger around, and she soon saw two horses and five riders silhouetted against the moonlight. *They're near the spot where I stopped the horse just a few minutes ago. Must have rejoined the river trail at the split.*

Ginger caught up to the children, and Clara and Thomas soon scrambled off their ride. The three older boys galloped away before Eva could light into them.

Clara gave her mother a tight hug. "Ma, that place was so cold," she said. "And evil."

Eva's little boy was crying. "Thomas, were either of you harmed in any way?"

He did not respond. She reached out to give his hands a comforting squeeze, but he yanked the right one back. A little corner of blue fabric extended from his closed palm.

ॐ❧

Back in camp, Millie settled Clara into the open wagon that served as their bedroom. After she wriggled down into the covers, the little girl said, "I'm sorry, Ma."

Millie gave her a tender kiss on the cheek. "No one's faulting you, child. I should have had the good sense not to trust Jezzie's boys. Rest up, we'll talk in the morning, Ducky."

"Isn't it already morning?"

Millie gave a little chuckle. "'Tis. But try to sleep a bit till the sun's full up."

As soon as her daughter was asleep, Millie stepped over the side of the wagon box and climbed down using the wheel's spokes like ladder rungs. The sound of snoring from the nearby Conestoga where Quincy and Jezzie slept grated like fingernails on sandstone. Millie hardened her resolve and headed for the covered wagon. She ducked under the wooden bows, then knelt next to her sleeping husband and his first, and favorite, wife. They were sprawled on top of several layers of quilts, each wearing naught but the cotton undergarment. His was flabby and loose like the aging man who wore it. She lay on her belly, the cotton fabric stretched so tight it seemed barely able to retain the woman's mountain of a backside.

"Wake up, you miserable frauds for parents!" Millie shouted.

Jezzie managed to roll over, but not without considerable groaning. Quincy's one deaf ear must have been a blessing of sorts, he snored on as if nothing had happened. Millie rolled him over and yelled into the good side, "Get yourself up. Now!"

After a half-minute of snorting and throat clearing, the two sat up, bleary-eyed but more or less awake. They made no effort to cover themselves, and Millie noted Jezzie's enormous breasts were fully a match for her hindquarters.

"What're you doin' here?" Quincy mumbled.

"Know what your boys been up to, Jezzie?" Millie demanded. "You even check on them afore you hauled yourself up here to sleep?"

Jezzie's expression was blank as a blizzard.

"I'll tell you where they been. They kidnapped my daughter and Tom Dunning and drug them out to the site."

"The Site?" Quincy gasped.

"The meadows. The one place no man in the Iron Mission will talk about," Millie said, "let alone ever go nigh."

Now Quincy was wide awake, his fleshy face showing concern. "Why did they . . . What'd they say about it?"

"Maybe you ought to ask them."

Millie expected her husband to reply, "in the morning" and drop back off to sleep. Instead, he pulled on his trousers and headed for the boys' tent, shirtless, his face fairly glowing red.

"And while you're at it, give them a switching for taking the little kids," Millie called after him. If he heard her, he gave no sign of it.

◛◚

In the grey predawn, Eva stirred the fire while Bennet sat nearby, nursing a hangover and a cup of tea. She looked up to see half-dressed Quincy Gale approach the Dunning camp, three groggy boys trailing behind like reluctant ducklings.

"Mornin', Bennet," Quincy called, without giving Eva so much as a nod.

"Uh, morning, Quincy. What's got you out so early?"

"My boys got somethin' to say to you."

The three Gale brothers carefully studied the dirt at their feet.

"Welcome, fellas. What's on your minds?" Bennet asked.

Sam Gale spoke for his younger brothers. "Sorry about what we done to Tommy, Brother Dunning. We didn't mean nothing by it. Just having a little sport, you know?"

Of course, Bennet had no idea what Sam was on about. Eva guessed all her husband knew for sure was that his head rang like a blacksmith's hammer on an anvil. "Boys'll be boys, I suppose," he mumbled. "Nobody got hurt . . . right?"

"Except for these three," Quincy said. "You can be sure as a gun I took a stick to them minute I heard."

Eva made no attempt to hide a smile.

After an uneasy silence, Bennet said, "All right, then. Thanks for the apology, and it'll never happen again, right?"

Eva forced herself not to laugh. *The man still has no idea what this concerns.*

Obviously relieved it had gone so well, the three boys replied in unison, "No, sir."

Sam winced when his dad slapped him on his hind end. "Get back there and help your ma pack up." The boys headed out at a lope. Quincy stayed behind.

"You know where they were, right?" Eva asked.

Bennet looked unfocused and a bit sheepish. "Not really."

Quincy hitched up his sagging pants. "They was explorin' up to the site."

"The site?" The word seemed to strike Bennet like the hooves of a mule. "You mean?"

"Yup. The mountain meadows."

Bennet's face went still paler. "They see anything?"

"Can't get them to speak of it. But something sure'n hell scared Old Nick out of all three of mine. You might ought to talk to your boy."

"Uh, I shall. Thanks to you, Quincy. And rest assured this goes no further."

Quincy nodded. "That'd be for the best." He touched his bare forehead as if it were the brim of a hat, then turned and started back without ever having acknowledged Eva.

~11~

Parowan - October 10, 1859

Tommy stood outside the door to Mama and Papa's room. Woobydog sat at his side, her tail happy wagging. "I know I'm never 'sposed to bother them when the door's shut," he whispered to his dog. "But this is serious."

He still shook from the dream that had scared him awake. In it, he'd peeked from behind his first mama's blue dress to see an old Indian on horseback. He had a big feather hat and a painted face. The horse galloped at them, and the chief grabbed Mama up without even slowing down. Tommy was left alone, but a piece of her blue dress tore off—it was in his hand.

I really have to knock. Maybe Papa won't be angry this time. Tommy raised his fist but froze when he heard a sound on the other side of the bedroom door. It was a thump . . . thump . . . thump, like when he jumped on his bed, which he was never supposed to do. *Were parents allowed to jump on the bed?* He'd remember to ask Mama. Then he heard Papa make a groan sound, and that scared him. He took a deep breath and rapped, soft at first, then a little louder. No one answered.

Tommy dropped his head to his knees and prayed in a small, quivering voice, "Heavenly Father, please make it daytime. Protect our family from Indians and Americans and any would harm us."

ॐ∽

On the other side of the door, Eva stared at the ceiling, deep in thought. At her husband's insistence, they'd just coupled. It was the best word she knew to describe the act. *Sexual congress* was not a term a proper Mormon wife would ever use, and it would be ludicrous to call it lovemaking. So Bennet and Eva lay on their bed, post-coupling, she deep in thought, he slipping into sleep.

"Bennet." No response. Eva gave his ribs a gentle nudge. "Bennet, we need to talk."

"Talk?" Her husband did not sound happy about being roused from half-slumber.

"Sister Hopkins saw his toes."

❧

Tommy woke to voices. He lifted his head off his knees. His neck hurt, but he put his ear against the door. He could hear some words, they didn't really make sense.

"Toes? Lottie?" Papa said.

"Hopkins . . . soldiers . . . little girl," in Mama's voice.

"Not . . . blood daughter."

"No less distraught."

"Do with . . . toes?"

I know I got a extra toe, but Mama always said it's fun to be a little bit special. Why are they fretting about it now?

"She knows . . . last of orphans," Mama said. "Thinks . . . still here . . . your father decreed."

"Decreed? . . . hasn't forgiven you. Anybody comes forward . . . hell itself to pay, and not just for . . . put . . . mission . . . prison."

"Prison?" Tommy gasped.

"Hopkins . . . angry."

"Army . . . the boy?"

At the word *army*, Tommy's tummy began hurting, and he started to shake so bad Woobydog snuggled closer to him.

She whimpered a little, but he grabbed her snout and whispered, "Shush."

There was a long quiet time, then Tommy heard his mother continue, "If Carleton . . . back."

"Bigger problems . . . child."

Prison? Army? Child's a problem? Tommy could not keep track of the scary bunch of words. He pushed his ear harder to the door.

". . . kind of problems?" Mama asked.

"Things . . ." Through the door, it sounded like Papa's voice kind of got sad. ". . . you don't want to know."

Their voices lowered, but Tommy'd already heard enough. *Mama and Papa don't love me anymore. I'm not their little boy, I'm a problem.* Of a sudden, the air felt cold as winter. Shivering so hard it hurt, Tommy stumbled on stiff legs to his bedroom. Woobydog tipped her head and watched him pull off the nightshirt and dress quickly in his daytime clothes even though it was still dark outside. He pulled on his boots, the laces were kind of blurry though his crying, but he tried real hard and finally got them tied. He put on his too-big wool coat. He felt that same old scratchy on his neck, but the coat seemed not to warm him. In the food area the sad boy found four chunks of hardtack and two yellow apples, tied them up in a cloth and pushed them deep into his coat pocket.

He tiptoed to the front door, and Tommy and his dog stepped out into the night. It was as cold and scary as Aunt Millie's cellar, and there was no Clara to pat his arm and tell him it would soon be all right.

❧⋙

In the bedroom, Eva listened. Her husband said nothing, but his uneven breaths and occasional throat clearing told her he was awake, no doubt thinking . . . and worrying. After about an hour, his breathing became more regular, then transitioned to soft snoring.

Eva had no such luck. She lay on her side, back to her sleeping spouse. The little candle had long since sputtered itself out, so she stared into the darkness, silently weeping, praying for her troubled husband and pleading for a way to keep her son safe.

It felt like an eternity, but at last the room began to change from black to gray. Eva pulled on slippers and a long coat for a quick walk to the privy. On the way back, she broke through a thin skin of ice and rinsed her hands in the bucket by the front door.

Once inside, the first order of business was to rekindle the fireplace. She laid two boughs of dried brown pine needles onto the gray ashes, then blew to revive the orange coals beneath. When the tinder caught, she carefully added a few sticks, then two short logs. Before long, the fireplace was crackling. With the same technique, Eva got a fire in the cook stove going. Soon the cast iron top glowed, and she set on a blackened pan full of water.

"Thomas, get up," she called. "Cornmeal mush is almost ready." No response.

"Woobydog, where are you? Go wake that boy of yours." Nothing.

Stretching and yawning, Bennet stepped through the bedroom doorway. Eva looked up from stirring mush long enough to say, "Wake up Thomas, please."

Bennet returned directly. "The boy's bed's empty."

"Empty?"

"Nightshirt's in a heap. Clothes and coat are missing."

"Woobydog?"

"Gone too, far's I can tell," Bennet said through a frown.

The mother's blood ran cold as snowmelt, and her breaths came in painful shudders. *Is this it? The moment I swore to my* boy would never come? Has my beloved son been taken from his rightful home? For a moment she wished for death, then a sliver of reason returned. Perhaps he just rose early and is nearby. "Outside, Bennet. You explore the orchard, and I'll search nearer the house."

Bennet searched their acre tree by tree. Eva checked the privy, the corrals, vegetable garden, and barn, growing ever more frightened—and angrier. Nothing.

After a few minutes, they met back on the front porch. Eva forced the thought of abduction from her mind. Thomas left fully dressed, including coat, with his dog. The facts argue for simply running away.

"This is your doing, Bennet Dunning," Eva barked.

"Me?"

"At times, I think you can't stand the sight of your own son. If I can see that, mustn't he?" She gazed at nothing for a few unendurable moments, then continued, "Has to be with Clara. Ride on over to Gale's and bring our son home."

Bennet turned to go, then stopped suddenly and twisted back, speaking in low, angry tones. "You got no idea what a man can nor can't stand to see."

Eva watched him without reply. Were there tears in his eyes?

☙◆❧

"It's disgusting enough to make a girl gag—but a good breakfast, I guess. If you're a pig." Clara walked out the cabin door carrying a bucket of kitchen slop. Squinting against the sun, she almost tripped over Woobydog curled up on her front porch. Next to his dog was Tommy, back against the log wall, sound asleep.

"Tommy!" she laughed. Woobydog stood, then leaned over her front paws and stretched, but her boy did not budge until the dog gave his cheek a couple of wake-up licks. "What're you doing here?"

He stood and rubbed his eyes. "Can't go back."

"You mean *home*?" Her friend looked to have been crying.

"Papa said I'm not his boy. I'm just the problem."

"What problem?"

Tommy shrugged his square shoulders. "I don't know. Something about prison and a army."

None of it made sense to Clara, so she directed her attention back to the drudgeries. "Come along, you can slop the hog for me," she said, then handed over the very full bucket.

When they reached the pen, Tommy leaned over the fence rail and emptied the mess. "Disgusting," Clara said with a wrinkled nose. The eggshells, brown fruit rind, and guts and feathers of last night's chicken dinner smelled near as bad as the dirty sow. Clara complained a lot about the stinky pig, but the truth was, she felt sorry for the lowly creature. The pig lived in the worst of all possible conditions, only to someday have her throat cut as the reward for becoming grown. "Remember when she was a cute little piglet, Tommy?"

"I 'member. I holded the baby in two hands. You wanted to name her Peggy."

"That's right," Clara said. "But Ma said giving the sow a name would just make it harder when it was time to kill and eat her." The girl shuddered. "As if I'd eat something that's been living in that mess."

They finished the chore, then walked back and sat on the cabin's front porch. "So, where you heading?" she asked.

"Fishing hole's probably the best."

"The one up the creek path?"

"I'll catch my food, and drink's not a worry."

"Think your mama's gonna miss you?"

"At least I won't be a problem."

"Why don't you tarry here for just now," she said. "You can help me with chores, and then we'll play. Lots of time to run away later—if you still want to."

Tommy's brow furrowed in thought, but before he could answer, Ma opened the cabin door. "Thomas? How did you—"

The boy took off running, Woobydog close at his heels.

☙❧

The quakies were mostly bare, but scrub oak still glowed orange as a fresh-washed carrot. Tommy and Woobydog hiked for about an hour, then stopped for a rest. The fall day was warming up, and the trail was mostly uphill, so Tommy took off his coat and tossed it onto a big flat rock. While Woobydog explored lots of smells, Tommy crawled up on the speckled granite and spread the coat out like a thick blanket. He was warm and weary and soon drifted off, his body determined to make up for last night's lost sleep.

Loud barking shocked Tommy awake. He sat up and looked around, reorienting himself to the day. The barking was Woobydog, of course. He looked up the trail to see her growl and charge, then retreat with a backwards hop and charge again. *Must be some critter hiding in that patch of scrub by the trail.*

He ran in her direction. "Leave it, Woobydog!" She didn't hear—or chose not to obey. "Come here, girl." Tommy stepped closer, but the dog kept charging and retreating. "That's enough fooling about."

He put a hand on her back, and Woobydog whipped her head around, biting him on the wrist. It was no more than a scratch, but Tommy was staggered. His dog had never, ever turned on him before—but there she was, hackles raised, snarling him a warning.

Tommy stepped in front of her, and the dog's head turned to follow. She barked and growled at him. "Woobydog, is that a marmot or—" Tommy heard the buzzing rattles and froze in fear.

The dog leapt forward, but too late. Tommy saw a brown-black streak, then felt a stabbing hurt. The sharp fangs of a rattlesnake poked through his pants, jabbing his right leg just above the boot.

Not a second after the big rattler released his leg, Woobydog bit onto the thickest part of the snake's fat body. The hard muscles were a big mouthful and the sound of the buttons on the snake's tail was like a screech from Hades, but Woobydog bore down until her powerful jaws tore through and her long top and bottom teeth met. She threw her head side to side, probably trying to stay away from those curved needle teeth. When she whipped the snake to her right, its head slammed against her side, and she let out a high yelp. Tommy was having a hard time seeing, but it looked like Woobydog may have been bit. For a few seconds, his dog stood over the dead snake to make sure it couldn't hurt Tommy more.

He thought for a moment to stand, but his strength was already failing him. With the last of his energy, he reached for where the hurt was and held tight with both hands. *Feels like I was branded, like a calf. Want to move my hands away, but I'm too much afraid to see. What if there really is a hot iron jabbing into me?* He finally mustered the courage to pull up his pant leg and look. To his surprise, it wasn't smoldering—all Tommy saw was dark red skin and two dots of shiny blood.

The strength to sit failed him, and Tommy sagged onto his back. He squeezed his eyes shut against the blinding sun and mumbled a prayer to the sky. "Heavenly Father, seems I'll be with you in, in, uh, real soon." Only the hurt of his leg kept him from falling into sleep, and words were now so hard to find. "Forgive me for, for leaving my . . . for running off. Tell

Mama I'm sorr . . . sorry. And help her know I'm in y . . . your arms. In the name of Jesus—" The fading child paused, found barely grit enough to add, "And if Woobydog is also 'bout to die, help me find her in heaven."

~12~

Clara heard the yelling first. "Millie!" Tommy's papa was pounding the cabin door with the heel of his fist. "Hello? Hello?"

She stepped around the corner and hopped onto the porch. "Hi, Brother Dunning. Looking for Tommy?"

"He here?"

Before Clara could answer, her mother stepped out. "Was a smidge ago. Thought you knew."

"He was gone when we got up."

"Tommy was here, all right," Clara said, matter of fact. "Stopped by on his way to running away."

Brother Dunning's voice got softer. "How'd the boy seem?"

"Awful huffed, but not hurt," Clara said.

Brother Dunning knelt next to her. "Know where he's off to?"

"Headed up the trace to our fishing spot." She pointed to the mouth of a narrow canyon that split the nearby foothills. "Up that little creek."

Tommy's pa mounted Ginger and reined her toward the foothills.

❧❧

From somewhere up ahead, Bennet heard sharp screams alternating with lower moans.

79

"Thomas!" he called out. His horse rounded a bend in the trail and Bennet spotted him flat on his back a few yards from a bloody snake carcass. Woobydog was limping around him in helpless circles but the dog stepped aside when Bennet dismounted and dropped to the ground. He knelt in the dust and placed a supportive hand under his boy's head. "Papa's here, Thomas." He thought his son almost smiled. "What happened? Snake?"

"Leg," Thomas said in a labored whisper.

Bennet slid the pant leg up and gasped at a lump swollen to the size and color of a prize plum. He looked closer and saw poke wounds centered in the angry skin. "God help us," slipped out of his mouth before he could consider the impact of the words on his terrified little boy.

Bennet was no stranger to snakebite, he'd seen several victims, even treated two of them. *Never knew a grown to die by a rattlesnake. But a fifty-pound child? That's a horse of a whole different hue.* He heard a whimper and looked up to see Woobydog pacing, her gait unsteady even for a three-legged creature. "Sorry, dog—can't be worrying about you just now."

Bennet drew a hunting knife from the sheath at his side and regarded it for a few seconds. A four-inch fixed blade set in a handle he had crafted from a section of elk antler, the knife was an everyday tool, streaked with dirt and speckled with dried chicken blood. He gave it a wasted wipe against his shirt sleeve. "This'll hurt," he said, voice cracking. "I'm so sorry, Son." With the knife's tip, he made a half-inch-deep cut from one puncture wound to the other. A quick spurt of blood seemed to relieve some of the pressure.

"Didn't . . . hurt," the child mumbled.

Thank the Lord. "Afraid this will."

He positioned both thumbs and forefingers just beyond the lump, then hesitated. *Stay strong, Bennet. You know you got to do it.* He ground his teeth while he pinched the angry flesh with both hands like a giant boil. Poor Thomas writhed in obvious agony but didn't make a peep. More goo oozed out, some of it snake venom, Bennet prayed.

Next he used the crusty knife to cut a two-foot length from the end of the lead dangling from Ginger's neck. He tied the rope as snug as he dared around Tommy's leg, just above the bite. "Hope I'm not too late with the strap." Bennet reckoned most of the venom was already in the blood, weakening the child's ability to speak or even cry out with what had to be godawful hurt.

Almost as if she knew how bad things were, Ginger held stock still while Bennet laid Thomas belly-down on her back just behind the neck. He steadied the boy with one hand, held the horse's mane with the other and hauled himself up and on. From behind, he pulled his son up to a sitting position, then wrapped his arms around the boy to secure him. *Kiss-kiss* got Ginger moving at a gentle walk, as fast as Bennet dared. Woobydog hobbled alongside, falling further behind with each step.

❧

Clara stood frozen, watching the horse come around the last bend. "Tommy!" she screamed at the sight of him. The little boy did not respond. His body looked completely wilted, propped up on Ginger's back by his papa's arms.

Ma ran out the door. "What in the—"

"Boy's snakebit," Brother Dunning called out.

Clara gasped. "Heavenly Father, don't let him die."

"Bring him inside, Bennet," Ma hollered. "Clara, get blankets from your bed."

She ran in, climbed to her loft, and tossed bedding over the rail. Tommy's papa gently laid him onto the soft blanket pile, then looked to ma with eyes that begged for help. She knelt next to Tommy and laid her ear against his chest, hoping to hear a strong heartbeat, no doubt. Next, she put a palm on his forehead.

Bennet looked to Ma with eyes so very sad. "I done all I could."

"He's still with us, Bennet." She patted the back of the father's hand. "You go fetch Evie, while we tend to your boy." She turned to Clara. "Poor Thomas's burning up. Fetch me a wet cloth."

Clara returned in a wink with the cloth. "Keep his head and face damp," Ma said. "It'll help with the fever." She gave a vigorous nod, then leaked a few tears as she pressed the damp and cool rag to the poor boy's brow.

"That feel good, Tommy?" He maybe responded, but with no more than a groan.

"Ma! He can hear me."

Ma shared a little smile. "That's wonderful, Clara Alice. You keep on telling him he's gonna be all right. Give him a measure of hope."

☜☞

Clara guessed an hour had passed since Ma sent Tommy's papa to fetch Aunt Evie and the wagon. For the entire time, she'd knelt at her best friend's side, cooling his brow and wiping his face, stopping only to rewet the little rag. With freshly dampened fabric, she gently wiped some crust from around Tommy's eyes. He opened them halfway and said, "Clara . . . where . . . are . . . we?" Never mind the voice was weak, it was the first time he'd said real words.

"Hear that, Ma?"

She was checking the bad leg and spoke without looking up. "Surely a good thing, Sweeting."

But the boy's bloated calf was not so good. With a quick glance, Clara saw the purple reached all the way down to his six toes, now plumped like sausages about to burst their casings. She reached back and took hold of the knotted tourniquet. "Ma, let's loosen the rope a mite and raise up his leg."

"No!" her mother fairly screamed.

Clara felt tears in her eyes. *Why is Ma so—*

"Sorry about yelling. But that would of a certain hasten the poison to his heart."

Clara squinted her teary eyes shut and nodded her understanding. Then she tugged the dreadful rope yet a little tighter.

Moments later, she heard the approaching wagon and left Tommy's side long enough to open the door. "They're here!" she yelled. *It took such a scary long time. But they're finally here!*

Aunt Evie jumped down from the wagon and hurried into the house. "How is he, Mil?"

"Holding his own."

She knelt next to her son and whispered through her tears, "You'll be good as ever, Thomas. I'm here to make sure of it."

Clara smiled, but she couldn't help but wonder, *are there things even a mother's love can't fix?* She stayed close as Aunt Evie gave her son a head-to-swollen-toes looking over. Her little chest pounded, and her mind swirled in fear and blurry confusion. *Could my best friend be in heaven before this dreadful day is over? How could I ever make poor Woobydog understand? Where did that dog get to, anyway?* There was just one thing she knew for sure, poor Tommy's leg looked even worse than just minutes ago.

Aunt Evie interrupted the girl's thoughts. "Thanks for caring for my son, dear Millie," she said. "I'd like to get him home—what do you think?"

Ma nodded. "Yes. Wait much longer, he may be too bad off to travel."

Brother Dunning readied the wagon, then hopped down, ducked back into the cabin and scooped Tommy up as gently as he could. Aunt Evie followed, while he carried the little boy outside and laid him onto the quilts and blankets that padded the splintery wagon bed.

Clara took a wide stance in the doorway. "I'm going with."

Ma stepped up and laid a hand on her shoulder. "Don't reckon Aunt Evie needs another child to look after."

"Tommy needs me, Ma."

Aunt Evie looked to Ma with reddened eyes. "Maybe could use some help."

Ma nodded. "Then I'll get her coat."

"You hop right on up there next to Thomas, Clara," Aunt Evie said. "Think he's going to need you by his side."

There she is! Before Clara could climb into the wagon, she heard a little whine and spied Woobydog lying on her side on the porch, thick hair matted and darkened with sweat. "What's wrong, girl?" The dog looked at Clara and struggled to stand, but one leg folded and Woobydog tipped against the rough log wall then collapsed back down. *Poor pup must be hurt pretty bad.*

"Woobydog get bitten, too?" Aunt Evie asked.

"Don't know," Clara said. She stepped over and scratched the animal under its chin. "Whatever it is, we'll mend you up, too." She looked up to see her Aunt Evie give a little nod of agreement.

It was hard, but Clara lifted Woobydog to the edge of the wagon. Brother Dunning took the good dog from there and laid her next to Tommy. Then Clara climbed in and made a place on her friend's other side. At least the three pals were together—for now. She held Tommy's hand, talking low, not stopping. "You're going to be fine. A strong boy like you will heal fast. Me and Woobydog are right here. You'll be home soon."

Clara thought for a moment that Tommy tried to respond, but even a smile must have been more than he could muster. After a while, when Clara ran out of encouragements, she asked, "What now, Tommy? Story? Song?" He surprised her, mumbling something too low to be heard over the thumps and rumbles of the old wagon. *He meant song,* she concluded, so she began a hymn that Ma had told her helped thousands of Mormon pioneers through discouragement and grief.

> *Come, come, ye saints, no toil nor labor fear;*
> *But with joy, wend your way.*
> *Though hard to you this journey may appear*
> *Grace shall be as your day.*

Tommy gave Clara's hand a weak squeeze. She squeezed back, then finished:

> *Gird up your loins; fresh courage take.*
> *Our God will never us forsake;*
> *And soon we'll have this tale to tell,*
> *All is well! All is—*

Sobs soon overcame the little girl. *But it isn't. Nothing in the whole wide world is well.*

~13~

Parowan - October 15, 1859

E va leaned over the bed and kissed her son's forehead. It seemed to her like months, but just five days had passed since they'd brought poor Thomas home. She felt warmth on her lips, but gratefully not the fiery heat from before. Eva wept softly, speaking to her beloved boy who was delirious—in, but mostly out of—consciousness. "You'll come back to me when it's time, my beloved. For now, it's perhaps a blessing you're somewhere else."

Without a second's prelude, the horrific memory slithered back. More evil and oppressive than the worst of those other times, something heavy wrapped around her like a physical presence, held her hostage to her darkest recollection. "Please, Lord, not again," she begged aloud. But God chose not to block the vision from her mind's eye.

A leather blacksmith's apron, the fire-blackened frock slippery with her son's blood. The hunched old man who wore it never had a day of formal training, but everyone in the Iron Mission called Heber Samuelson "Doc" and trusted his medical advice. Four days prior, Eva had watched in terror as the blacksmith-surgeon inspected the dark, bleeding cavity where a third of her son's calf had sloughed away. "Boy'll be dead in two days if I don't take it." Doc Samuelson stated it as simple fact with neither apology nor evidence of compassion.

An hour later, he sawed off Thomas's right leg just below the knee. How could her poor husband have endured it, he and Grandfather Dunning holding the child steady while the butcher did his deed? But Bennet said throughout the unimaginable ordeal, their son did not scream nor cry out. It seemed the little boy's unconscious state was indeed a blessing.

Bennet stepped into the bedroom that he and Eva had given up to Thomas, and Eva's mind jumped to the present, grateful to have been pulled from her waking nightmare. He stood next to Eva, her body quivering when he laid an arm around her shoulder. "Any better?"

"Seems the fever broke."

"Doc Samuelson said that's a good sign, right?"

She managed a feeble nod. "He did."

Bennet cleared his throat, then said, "Eva, my father is here."

She responded with a noncommittal hike of her shoulders.

"He'd like to see the boy."

"*The boy*? Again?" Eva wriggled out from under her husband's arm, then stood to face him. "How about *Thomas*, or *grandson*?"

Bennet's response conveyed neither anger nor sarcasm, "My father would like to pay Thomas a visit. May he see his grandson, Eva?"

Her head sank. "Of course. I'm sorry. It's just been so—"

"Painful. I know." He kissed her cheek then stepped out to fetch his father.

Warren Dunning entered the bedroom behind his son, and Eva stood. She immediately noticed the bishop wore his dark, vested suit and a somber expression, suggesting to Eva that this may be more a bishop's errand than simple visit from a concerned grandfather.

Bishop Dunning stepped to Eva's side and patted her shoulder in that condescending way that made her gut churn. "How are you faring, Sister Eva?" he asked in a cloying tone.

"I'm well." She paused, then continued. "Your grandson is still fighting for his life."

Father Dunning seemed unaffected by what Eva had intended as obvious sarcasm. "But Bennet said he's doing better."

"Fever finally broke," she said.

"Thanks be to God."

"Amen," Bennet added.

"Sister Eva." The Bishop motioned for his daughter-in-law to sit down, then stood next to her at the edge of the bed. "Do you see the Lord's hand in this?"

"God's hand?" Eva blurted. "How can you even—"

"It seems He's given us a message that we erred in not returning the boy to his own people."

Hot blood rose into her neck and face, and angry words escaped her mouth. "If you're saying God sent a serpent to plague my son for what I—"

"For what we all did. And I didn't claim it was a punishment. Perhaps a gentle reminder that we are not the child's rightful wardens."

"Gentle reminder?" Eva leapt to her feet, glowering at the pious old man. "Maybe, just maybe, this *was* a message from God. And the message is, 'My daughter Eva, it is so important for *you* to raise your son—for Thomas to be taught the gospel of Jesus Christ among the saints—that I have sacrificed his leg to make sure it is so.'"

Her logic seemed lost on both men. Warren spoke first. "Whatever does losing his leg have to do with the boy staying here?"

"It was his right leg, his right foot." The men regarded her with blank stares. "The army is looking for a boy with eleven toes. The boy, my Thomas, now has but five."

For a moment, neither man had a response. Then the bishop spoke. "Dear girl, do you truly believe God would take his leg to keep him here?"

"The God I know and love, the God who delivered Thomas to our keeping, would do no such thing." She leaned in, staring deep into her father-in-law's eyes. "But the thought's no more far-fetched than the Creator of Heaven and Earth inflicting unspeakable agony on a little boy . . ." She paused for breath and courage. ". . . to teach us a senseless lesson."

"Sister Eva." The bishop cleared his throat and, in a voice, thick with pomposity said, "Your husband and I have talked the matter over."

"My husband?" She turned and fixed her glare on Bennet. "The matter?"

"The boy is welcome to stay if . . ."

There was a long and awful pause, then Father Dunning continued, ". . . if you agree to Bennet marrying Widow Shand."

Eva gasped. The conversation had taken such a sudden turn—from preposterous theology to despicable blackmail—that it took her a few seconds to recover from the whiplash. When she finally caught her wind, she broke into uncontrolled laughter.

The bishop's forehead wrinkled with apparent confusion. "Sister Eva, I fail to see—"

"The joke? The pathetic, bad jest?" Eva locked her eyes onto her husband, a man so cowardly his father had had to make the threat. "Marry the cow," she laughed. "Jab her with that whore pipe every night. Why should I give a good God-damn?"

The profanity seemed to startle the men into silence. Eva knew with just two words she had trampled a commandment of God as well as the law that Brigham Young had declared for his Utah Territory. *But right now,* she thought, *I truly do not give a good God-damn.*

After nearly a minute of stunned silence, she continued in softer tones, "Please leave now. Both of you." She stayed strong until the awful men left the room, then hung her head, bitter, frightened tears trickling from her cheeks and onto her sleeping son's nightshirt.

~14~

Carrollton, Arkansas - March 12, 1860

R uby turned the old wagon onto Carrollton's Center Street. Now half a year since the Buggy Parade, a dozen townsfolk walked the street, about their daily doings with no apparent thought of events which so recently had hallowed the ground. Above them, a few decorations remained in place. Tattered and faded, what bunting had endured still held the joy—and aching—of the remarkable day.

After stopping the two-horse team, she thought to hand the reins over to her husband seated next to her. But she hesitated. "Sure you'll be right without me for a while?"

After a long siege of pneumonia, Harold was finally well enough to get dressed without her helping and to take meals at the kitchen table. But the short wagon ride to the Carrollton coach station was a big step—the first time in a month the man had ventured further from his house than the backyard privy.

Harold smiled. "Hop on down. I'll be right as rain, time you're back."

Ruby leaned over and kissed the stubbled face of her best friend, the man who'd swept her off her feet those years ago, when both were thin and limber. Time had thickened them both, writ lines and furrows in their skin like maps of memories made together. They'd cherished and protected one another for so long, it pained her to think that the day would surely come when one would be called home to Jesus, the other left to face the dreary world alone.

She climbed from the seat and retrieved her travel case from the wagon bed. "Don't overdo it, old man," she chuckled. "I'll be home in a week." She took a few timid steps, then glanced back to see him giving her a little get-on-with-it wave with the back of a ham-sized hand.

Ruby turned to confront a heavy wooden door adorned with a striking design: a black circle over a dark red diamond. Gold leaf lettering filled the ring: *Wells Fargo & Co. Express.* She pulled it open and walked inside.

The man behind the desk raised his head. "Good day, ma'am," he said and looked her up and down. She cared not a whit, but idly wondered what he saw. *Plain* was the word most likely to describe her. Her dress was clean, in good repair—and plain. In color and arrangement, her graying hair was unadorned, and most would say her face was unremarkable. But blessed with height above most men, she was impossible to ignore.

Ruby acknowledged him, then parted with two dollars for the three-day trip. "Highway robbery," she said.

The agent looked a bit put off. "That joke's pretty much wore out here, ma'am."

"Uh, sorry," she managed. *Look at you, Ruby Seddon,* she smiled to herself. *Making a joke and not even knowing it.*

"Coach'll be here in an hour or so," the agent said. He pointed to a wooden bench polished with use. "Make yourself comfortable."

As soon as she sat, Ruby thought, *This uneven hunk a ironwood's anything but comfortable. Guess he's the one just made a joke.*

જેન્ક

An hour-and-a-half later, the coach stopped in front of the little ticket office. The driver loaded Ruby's case onto the roof compartment of the red and gold Wells Fargo stagecoach, then took her elbow and helped wedge her into the last available space—between two large men who seemed ignorant of the fact most folks bathed themselves every week or two. The rig rocked to one side when the large man climbed back to the driver's perch. There was a loud whistle and the clomps of six horses taking their first steps. She took in breath as deep as possible, crushed as she was between two men the size of prize hogs. *Putting it in the best light, I'll have plenty of time to plan for my big meeting with Senator Mitchell.*

મ

Funny they call it Little Rock. Nothing little about this here city. The unpleasant trip had gone by quickly, and Ruby now shared a proper board sidewalk with what felt like half the town. The early spring air was cool and carried the unmistakable smell of bread baking somewhere nearby. She turned a corner, and the grandeur of the Arkansas Statehouse suddenly revealed itself. A two-story cube the size of a mansion jutted out from the center. Along its front stretched a marble portico, the overhanging roof supported by four columns. Behind the main hall, long wings stretched to the left and right. *Building looks so fresh and clean, it could have been whitewashed just yesterday.*

Ruby was soon inside, seated comfortably on an upholstered couch in a small anteroom. She waited patiently for her time with the senator, and after about ten minutes, the tall wooden door groaned open. A squat, white-haired woman stood in the doorway, smiling graciously. "Welcome to Little Rock, Mrs. Seddon." She gestured to the open doorway. "The senator will be pleased to see you now."

Ruby stepped into the office, and the secretary left, closing the door behind her.

Senator Mitchell stood in front of a wide oak desk, a welcoming smile on his face. "Good afternoon, Mrs. Seddon. It's lovely to see you again." He took her hand in both of his and gave it a firm shake, then gestured to a nearby chair, finer than any she'd ever imagined. "Please set down." After the wooden stage seat, it felt like sinking into a pale blue cloud surrounded by oak shelves polished to a shine and filled to the ceiling with more books than a body could read in two lifetimes.

The senator stepped around and took the big chair behind the desk. "How're the town's children faring?"

"Ain't been easy for them, Senator, what with all they been through."

He gave a sympathetic nod. "Been sorely troublesome for my Prudence and Georgia Ann, too. It maybe gets a bit better every day."

"Anyways, thanks to you for agreeing to see me, Senator."

"Ruby, may I call you Ruby?"

"Of course, sir."

"Back in Carrollton I promised to tell you if I received more information."

"I assumed that's why you invited me here, sir."

"Two things will surely be of interest to you. First, the rumor I spoke of back then persists. I emphasize that it has not been confirmed, but a few continue to share stories that there's one last of our young'uns still with the Mormons."

"How old?"

"According to the gossip, a boy. Most likely six or seven."

"Marvelous! I just need to travel to the Utah Territory and fetch my Levi."

Mitchell shook his head. "That may be a fair bit harder to do than speak it, Ruby."

"Sakes alive, it don't sound easy."

Senator Mitchell's gaze seemed to reach beyond the room. He clasped his hands as if in prayer, chewing softly on his thumbs, nervous or deep in thought. Or both. "There's another important scrap of information," he said.

"There is, sir?"

"Major Carleton's thinking more and more about the possibility our folks was killed by the Mormons, not Injuns."

"There's been that kind of talk for more'n two years."

"Indeed." Mitchell nodded. "And if it's true, the Mormons will do anything to try and hide their secret. Handing over your grandson would be tantamount to a confession they lied to Carleton before." Mitchell paused for a moment to rub his temple. "How old's your boy?"

"Levi was three when his folks was killed. So, six by now."

The senator's brow furrowed. "Old enough to remember what happened, perchance. And if they thought young Levi could give testimony against them—"

"As God in Heaven is my witness, Senator, I will rescue that child and wreak vengeance upon them Satan's spawn that killed his ma and pa."

Mitchell regarded Ruby without speaking. She guessed he felt the same white-hot mix of love and hate, fear and determination that coursed through her own veins.

"I believe you will," he said, then gave his silvered head a deliberate nod. "I honestly believe you will, Ruby." A moment's pause, then, "And I've a bit of an idea as to how you might proceed."

"I'm one big ear, Senator."

Mitchell sucked in a long breath, then began. "Few years back, on a trip to Chicago, I met an extraordinary man named Allan Pinkerton. Mr. Pinkerton was the first detective on the Chicago police force."

"Detective?"

"Investigator, a man who solves crimes. He's created a private detective agency. If anybody can find your grandson, Pinkerton can."

Ruby's face fell. "Private? Means I'd be obliged to pay him?"

"That's right."

The woman's chin sank to her chest. "Got to be honest, Senator. Harold and me's poorer'n Job's turkey."

Mitchell brushed the words away. "Maybe we can help each other."

"Not following your thinking."

"You talk to Pinkerton about your boy. If he reckons he can do something, I'll cover the fee, if . . . if as part of the investigation he can substantiate who murdered my family."

"You want the killers' names?"

"If possible. But mainly I got to know, once and for all, if it was Injuns or Mormons put my kin out of the way."

Tears filled Ruby's tired eyes. "Me too, Senator Mitchell. Me too."

"Can you board the train in the morning?"

Ruby's poor mind was fairly spinning. "*Tomorrow* morning?"

Senator Mitchell nodded. "I've already written to Pinkerton. Miss Finch will provide you pen and paper for a letter of explanation to Mr. Seddon."

A foggy mix of dread and anticipation now swirled through Ruby's head. But there was, of course, no answer other than, "Yes, sir."

"I suspected that might be your response." He slid a beautifully written document across the desk. Ruby picked the sheet up and scrutinized it—the words may as well have been Latin.

"Can you—"

"I can read it good enough, Senator. But I ain't no Blackstone lawyer."

Mitchell chuckled. "Fair enough. It's my promissory note affirming payment to Mr. Pinkerton. One thousand dollars to be used for expenses, an additional two thousand upon successful completion of the engagement."

"Land sakes!" Ruby gasped. "That's a fortune."

"Remember, Ruby, this assignment is as much for me as it is for you. Five of my beloved family members were murdered, and I've sworn the killers shall not go unpunished."

"Amen," she said with a solemn nod.

Mitchell pushed a second item, an envelope, across the wide desk. Ruby opened it to find more cash than she had ever seen at one time.

"Senator Mitchell, I can't rightly—"

"Travel in safety and comfort, dear Ruby. God speed you on your errand and may He reunite you with your precious Levi."

~15~

B alancing the well-worn family Bible on her lap, Ruby settled onto the train's wooden seat. Reading was to be her comfort as well as a way to pass time on the long journey, but the train was too loud to concentrate, and the words jumped and blurred with the constant lurching. She rubbed her gritty eyes, closed the book, and leaned her elbows on it like a small table. Hands clasped under her chin, she prayed in silence.

Oh God, most kind. I praise you, God and Creator of all. I confess before you that I'm weak and unworthy, in need of the atoning sacrifice of Jesus Christ, Savior of everybody what praises His name. Dear Lord, help me come safely to Chicago to meet Mr. Pinkerton. Guide his heart and bless the man to discover some way to return my grandson, Levi Cantrell. I'm sure you remember—you showed me the boy in a dream. Through the sacred name of Jesus— Wait, hold on a mite. I'm gonna stop talking, I mean thinking, now, but I want to stay in my prayer, if that's all right by you.

After half an hour of silent meditation, Ruby's breathing slowed to match the rocking of the train.

☙◦❧

The coal-fired steam engine was noisy, but for Ruby that was not the worst part of the trip. The train traveled through a cloud of its own smoke, dark with soot. The windows stood open throughout the daylight hours, and everything and everyone in every car became coated with a fine layer of the vile black powder.

Every three or four hours, a uniformed conductor walked the length of the train announcing an upcoming stop for fuel and water. Mostly the breaks were short, no time for much more than a turn in the station's toilet and to maybe buy a slice of bread and a few dried apricots. During the longer stops, Ruby hurried to brush off her clothing the best she could, then wipe the grime from her face and hands with a handkerchief dampened in the station's rain barrel.

After three long days and nights of this routine, the train finally stopped in St. Louis, roughly halfway between Little Rock and Chicago. The boilerman bled off pressure in a long, loud hiss. Ruby hefted her single suitcase, tucked the Bible under her arm, and stepped onto the wooden platform into nightfall and a cloud of condensing steam. The conductor'd announced a thirty-minute stop, but Ruby would not be reboarding. Deep in one of her dress pockets she had a ticket for the Chicago Express, leaving at 8:30 the following morning.

Ruby had never before had the money nor the occasion to rent a hotel room, but Senator Mitchell made her promise she'd spend the twelve-hour break sleeping in a bed rather than on a wooden bench at the train stop. In spite of the senator's insistence, she may well have caught a nap at the station and saved the money for later—but she felt the coal grime in every fold and wrinkle of her aging skin. She would be happy to rent a room, so long as a bath was included.

It was full dark outside, but navigating by gas streetlamps, Ruby soon stood in front of a plain looking place called The Station Hotel. Coal oil lamps from some of the rooms illuminated enough windows for Ruby to gauge the three-story building as less than a third the size of the Arkansas statehouse. But all she needed was one room with one bed—bath included.

She stepped out of the early spring chill and into a cramped hotel lobby furnished with two identical sofas of dark walnut with red brocade and gold trim—nicer than the otherwise humble hotel deserved.

Behind a wooden table, the clerk set down his book and stood. He was about forty, dirty shirttail half untucked, dark trousers straining against an overhanging belly, his careless appearance in contrast to the fine furniture. Over the top of bent wire-rimmed spectacles, he regarded Ruby with eyes crinkled with what looked like suspicion. "Good evening, ma'am," he said without a hint of warmth. "Welcome to St. Louis."

"Likewise. I mean, thanks to you. How much for your smallest room?"

"They're actually all about the same size. Fifty cents for one night."

I expected the big city to be expensive, but four bits? "That include a bath and a steak dinner?" she joked.

The deskman seemed unamused. "No dinner. Bath's another quarter."

"Can I get me a bath but not a room?"

He shook his head. "No ticky, no laundry."

"Speak English, boy," Ruby shot back,

The look on the man's face said he didn't take kindly to being called *boy*. "My, oh my, look at the time. In thirty seconds, the price doubles to a buck-fifty."

Ruby flushed with anger but considered her alternatives before responding, "Towel's included, right?"

"That'll be an extra—" Her steely glare stopped him mid-sentence. "Towel's included."

"Best get on with it, then," she said through gritted teeth. Ruby turned her back to the man and fished a dollar from its hiding place. She swiveled around and paid, then tucked the two-bits change next to the train ticket in her pocket.

After recording her name and address in the log, the proprietor handed her a triple-notched skeleton key. "Room 225. I'll bring your luggage up."

"I dragged this lot from Carroll County, Arkansas," she said with a shake of her head. "Ought to be able to heave it up a flight of steps."

Ruby struggled with the narrow stairway, but the climb was less daunting than facing a man expecting her to tip him the change she had just put away.

He called after her, "Tub's in the basement. It'll be ready in ten minutes."

The room was sparse, no furniture but a narrow steel-spring bed with graying comforter—a porcupine of feather quills. Ruby unpacked a change of clothing and laid it on the bed. It was still a few minutes until the bath was ready, so she checked the letter and the money. Both were exactly where she'd concealed them.

❧

In the dim light of a single lamp, the basement room was eerie and damp, smelling of molded straw that lined the floor. "A downright dismal space. But I reckon the bathtub's down the basement for a reason—water don't usually run uphill."

Shivering against the cellar's chill, Ruby placed her clean clothes on a small table near the bath. "Am I taking a bath or getting pickled?" She laughed aloud. The "tub" was half a wooden barrel, its graying staves hugged tight by deeply pitted iron hoops. It was already filled with clean enough looking water, so she undressed. She stepped up on the nearby stool, raised her leg—then changed her mind and brought it back. Instead, she dangled a hand in to test the temperature. "Ooh!" she gasped. "That there's 'bout half-a-minute short of a iceberg."

Ruby steeled herself with a deep breath. "Guess I paid the quarter to clean up, not for a warm soaking. Best git gittin'." She climbed in and washed as well as she could with the small handkerchief and no soap. Two shuddering minutes later, Ruby stepped out of the darkened bathwater, dried herself off, and quickly dressed in fresh clothing.

On the trip back to her room, she noticed the disheveled clerk was not at his station, so she let go the damp and darkened towel on the floor next to his desk.

Back home in Carroll County, the only sounds after dark were crickets and the occasional baying hound. St. Louis, however, was a long way from Arkansas. For most of the night, horses, carriages and chatty folk passed just below Ruby's open window. Normally the hullabaloo would have made it impossible to sleep, but after three nights of restless dozing on a hard train seat, she soon gave in, not so much as turning over until light woke her.

After the bath and a full night's sleep, she felt energized—ready for whatever was to come.

~16~

Ruby stowed the valise under her seat on the Chicago Express. A uniformed conductor entered the car and called, "Tickets please." She gave him a satisfied grin and produced hers from one of two deep dress pockets. The man punched and returned it, and Ruby leaned back into the seat she shared with the big Bible.

A slender woman, likely in her late forties, stopped at Ruby's section. She wore a deep blue dress with white bib and frilly cuffs of first-rate linen. It was the finest clothing Ruby'd ever seen—and she'd been to Little Rock.

"May I?" the city gal asked, pointing to the empty seat directly across.

"'Course," Ruby said.

She sat herself down and said, "Good day to you, madam," with a kind smile.

Ruby smiled back. "A good day it is." She patted the bench. "Seats on this train's upholstered. Should make for a comfy ride."

Her travel mate nodded. "But still a long one."

"Three days till Chicago, ticket man said."

"I'm afraid so."

"That's just fine by me." *Got lots of thinking and planning to do. And of course, my Bible reading.*

"By the way, I'm Mrs. Martha Goring." She leaned forward and extended a hand, smooth as a baby's.

"Ruby Seddon. Pleased to meet you, Mrs. Goring."

"Please call me Martha. Do I distinguish a southern accent?"

"Born and bred in Arkansas. But it seems to me you're the one with the accent."

That gave Martha a small chuckle. "Moving north to escape the war, Ruby?"

"Ain't no war, so far as I know."

The conductor called, "All aboard," and the train began to move in fits and starts so jerky it seemed the locomotive had not fully made up its mind.

Martha cleared her throat, a sure indication she had more to say. "My husband says a war between the states is coming—very soon."

Ruby smiled without speaking. *Bite your lip, Ruby Seddon. No way you're getting into that chinwag.*

⌘

The train had been underway about three hours, time Ruby'd spent staring out the window and mentally practicing what she planned to say to Mr. Pinkerton. She yawned, more from boredom than fatigue, then reached for the Bible next to her. *May's well start with the Ten Commandments.* Ruby quickly turned to Exodus 20. She drew a sharp breath—the commandments were still there—Senator Mitchell's letter and the hidden money were gone.

"No!" she yelled, waking Martha. "It just can't be." Ruby fanned wildly back and forth through the pages. She stood, held the heavy book by the spine and shook it. Nothing dropped out. Not only was the cash gone, there was no promissory note. The source of her financing had disappeared along with the address of Pinkerton's Detective Agency.

"What's wrong?" Martha asked.

"It's gone!" Ruby gasped. "He stoled it!"

"Stole what?"

"Everything. Well, all but my last twenty-five cents, which I'll surely require to feed myself these next three days."

Martha came across to the empty seat next to Ruby. She put a comforting arm around her shoulder, then offered a dainty handkerchief. Ruby hesitated at first, but she finally took the delicately embroidered cotton and began to mop her tears. She spent the next hour sobbing her way through a story beyond anything Martha Goring could likely have imagined.

When Ruby finally took a breath, Martha interjected, "High time we rid this great country of those twin relics of barbarism— polygamy and slavery."

"How's that?" Ruby asked.

"I'm traveling to Chicago for the convention."

Ruby was no more enlightened.

"Republican Party," she said. "Can't vote, of course. But I'm going to show support for Mr. Lincoln."

Ruby felt the hair on the back of her neck stiffen. She and everyone she knew held Abraham Lincoln in the uttermost disdain. He was not simply misguided, the man embodied evil, determined to start a war that would force brother to fight brother to the death.

"When he's elected, he'll finally free the slaves and hopefully end the barbarity of polygamy. It sounds like your poor grandson is a victim of both."

"A veritable fact. I've good reason to believe the boy's being held slave in the home of some filthy Mormon priest and his harem of whores, uh, pardon the language."

Martha looked at her, kind eyes welling up. "I'm so sorry. I wish there were something I could do to help."

Just told you I'm flat broke. How about borrowing me a dollar or three? Ruby was too proud to ask, and Martha did not offer.

☙❧

After three long days and nights on the train, Ruby and Martha stepped down into Chicago's Union Station, a scene of barely controlled bedlam. Hundreds, maybe thousands, of people bustled about, each well-dressed traveler with a case and, Ruby guessed, their own story about what they were running from or heading to.

Martha embraced Ruby and spoke into her ear, "May God bless you with success." Then Martha melted into the crowd, swept away into a fearsome new world Ruby could never have imagined. Weighed down by dread far heavier than the Bible and suitcase she carried, Ruby picked a direction at random and began moving. After ten frustrating minutes elbowing her way through the throngs, she sat down on her case and sobbed. *Five hundred miles from home, more alone than you've ever been, and five cents to your name. What you gonna do now, you wretched, soot-covered soul?*

She wiped her eyes and started walking again—no destination, just a powerful need to get further from the train station's crowds, find somewhere she could think more clearly. After half an hour, she stopped and looked around. Tall buildings, more than she could have thought possible, loomed side by side in unbroken canyon walls. Unbelievably, the wide street still bustled with pedestrians, people on horseback, huge wagons and men pushing sideless wooden barrows heavy with burlap sacks. A policeman stood in the spot where another street crossed hers, blowing his whistle and waving his arms, mostly unheeded by the mob.

Dodging traffic, Ruby finally managed to get across the busy street and enter the front door of the rickety looking Lake Hotel. Against the far wall was a cage that held a small man with a green eyeshade and long sleeves held up by arm garters. "How long?" the man asked without looking up.

"How long for what?"

He leaned left and spat into a tarnished brass spittoon. "How long, as in how many days you staying?"

"Oh. Won't be needing a room. You know the offices of the Pinkerton's Detective Agency?"

He thought for a moment. "Could be somewhere on West Water."

"I'm new in these parts. Where do I—"

"Other side of the river."

"How do I get there from here?" she asked. The ill-mannered man just picked up a quill and went back to his paperwork without ever having looked up.

Ruby found the bridge without much fuss. It was less than thirty yards end-to-end, but the traffic was clotted and slow, and it took twenty long minutes to carry her things across. The endless crowds were not all that made the crossing disagreeable— the foul-smelling river below seemed the final destination for the contents of the city's privies.

She made it to the other side without incident, turned right at the first street and immediately encountered a noisy cluster. Many carried signs: *Honest Abe for President, Nominate Wm. H. Seward.* The chanting and yelling were painful to Ruby's ears, and she skirted the gathering the best she could. As soon as she'd escaped the throngs, she caught the attention of a young woman pushing a baby carriage. "Pardon me, Miss. You know if this here street's the West Water?" The woman stopped, but Ruby noticed she kept some distance between them. "Looking for Pinkerton's Detective Agency. Supposed to be on West Water."

"Yes, you're on West Water," the woman said, a bit of nervous tremor in her voice. "I think Pinkerton's is somewhere in the fourteen-hundreds."

Ruby was stumped. "Not sure what that means."

The woman pointed left. "The address, the number on the building, is south fourteen-something. Please excuse me, I have an appointment."

"Of course, thanks so much for—" The young mother was already out of earshot.

It's on this here street. Sounds like I just have to walk down along the river for a bit. Be there in a jiffy, no doubt. Ruby began walking, buildings to the left, the road and waterway on her right. As she strode, she looked for numbers on the buildings she passed. *Praise the Lord, 1501. Got to be nigh unto it now.*

The next door began the 1400s, but it turned out Pinkerton's was nowhere in that block. *What you going do now, Ruby gal?*

She pulled open a heavy door marked *First Chicago Bank, 1393 N. West Water* and stepped through. Just inside, she encountered a burly man, heavily armed and wearing a constable-looking uniform. "Excuse me, sir," she said.

Something—coal-darkened clothing or perhaps her manner of speech—caused the guard to straighten up and rest his right hand on the butt of a holstered pistol. "Do you have business with the bank, ma'am?" was his measured reply. *Lordy, I know I look more'n a bit disheveled, but felonious? The man seems to be thinking on shooting me.*

"No, sir." Ruby noticed the guard's back stiffen even more. "Just a question. You seem like a fella might know where I can find me the Pinkerton's Detective Agency. My business is with Mr. Pinkerton."

The man's bearing immediately softened. "The private eye? Yes, ma'am. It's a matter of fact that I've been there myself a few times—intending to become employed." Ruby encouraged him with a smile, and he continued, "Pinkerton's is on this street, West Water number 1425."

"That just ain't possible," she said. "Walked this entire block two times and found hide nor hair of them."

The big man broke into a friendly laugh. "This is *North* West Water, ma'am. Mr. Pinkerton is 1425 *South* West Water."

Ruby scratched her head in consternation. "North, South, West—can't make a lick of sense out of any of it."

"It's easy enough," he said. "Just keep going south." He pointed in what she assumed was a southerly direction. "The numbers will count down to naught, then start back up."

"Right strange, but I reckon I got it," Ruby said. "How far is it to the Pinkerton's, then?"

"Can't be much more than three miles. You can hail a hansom right out front—cost you maybe ten cents."

She nodded. "Much obliged. You have a blessed day, now."

Ruby carried her luggage back out to the street. *Three more miles, huh? Riding in a buggy would be nice.* Then Ruby reached deep into her pocket and fumbled with its meager content. She gave a resigned shrug. *Guess a bit more a walking won't do me no hurt.*

~17~

About an hour later, Ruby stood in front of the door she was seeking. The words "Pinkerton's National Detective Agency" formed the shape of a wide-open eye. Inside the oval, in smaller lettering, "We never sleep." Ruby gripped the door's latch but let go before turning it. Her brow wrinkled with fret.

What am I going to say to the man? Got no appointment, the Senator's letter of introduction's lost. She gave her damp and gritty face a light feel, then glanced down, in a mood to match the dark of her coal-dusted clothing. Ruby sagged under the weight of fear and fatigue—and sheer hopelessness. *I'm filthy as a chimney sweep. If Mr. Pinkerton'll even talk to me, can't imagine he'll take this old lady serious. Best just hang up the fiddle and high-tail it back to Arkansas where I belong.*

She plunged a hand into her pocket. The second half of her roundtrip ticket was still there. All she need do was turn around and—

She swiveled to her right, and into a glint of sunshine mirrored from a nearby window, a cheering warmth upon her cheek. *God's grace, of a certain.* She filled her lungs with air and courage. *You're not here for yourself, Ruby Seddon. You made the awful trip for that sweet young boy so far away from kith and kin.* She turned the latch and stepped inside. The little foyer was empty but for a couple of chairs. Not a person on sight. "Hello?" Ruby called out.

A door opened and a man appeared. "Allan Pinkerton, at your service."

She held out a hand and he shook it with vigor—and a strength she'd not expected from a man his size. "Hello, Mr. Pinkerton. I'm Ruby Seddon out of Arkansas."

He ushered her into an office, small but smartly furnished. "Please sit, madam," he said, motioning to one of two visitor chairs. Mr. Pinkerton took his seat behind the desk.

"'Tis a pleasure to finally meet ye, Mrs. Seddon." The man Senator Mitchell had said was a former Chicago policeman was six inches shorter than Ruby but made a larger-than-life impression. He was middle forties, apparently not yet in need of spectacles. She looked into his piercing brown eyes and thought, *It'd be a rough cob that could lie to that man.*

"Pleasure's all mine, Mr. Pinkerton. Hope you can excuse my appearance."

He cast a knowing look. "Came straightway from the railway terminal, did ye, Mrs. Seddon?"

Ruby managed a little smile. "That I did, sir. And I'd be pleased to have you call me Ruby."

"Well, Ruby, coal dust or none, you're sure bonny enough to brighten this humble office." He spoke with more than a hint of . . . something.

Ruby fought back a tear. "I'm frankly stunned by your warm reception, sir."

"Received a telegram from Mitchell the week before." Mr. Pinkerton gave a friendly laugh. "Been expecting ye any day."

Ruby looked quizzically at the smaller man. "Your manner of speech is new to me, sir."

Pinkerton nodded and smiled. "I'm born a Scotsman. Came across at age twenty-three. Now twenty more years along, I'm surely too old to be changing my ways."

"That's a thing I understand," Ruby chuckled.

Mr. Pinkerton stood in response to a knock. "Please excuse me, madam." He opened the door to reveal a woman with long, walnut brown hair. She was in her late thirties, about

Ruby's height. But where Ruby was thick and sturdy, the woman at the door was whip thin, her face drawn and narrow.

"Mrs. Seddon, this is Mrs. Kate Warne, my employee." Kate stepped closer and shook Ruby's hand with a strength that seemed unlikely for a woman so slight of frame. Pinkerton pointed to a third chair. "You've come at just the right time, Kate." Ruby expected Mrs. Warne to produce paper and pen and commence taking notes. She did not.

"We've a bairn to find." Pinkerton slid forward in his chair and gave the back of Ruby's hand a reassuring pat. "So, let's get down to the brass tacks."

"First off, I got to tell you I ain't got the Senator's promise note," Ruby said. "Some piece of human trash in St. Louis stole it."

The detective's eyes seemed to brighten at the mere mention of a crime. "Who took it?" Pinkerton asked.

"Hotel clerk, I'm guessing."

His eyes went even brighter. "Used a master key whilst you were out?"

"Likely so, Mr. Pinkerton. In any case, my money and the note's gone for good."

"Yes, of course. But worry yourself no more, dear lady. I know the senator to be a man of his word." He paused for a moment, then said, "On with the business at hand. Tell me about your grandson so we can devise a strategy that'll get the wee one back home where he surely belongs."

Over the next half-hour, the three ignored the sounds of rowdy men and the smell of sweating animals and their manure that entered from an open window. Pinkerton took copious notes, while Ruby recounted the story. Then she spent another hour answering a heap of questions from Mr. Pinkerton and Mrs. Warne. At the end of the ninety minutes, Ruby was still not certain why the other woman was in the room.

"Let me recite the very real challenges we face," Mr. Pinkerton said.

Ruby prayed the list of problems would be short.

"First off, I've no agents anywhere in the West. Secondly, every single one of my men here are—" He stopped himself as if he were about to reveal some secret. "Are currently engaged. The third problem is the danger. We'd be conducting an investigation in a land ruled by a tyrant. Best believe Brigham Young has eyes and ears in every nook and cranny of the Utah Territory. And if rumor is truth, he'll not think twice about hanging anyone taken for a traitor."

Ruby's head sank. "Sounds pretty much impossible."

Pinkerton walked around the desk and placed a hand on Ruby's sagging shoulder. "It does appear as black as the Earl o' Hell's waistcoat. But that's why Mrs. Warne is here."

Ruby's thoughts swirled in confusion. *Earl a Hell? Don't reckon that's in my Bible. And I'm still not sure what this woman's—*

"Five years ago," Mr. Pinkerton said, "recently widowed Kate walked into this office and asked for a job. When I hired her, she was the first woman detective in all the world, so far's I ken. And she's proven over and again to be one of my finest."

"Thank you, sir," Kate said. Then she turned to Ruby. "I think as a woman I can work myself into the midst of the Mormons without arousing suspicion." Ruby was stunned but managed to give Kate her full attention. "With the travel, it will take some time, several months. Can you be that patient?"

Ruby clenched her teeth in sheer determination. "I'll do anything to rescue my Levi."

"That's the spirit," Pinkerton said. "As they say back home, 'Tis a lang road that's no goat a turnin.'"

Ruby gave a palms-up shrug. "Meaning?"

"Things will surely change for the better."

Ruby cracked a smile. *Man's got a way with them Scottish words of his.*

"You'll need to stay another day or two to work out some details with Kate," Mr. Pinkerton said. Can ye do that, then?" Ruby heard confidence in the man's voice.

"Actually, I— Of course," she said.

"There's two more things." His tone became more serious. "And they're important."

"I'm one big ear, Mr. Pinkerton."

"First, we don't know to a certainty the child's alive."

"He is," Ruby said. "I just know he is."

Pinkerton closed his eyes and massaged the bridge of his nose. "In any case, Kate can't bring the boy directly back to you."

"Did you say *cannot*? Then why're we even—"

"Kate's not blood kin," he said. "For her to just grab the boy up'd be kidnapping, plain and simple."

Ruby felt like she'd been kicked in the belly. "But this whole thing's about getting him back!"

"And that we shall—but it's going to take time. Kate'll have to locate him first, get the lay of the land, so to speak. Then at some point, a family member will need to go to the Utah—and it'll be rightly perilous."

Ruby leaned forward and glared at Allan Pinkerton. "I weren't born in the woods to be scared by no owl. Let's make it one trip—me and Mrs. Warne together."

"Kate'll be going in disguise," he said. "Not sure how we'd make that work for you."

"But I could—"

"Why don't you get some rest and we'll talk more tomorrow. Where're you staying, Mrs. Seddon?"

She looked up. "Still answer better to Ruby."

"What's the name of your hotel, Ruby? I'll arrange for a carriage."

"Got no hotel." She tried not to cry, but at that moment, three sleepless nights on a train, the stress of the larceny, and all the rest caught up with her. Ruby began to weep.

"Boardinghouse, then?"

Ruby sobbed quietly but did not respond.

Allan Pinkerton pulled his chair around next to hers. He took her hand and fixed her with those fierce eyes. "Of course—your money was poached along with Senator Mitchell's letter."

She nodded.

"Well, that's an easy repair." He stepped to a safe along the wall behind his desk and withdrew some bills. "Will twenty dollars keep you comfortable for a few days, then get you safely home again?"

"Can't take your charity."

"It's none of the sort, dear woman. I design to add it to the good Senator's bill," he said, a bit of twinkle in his brown eyes. "With a bit of interest."

Kate put her arm around Ruby and helped her up. "I'll ride along and make sure you've got a comfortable bed and a warm bath for the next two nights. And Mrs. Seddon, er, Ruby . . ."

"Yes?"

"Speak as little as possible. And if you're asked what brought you to Chicago, say you are escaping the South."

"But I'm not—"

"Feelings in the city are running high just now," Kate said. "You're of no use to your grandson if you don't live to bring him home."

"Chicago's near hell on earth, but after a bath, I can endure it two more days—with my mouth tight shut. Most likely."

~18~

Parowan - April 12, 1860

B ennet Dunning sat proudly astride Junior, a thick-chested stallion just over sixteen hands. Chestnut brown with random splotches of white, the big horse was the finest of the Shand's livestock holdings. From high in the saddle, Bennet prayed to the open sky. "Lord, I vow to be a good steward of these things you're about to bless me with. In the name of Jesus Christ. Amen."

As his eyes surveyed the home and surrounding property, Bennet's mind roamed back to events that had set the stage for his upcoming marriage. In January of 1851, Edward and Naomi Shand arrived in Parowan as part of a select group of Mormon immigrants. That first company included experienced metal workers from England, sent by President Young to mine and smelt the iron ore found in the Three Peaks area, red-dirt hills seven miles west of town. There was also a contingent tasked with building a wooden fort without delay.

As head of the Deseret Iron Works, Edward was a respected and well-to-do member of the community. But after just six years, tapped out deposits and workers longing for the green hills of their homeland shuttered the mine and smelter. The death of the industry did not mean financial ruin for Brother Shand, however. He'd invested well and soon moved from iron to overseeing fifty productive acres of grain and a herd of prime

Texas longhorns, possessions soon to be under Bennet's control.

Bennet reckoned Naomi's first husband made one miscalculation—and it proved deadly. Months after operations shut down, Edward returned in hopes of salvaging some abandoned equipment. He was deep in an underground shaft when he probably heard a heavy booming, thunder from a late summer storm. The resulting flash flood filled the mine with muddy water and deadly debris. Along with his lands and livestock, Edward Shand left behind a wife and three children.

He also left a sturdy two-story home built of fired adobe bricks, dark orange like the surrounding soil, designed according to traditional architecture from Coalbrookdale, Edward's hometown in England. Bennet found his new home pleasing to look upon—symmetrical, with double front doors that opened into a large central hall with massive fireplace. Identical wings ran right and left from the big hall, terminating in gabled rooms, each with its own fireplace.

It was a home well suited to their wedding celebration planned for the next afternoon.

დ√ა

A quiet but conspicuous presence seated at the head table on Bennet's immediate left, Eva Dunning picked at the meal of roast chicken and early garden vegetables. *A guest at my own husband's wedding. How perverse is that? Let me count the ways.*

The main hall in the home that Edward Shand built held the wedding party, mostly family. Nineteen adults sat around two more tables in the Shand's central hall. Four children, Naomi's three plus Thomas, sat at their own table. His new crutch propped against the back of his chair, Thomas ate without looking at or speaking to his new siblings.

After teenage girls cleared away the dishes, Bishop Dunning stood. "Brothers and Sisters," he said, holding up a crystal wineglass of unfermented grape juice. "I propose a toast to the happy couple."

"Hear, hear," one of the men called out.

Not really a couple, Father Dunning, Eva reflected. *There are three of us in this marriage, remember?*

"May their union bring immeasurable joy in this life and for eternities to come." His first wife, Genevieve, had died giving birth to Bennet, but to Warren's right sat his two current wives. Each was younger than he by at least twenty years, and each had the sad, resigned eyes of a woman twice her age.

Dunning touched his glass to his wives' with two little clinks. Once he'd taken a sip, the partygoers followed suit. "Now it's time for the young'uns to run outside and play," he announced.

Naomi's children were up and gone like a shot. In silent sorrow, Eva watched little Thomas struggle with his crutch and finally hobble out. As soon as her one-legged son had closed the front door behind him, Warren Dunning resumed, "And one more thing. May Bennet and Naomi be fruitful and multiply." He gave an exaggerated wink. "This old man needs some grandkids. Now let's clear out of here so they can get that part started."

The guests shared a hearty laugh, but Eva fought back angry tears. *Did you somehow forget you already have a grandson, Father Dunning? Were you not the one who brought Thomas to us and commanded that we rear him as our very own?*

❧❦

Tommy sat in the dirt, back resting against the home's brick wall. *Sure wish Aunt Millie was here—and Clara, of course. She's the only one who'll play with a one-legged boy who can't jump nor run.* He missed having Woobydog at his side, too. But at least she was fixed up. His dog had recovered from the snake attack in just a few days, something about a "dry bite," Papa said.

From his seat on the ground, Tommy watched Naomi's sons, twelve-year-old Karl and seven-year-old Kyle, in a confusing argument. "Liar," Kyle said. He gave the older boy a shove to make his point. "They don't do that."

Karl punched his brother in the chest so hard he nearly fell over. "Sure do, he said. Sticks it right inside her."

Kyle rubbed his sore chest and shook his head. "How could he even—"

"First it gets real stiff. You'll understand when you're a measure older," Karl said.

Like he's so smart, Tommy thought.

"Still don't believe it."

"Neither do I," Tommy whispered to himself.

Bess, the boys' older sister, arrived near the end of the strange chatter. "Tell him, Bess," Karl said. "Tell Kyle where babies come from."

Big sister wrinkled her nose in disgust. "I'm not talking about any of that with you miserable shoats." She pointed to Tommy. "Why don't we see what Pegleg has to say about it."

"Pegleg! That's funny," Kyle said. "Pegleg! Pegleg!"

The Shand boys laughed uncontrollably.

"That name's just stupid," Tommy muttered.

"What'd you say?" Bess demanded.

"Doesn't even make sense. I got a crutch, that's nothing like a wooden leg."

"Hey," Bess called to her brothers. "Guess the kid don't want us calling him Pegleg." The boys approached Tommy, but Bess got there first. He tried to stand, but the girl pushed him back down. The brothers laughed when she leaned into his face. "You're Pegleg now, boy. What we say goes." She reinforced the message with a hard slap to Tommy's cheek. "Best get used to it."

Tommy was tingling all over with anger, and when she turned her back on him, he grabbed up his crutch. From his sitting position, he swung it around such that the heavy wood caught Bess behind the knees, and she folded in a howling heap.

"What in blazes?" Sister Shand walked out the front doors just in time to see Tommy attack her daughter. Mama and Papa were right behind. She hiked up her white skirts and came at Tommy. He saw scared on Mama's face, she also set out on a run, but too late to help.

From the corner of his eye, Tommy saw Sister Shand's clenched fist fly at his temple, then the world went fuzzy gray. "Don't you never strike a girl," he heard through the fog. "Never. Learn how the world turns, boy," she hissed, "or suffer the consequences."

She clubbed him again.

Strangely, the second blow seemed to clear Tommy's vision just a bit. He saw his mama take a long leap, ramming her head into that other woman's big chest. Sister Shand went to the ground, and a short but angry wrestling match followed.

Tommy looked on helplessly as his papa's strong hands grabbed Mama by the back of the collar and yanked her off the woman who had hurt him. "What is the matter with you, Eva?" he yelled.

The fight lasted less than half a minute, just long enough, Tommy noticed, to destroy the white wedding gown. Sister Shand stood up and pointed a fat finger at Mama. "That woman is full-on daft," she screamed at Papa. "You'd best do your husbandly duty and keep the sow in her sty." She took a breath, then tried to dust herself off—it didn't really help. "The boy's got to have a firm hand," the angry woman said. "And if needs be, I'll provide it."

"Thomas, you go on into the house," Papa ordered.

Tommy was still real dizzy, scared and confused about everything. *Had Mama really just got in a fight with Papa's new wife? What would happen later, when they all got home?*

"Now, Thomas!"

He gathered up his crutch and hobbled back inside.

⌒⌒

"You heifer," Eva spat. "Touch my boy again and there'll be the devil himself to pay."

A mean smile split the bride's soiled visage. "*Your* boy? From what my husband tells me, he's no more yours than mine."

Eva exhaled in a ragged gasp—a physical punch could not have emptied her lungs any quicker. Unable to speak, she could only stare at the man who had violated a sacred confidence. That her husband would be spending this night coupling with another woman was appalling. But he had casually provided the witch the one spell that gave her power of life and death over her son—and that was unforgivable.

Probably sensing he had to do something, Bennet shook his finger at her like a school marm scolding an unruly child. "You get on home, Eva, and take the boy. I'll deal with this later."

In that moment, the last bit of hope that Eva harbored, the thought that perchance she and the new woman might coexist in peace, vanished. As she seethed in silence, Eva made herself a solemn vow. *Bennet will never again share my bed, and the day Naomi lays another hand on Thomas will be her last on this mortal coil.*

⌒⌒

"You take it from here, girl." Eva let the reins hang limp, and the loyal mare trod on. It was almost dark, but she was confident Ginger knew the way back home from the wedding. Pulling the buckboard required extra energy, and the horse ambled along even slower than usual. Thomas nuzzled his bruised head up against Eva for a few minutes. He had to be hurting—and worn thin from the awful day. She almost smiled when he eventually scrambled back into the wagon bed, soon snoozing peacefully on the cozy quilt pile.

She propped her feet on the slanted footboard and rested elbows on her knees. Closing her eyes, Eva felt the sprung seat sway her body gently in perfect time to the soft thudding of Ginger's hooves. She was weary but dared not sleep. Now was the time to think, to devise a plan. There had to be some way to spare Thomas—and herself—from the inevitable misery that was otherwise their polygamous future.

Divorce was common on the western frontier and not unheard of among Mormons, especially polygamists. She had considered it many times over the past weeks. *But after the divorce, then what? I'd surely be a pariah in our little community. That I could endure, but divorcing Bennet would mean expulsion from his home. And as easily as old Bishop Dunning gave Thomas to me for safekeeping, he would surely pass my son to another family—or left with Bennet to be beaten and bullied by Naomi and her evil offspring.* She shuddered at a third possibility. *Send Thomas back to Arkansas.*

Think. I have to do something. But what? She rejected possible moves as quickly as she conceived them, and with each bad idea, more anger addled her mind. "Oh, God, what am I to do?" she called to the stars. "Am I unworthy of your help? Are you busy with someone more deserving?"

In spite of scriptural assurances, she heard no still, small voice, felt no burning in her bosom. Whatever the reason for

God's silence, Eva knew one thing: She and Thomas were on their own.

She picked up the reins and laid them across the left side of Ginger's neck. The weary horse balked, then finally turned herself and the little wagon around, headed in the general direction of California. Eva knew this new plan was one that, in her desperation, she had failed to think through completely—or perhaps at all.

Ginger pulled the wagon for two more hours, then stopped. They were only a few miles closer to San Bernardino, but that was not the aging mare's problem. The horse understood naught beyond hunger, thirst and fatigue, and it was clear that Ginger would not be taking another step until those privations were reduced.

"I understand, girl. Rest now. In the morning, I'll find you all the grass and water you want." Eva stepped around the seatback and flopped down on the quilts next to her son, soon falling into prescient dreams.

❧

"Sister Dunning, you unharmed?"

Eva sat up and opened her eyes to see a young man in the uniform of the Militia, a private police force created to defend the Saints against the oft-preached imminent invasion of the U.S. army. In the meantime, militia men stayed busy enforcing the laws of the theocracy, as written and interpreted by President Young.

"Mama, where are we? Who are those—"

"All is well, Thomas. No doubt these men are here to help us." She emphasized the second sentence, speaking loud enough for the soldier to hear.

There was a second man, older. He said, "That's right, Sister Dunning. Someone was concerned. Thought you might have got lost traveling home last night. We're sent to check on your wellbeing."

"Who was that, so concerned about my wellbeing?"

Both men feigned temporary deafness.

"So, are you?" the younger man asked.

"Am I what?"

"Safe? And on your way home?"

Eva gave barely a laugh. "You can see we're safe enough. But I might've gotten a bit muddled as to direction," she lied. "Would you be so kind as to point the way back to Parowan— New Town?" *Guess 'New Town' was unnecessary. Whoever these boys are, they surely know I don't live inside the fort.*

"Yes, ma'am." He gestured in the direction from which the wagon had come.

"Thank you, brethren. You were the answer to my prayers." *At least to the part about what* not *to do.*

"You're welcome, Sister Dunning." Wearing a self-satisfied smile, the younger man gave his horse a bit of a kick. "It'd be our honor to accompany you home, ma'am. Could be Injuns about."

The Mormons and local Paiute Indians were trading partners, currently on friendly terms. But there was no use arguing with their thinly veiled demand. She turned the buggy and fell in behind the mounted soldier. The partner kept his horse close behind the errant wagon.

Eva and Thomas finally pulled up in front of their home. She helped him into the house, then led unhitched Ginger and led her into her corral. Eva dumped two pails of fresh water into a wooden trough, then while the horse slaked her thirst with loud slurps, Eva tore up sweet green grass from a tiny patch nearby and tossed handfuls on the ground nearby. Ginger gave her benefactor a brief look, and in her huge brown eyes, Eva thought she read *thank you.*

"You're welcome. Sorry about last night, girl. Of course, we weren't going to California. But believing it—even for a few hours—might just have kept me from doing something foolish—well, yet more foolish."

~19~

Parowan, Utah Territory - September 10, 1860

N ot one single time in most of five months?" Millie asked, then blew across the top of her steaming teacup. Thomas and Clara were outside the Gale cabin, gathering eggs while their mothers enjoyed a private moment inside.

"Haven't allowed him in my bed since his wedding to that milk cow," Eva answered.

"How's he taking it?"

"He's not taking it, Mil, 'cause I'm not giving it."

Millie laughed and gave Evie a playful slap on the knee.

"Showed up a couple of nights, and I sent him packing. We've no chance of conceiving a child, so he can get what he wants somewhere else."

"What about—"

There was a rap on the door, and the women looked at each other in surprise. Visitors were rare this far beyond the fort.

"Who in all nature might that be?" Millie said. She stood and walked to the door, a curious Evie directly behind. Millie opened it to see a man, maybe thirty years old, at least six feet tall. His angular face was clean-shaven—even smooth—and shirt sleeves were pushed up to the elbows exposing forearms like braided hawsers.

Millie suddenly realized she'd been staring a bit too long.

"Sisters." He slid a red bandana off his head to reveal an unruly shock of straw-colored hair above eyes blue as robins' eggs. "Is one of you the sister Gale?"

His speech was magical, British. Millie almost gasped. *He sounds so much like Sean.*

"Sister Gale?" he repeated.

When she finally spoke, Millie's voice cracked a bit. "I . . . I'm Sister Gale. And this is Sister Eva Dunning."

"Good day, Sisters." The man's smile was broad and sincere. "Brother Peter Wilton at your service. Your husband sent me to cut and reap the wheat, Sister Gale."

It took Millie a moment for the words to make sense. "Quincy usually sends his boys."

"Brother Gale's got his sons busy with other fields, asked me to get this crop in before the birds nick it. He said you and your daughter'd help gather—if that's not a burden."

"No burden." Millie smiled. "Just a surprise."

The field in front of Millie's cabin was only about half an acre, but after the near-famine of 1857 and '58, President Young told his people to grow grain on every available plot and build up a surplus where possible. Quincy's boys had sowed wheat in the little field the past two years.

"Brother Wilton," Eva said, "how is it we've never met you before?"

"President Young called me to emigrate from England. I worked with the iron back home."

"Yes, but—"

"Since the ironworks shuttered, I've traveled about the territory for work. A bit of smithing here, farm work there. Whatever a fellow can find."

Millie flashed a too-friendly smile. "Well, Brother Wilton, I'm obliged to have your help with the reaping."

Clara ran around the corner of the cabin. "Ma, when're we gonna—" She stopped mid-sentence and gaped at the stranger. "Gosh! He's real handsome."

"Clara Alice!"

"Too forward?" Clara asked.

Millie raised an eyebrow and nodded.

"Sorry, Ma."

The handsome man couldn't hold back a laugh.

"Clara, this is Brother Wilton," Millie said. "Brother Wilton, my daughter Clara."

Brother Wilton bowed. "An honor to make your acquaintance, young Sister Gale."

Clara cast a sideways glance, perhaps to see if her ma noticed her face reddening. "I'm sorry about, you know—"

"No apology necessary. I'm flattered."

☙❧

Millie glanced up at the red bandana drenched in Peter Wilton's head sweat. It was halfway through September, but the wheat field was bright and summer warm. Millie and Clara followed at a safe distance, gathering the sheaves and tying up each bundle with a bit of bark hair stripped from a cedar fencepost, then leaning them together in teepee-shaped shocks topped by heads bowed with heavy kernels.

White shirt also darkened with perspiration, Brother Wilton rotated his tapered back at the waist, sweeping the scythe through grain the color of his hair.

Struggling to ignore a deep ache she'd not felt in years, Millie forced herself to look anywhere but at this magnificent fellow.

☙❧

Three hours later, Millie watched as Peter Wilton stopped to survey the results of their labor. "What do you think, Sisters Gale? A good start?"

Before Millie could answer, Clara blurted, "I'm thirsty."

The handsome man let out a deep rumble of a laugh. "Me, too," he said in a feigned whine. "Time for a tea break, Ma?"

"Tea?" Clara said. The word seemed to surprise her.

"Just a manner of speaking. 'Tis actually water I think we're all in need of."

"Take me a minute to fetch it," Millie said. "Can you keep up on your own, Clara?"

"Yes, Ma." Her voice was edged with sarcasm beyond her years. "I know I'm just a child, but I can stack sheaves for another minute or so."

"Not me," the man said in a mischievous tone. "I propose some sitting in the shade—posthaste."

Clara ran up and hugged him. "If Peter's ready for—"

"Clara Alice Gale! It's Brother Wilton to you."

He shot Clara a little wink.

"Yes, of course, Mother Dee-uh," Clara said in a terrible attempt at an English accent.

❦

Clara led Brother Wilton up the four steps to the front porch. "Careful of the last one," she called back over her shoulder. He stepped over the top plank, a ragged gap separated it into two halves. They sat down with backs against the log wall, the overhanging roof providing blessed shade. "Better now, Brother Wilton?" Clara asked.

"Indeed. This is more to my liking." He smiled, and she offered a toothy beam in return.

Ma stepped out the door, a blue jar of heavy crockery in her hands. Brother Wilton stood to help. "Set yourself back down this instant, Peter Wilton," she said. He hesitated a moment, then shrugged and retook his spot. She set the pot down, stepped back inside, and soon returned with three mismatched china mugs. Ma dipped a mug into the jar and handed it to Brother Wilton. He emptied it without taking a breath. "That's marvelous, Sister Gale. How could it be that it's so cool?"

"My own secret," she said.

Clara rolled her eyes. "Not much of a secret. We keep it in the root cellar—it's always cold in there."

Ma handed Clara her drink, then took Brother Wilton's mug and refilled it. "Drink up, you two. Water won't stay cool in this heat." Then she disappeared back into the house.

"How often does your father visit, young Sister Gale?"

Clara laughed at the last two words. "I'm not your sister."

"You're someone's sister. Brother Gale has three sons, right?"

She nodded. "But I don't claim them as brothers."

"Half-brothers, then?"

"Nope. My pa died a couple of months after I was born. Quincy took Ma to wife soon after." There was a long pause, then, "Never."

"Never?" The word seemed to catch him off guard.

"Quincy never comes around."

❧

An hour later, Millie gave Brother Wilton a furtive glance. He stood, hands on narrow hips, surveying the field. The air smelled of clean, fresh straw—all the grain was cut, and two hundred shocks stood waiting to be loaded. Millie tried to pretend that the hours had not passed too quickly for her. "Compliments on a job well done, Brother Wilton."

"And to both of you." He regarded the neatly napped ground a moment longer. "Quincy intends for me to gather and deliver it to the threshing floor soon as his wagon is available."

Millie felt her face warm at the mention of his return. "We're happy to help with the loading."

Brother Wilton smiled, doffed the red bandana, and bowed deeply. He stared at Millie—perhaps too long. "Till then, dear sisters," he finally said, "parting is such sweet sorrow."

"Wait!" The instant the word left her mouth, Millie realized how desperate it must have sounded. "I . . . I mean, least we can do is feed you dinner."

He flashed a smile. "A bit early, don't you— Oh, that's right, 'tis luncheon you refer to."

Millie turned her palms up. "You hungry?"

"To be honest, I am quite peckish."

"That mean hungry?" Clara asked.

"It does," Brother Wilton said. "And I'd be pleased to stay, if it's not a burden."

"How can I help, Ma?"

"Fetch three big potatoes and some apples from the cellar." Her daughter turned to go. "Clara, wait."

She stopped and looked back. "Yes, Ma?"

"Reckon there's also a few tomatoes still in the garden." Clara hurried off.

"A lovely girl." Brother Wilton stood and rolled his neck. "She must be quite a comfort to you."

"Comfort?"

"Guess I meant to say good company. You are rather isolated here," he said, gesturing to the endless desert just beyond the field.

"Clara's the best thing in my life. If it weren't for her, I'd . . ." Her voice trailed off.

Brother Wilton sat back down, riveting Millie with the deep blue of his eyes. "Tell me about her father."

"Quincy?"

"No." He shook his head slowly. "Clara told me her father passed soon after she was born."

Millie shook her head. "Well, ain't she the little chatterbox."

Brother Wilton smiled and nodded his agreement.

"Sean was an English sheep man when he joined the church—raised Galways. We met and married in Great Salt Lake City, then President Young called us to move south."

"How did he perish, if it's not too painful."

Millie sighed. "Horse lost its footing in a loose rockfall." She pointed a thumb behind her. "Up Parowan Canyon, not far from here."

"I'm so sorry. How you must miss him."

I miss him beyond what human tongue can tell. Millie sniffed, felt her eyes well up. "I have our Clara."

They looked at each other without speaking for a few moments, then Millie said, "Tell me about your wife, Brother Wilton."

"Not a bit to tell, really."

"Nothing?"

He smiled. "Not married. Never have been."

Millie's heart missed two beats. "But surely—"

"Damned polygamists got all the good ones," he said. "Please forgive the profanity."

Millie's laugh was long and loud. "Those damned polygamists!"

❦

Peter Wilton sat in Sabbath worship service among families from throughout the northern half of the Iron Mission. He fought to keep his mind from wandering while William H.

Dame, President of the Parowan Stake, continued the afternoon's sermon with a deep, booming tirade against the United States government. He finished with a grim warning that apostates—those who did not obey the Prophet's edicts without questioning—would be driven out from among the saints. It was nothing new, but today the last bit got Peter's full attention. *I must find some way to purge these doubts I've been having.*

The session ended in a rousing hymn and a long benediction, then Peter followed two hundred women and children in their Sunday dress out the twin front doors, down the steps, and into a fine fall day. Most of the men remained inside, clustered in small groups, no doubt deep in discussion of everything from the weather to how to deal with "cousin Lemuel," Mormon vernacular for Indians. Peter needed fresh air.

Once outside, he stood admiring the stone structure. The Rock Church was the largest and finest building in Southern Utah. It was constructed of local material, pale orange sandstone on the long sides and smooth gray river rocks in front and back. The huge uncut stones, mortared and fitted together like a jigsaw puzzle, made Peter think of the soaring cathedrals back home in England. The church's roof was sharply pitched. Protected by thousands of overlapping wooden shingles, it also boasted a rounded cupola topped with a short steeple. Like other Mormon houses of worship, no cross adorned the building, inside or out.

Peter spotted Sister Gale and Sister Dunning standing in the shade of a spreading willow tree, talking and watching their youngsters enjoy what must have been a rare chance to play with other children. The game was tag, with one apparent modification to the well-known rules. Anyone chasing the one-legged boy hopped on one foot.

"Good afternoon, Sisters. How did you enjoy the conference?"

"Good day, Brother . . . uh, I'm afraid I've forgotten your name," Sister Dunning said.

"Wilton, Brother Peter Wilton."

"Brother Wilton, of course."

"Brother Wilton was gracious enough to cut our wheat last week," Sister Gale said.

Peter thought he heard something odd, perhaps mild embarrassment, in her voice. "Yes. Nice to see you again, Sister Gale," he said. They looked directly into one another's eyes, holding the handshake perhaps a smidge too long. "Miss Clara appears to be enjoying herself."

"True enough." The girl's mother pointed her chin in the direction of the noisy play. "Over there breaking the Sabbath, I suppose."

Peter chuckled. "I rather suspect the good Lord loves the sound of children's laughter. Well, best be going." He turned to leave, then pivoted back. "Not certain when I'll next have the use of Brother Quincy's wagon. Sorry."

"No problem. I'm— We're to home pretty much all the time.

�❧

Eva waited until Brother Wilton was out of earshot, then said, "You're blushing."

"Just the heat of the day," Millie said.

Eva flashed a wicked smile. "It's heat, all right. What's going on, Mil?"

"Nothing. I told you, he cut the grain last week. Me and Clara gathered and stacked it. That's all."

"Hmm," Eva said with a sly grin.

"Don't you go judging me, Evie Dunning. I can look at the tree without picking a peach."

"Not judging, Mil. That's a fine-looking tree. And the way the man talks. . ."

Millie averted her friend's gaze. "Sounds a bit like my Sean," she said.

"Where's his wife?"

"Never married."

Eva's eyebrows arched in concern. "That so?"

Millie leaned in closer and whispered, "Honest, Evie, I been praying to rid myself of impure thoughts." She stared off at nothing in particular. "But—"

Eva's expression became solemn. "Ponder hard the consequences." She fixed Millie's eyes in a deep stare. "Think about Clara."

~20~

Parowan, Utah Territory - September 11, 1860

Millie stepped out of the root cellar and into the late summer sun. She set a basket of withered yellow apples on the ground, then struggled to close the door back flat to the dirt. That done, she picked up the fruit and began the walk to the cabin. *Thomas will surely be surprised when Clara brings two pies for his birthday tomorrow—a whole one just for him. Hard to believe the boy's already six, and Clara'll soon be eight, old enough to be—*

"What in blazes?" She spotted something that stopped her still as a stump: a handsome blue roan approaching the homestead at a trot. The horse bore Peter Wilton, his tan cotton shirt snug around the narrow-waisted torso, a four-foot pine plank under his right arm. Her face broke into a broad grin. *Don't run, Millicent Gale. That would be unseemly.*

The short walk down the hill and past the pigsty seemed to take forever, but Millie finally reached the front of the house where Brother Wilton stood waiting, the board leaned against the nearby porch. "Good afternoon, Sister Gale," he said.

"Brother Wilton, so nice to see you."

"Miss Clara about?"

"Spending some time over to Sister Dunning's place."

"Sorry to have missed her." Brother Wilton handed Millie a small cotton bag. "I brought her a bit of sweet—rock candy of my own making."

"Then I'll thank you on her behalf," Millie said. "I, uh, I expected you'd come with a wagon."

"Oh, of course." He gave an agreeable little laugh. "I just stopped by to tell you I shan't have the use of Brother Gale's wagon until Tuesday next."

She nodded. "That's very kind, Brother. But you really didn't have to—"

"Also of a mind to repair that broken step." He pointed to the splintery gap dividing what had once been the topmost of four treads.

Millie cocked her head. "It's something I planned to get to someday."

Brother Wilton's grin showed two rows of impossibly white teeth. "Seems someday is today." He nodded in the direction of the weathered saddlebag. "I've brought the wood and the necessary tools. May I begin?"

Millie hiked her shoulders. "Not gonna tell you no."

Brother Wilton stepped to the roan and pulled a saw, hammer, and a few precious iron nails from his bag. Millie took her basket into the cabin and began peeling apples for two pies.

Twenty minutes later, Millie heard rapping at the open door. "Done," Brother Wilton called into the house. "Come look."

"So soon?" She stepped onto the porch and inspected the repair. "That's wonderful! How can I thank you?"

"No need. In fact, it's I who should be thanking you for letting me provide a bit of Christian service."

"I, uh . . ." she stammered. "Then I guess you're welcome."

Brother Wilton picked up his bulging leather bag. "I'll be back on Tuesday to collect the wheat."

"Please don't go," she blurted. *That came out all amiss, Millicent. Settle yourself down.*

Brother Wilton stared at her in apparent confusion.

"I mean, there's an apple pie in the oven. Hoped to serve you a slice—or two." *Young Thomas will surely be content with half a birthday pie to himself.*

"That's extremely kind, but—"

"Needs another thirty minutes baking," Millie said. "Folks who've eaten my pie would tell you the wait's a small price to pay for such an indulgence."

"You've convinced me," Brother Wilton laughed. He sat and leaned back against the dark log wall.

"Meantime, I'll fetch you water from the cellar." She hiked her skirt, then tested the new stair with one foot before stepping on it with her entire weight.

"Don't trust my work?"

Millie felt her cheeks warm a bit. "It's just habit."

He broke into a hearty laugh. "A bit of a josh, Sister."

She added her laughter to his. "Suppose I deserved it. Anyway, I'll be back directly."

Brother Wilton stood and said, "Tell me where the cellar is. I'm happy to get it."

"Peter Wilton, you set yourself back down this instant. It's my turn to provide a bit of that Christian service you were speaking of." Then she stepped back into the cabin for the blue crock.

A few minutes later Millie came around the corner of the cabin, walking slowly so as not to slosh water from her jar. Peter seemed to sense that her arms were starting to cramp. He hurried to her side and took the burden, then carried it up the steps and carefully set it on the porch.

Millie was soon back with two cups. She sat down between the crockery and the man, then dipped one into the container and handed it to Brother Wilton. He drained it in three gulps. "Refreshing. Thank you, Sister Gale."

She refilled his cup and dipped one for herself. They sat and sipped without speaking for more than a minute until Millie broke the silence. "Tell me about England."

Brother Wilton stared into the distance while he replied, "It's as different from this desert as different can be. More shades of green than you'd even imagine. Of course, the weeks on end of rainy weather can make one feel quite gloomy. Still, my heart often aches to be back among so many lush and growing things."

Millie's thoughts briefly wandered. *His accent is so much like Sean's.* "I speak the king's English," Sean once said. "You seem to be the one with the accent."

"Sister Gale, are you well?"

Her mind was yanked back to the present. "I'm fine, thank you. Sorry. So, uh, are your parents still living? Brothers or sisters?"

"No siblings. My mum and dad are still alive, so far as I know."

"You're not certain?"

Brother Wilton's wide shoulders lifted in a shrug. "They cut off all contact six years ago, when I was baptized into the Church. But I'd like to hear more about Sister Millicent Gale."

"In due time," Millie said. "You've never married?"

"Came close some years ago, but no."

"Came close? Sounds like a tale needs telling."

"Well before I'd heard of the Mormons," he said, "I determined to emigrate to America. Alas, she was a girl unwilling to leave home and family so far behind."

"But you cared for her enough to marry?"

Brother Wilton gave a noncommittal tilt of the head. "It was all a very long time ago—and thousands of miles from Zion."

It was clear there'd be no more discussion of that topic, so Millie moved on. "Is Zion what you expected?"

He shook his head as he spoke. "Honestly? I expected naught the likes of this barren, lonely place. And you?"

Millie gave a knowing nod. "I thought the Great Salt Lake City was desolate. But the Iron Mission . . ." She took a deep breath and let it out with the saddest of sighs. "We are well and truly beyond the edge of the civilized world."

After a stretch of quiet, Brother Wilton said, "You are blessed to have a wonderful daughter."

"Mm hm," she nodded. "Even trapped in this wilderness, my life's a joy because of Clara." Millie felt her face melt into a smile. "Can you believe she's near halfway through reading the Book of Mormon?"

"Not at all surprised, she seems remarkable in many ways." He paused for a moment, then said, "I've prayed to someday have my own little family. If I'm ever blessed to raise a daughter, I couldn't ask for more than that she be just like our Clara.

The word *our* pierced Millie like an arrow. Bereft of speech, she stared at the perfect man before her.

"*Your* Clara, sorry to have misspoken," he quickly corrected.

Millie averted her eyes, staring out at the endless sage. "Thank you, Brother. Those're among the kindest words I've ever heard." *Dear God, please take away what I'm starting to feel.*

∂∽

Millie watched Brother Wilton chew his first bite of pie. "Worth the waiting?" she asked.

His eyes rolled skyward in apparent rapture. "Indeed." He swallowed, then continued, "Ambrosia."

Millie threw back her head and laughed. "Food of the gods."

"That's right." The man looked confused. "But why is that so—"

"It's what Sean used to call my pie."

"Though I never met the fellow, I can tell he had unfathomably good taste."

"Man did love his pie."

Brother Wilton's reply was barely above a whisper. "And you, I'll wager."

Millie felt her eyes well up and she turned away in the hope that Brother Wilton might not notice.

❧

That night, Millie Gale lay on her bed for hours, trying not to think of Peter's kindness—and his ice-melt eyes.

Four miles away, Peter Wilton stared into the darkness above his bed, trying not to imagine what his life might have been had he met Millicent before she became old Quincy Gale's extra wife.

~21~

September 18, 1860

Millie sat in her rocking chair in the shade of the cabin's covered porch. Brother Wilton perched on a nearby stool. Quincy's wagon sat in the field, piled high with sheaves of wheat reflecting the yellow sun of an autumn afternoon.

"We did it, Sister Gale." His voice was low, husky from hard work.

"We're a real good team."

"Where's Miss Clara today? That's twice I seem to have missed her."

"Over to the Dunnings again. Whenever she can, Eva teaches the children reading and figuring."

They sat in silence for a bit, a tiny breeze delivering the sound of buzzy insects and the smell of earth and straw.

"Don't take plural wives." The moment Millie heard herself speak, she knew she should not have.

Brother Wilton looked puzzled. "What's that, you say?"

She felt her cheeks burn. "I'm so sorry. It's not my place to speak a single word."

He broke into a low chuckle. "But now you have, and I think I'll hear more."

"My meaning is just, well, the woman you marry should have you for herself . . . deserves to have you for herself."

"That's, umm, that's kind of you to say."

Torn between shame and a deep need to unburden herself, Millie stared down, shaking her head. "Forgive me. That was unseemly."

"Not any problem." He sat in thoughtful silence for a few moments, then said, "If I may be so bold, do you sometimes wish you could have Brother Gale for yourself?"

"I should not be talking about such things."

More silence.

"No," Millie continued. "No, I don't want Quincy to myself. I don't want him at all. Never did."

"That saddens me to hear, Sister Gale."

A deepening need for male companionship overwhelmed her unease. *Just talking to this kind man gives me a measure of joy I've not felt since losing Sean. Surely there's no harm in conversation.* "Call me Millie, Peter. Please." She flashed him the suggestion of a smile. "No one's around to hear."

He reached over and laid a hand on the back of hers, then looked into her eyes and spoke her proper name. The way he said *Millicent* made her feel like melting butter.

"Peter." Her tears began.

"Perhaps I should go now," he said.

"No, Peter, please." Her shoulders heaved with silent sobs. "I'm so alone."

Peter knelt in front of the rocker. Millie's hands rested on her legs, above the knees. He placed his hands on hers. "Millicent, I—"

Slowly, she drew her hands away, leaving his palms against the tops of her thighs. Instead of removing them, he commenced a gentle massage. Without conscious thought, Millie leaned forward, put her hands behind his neck and kissed him. He did not resist, so she nudged his head toward her lap.

She stood, and for the briefest of moments, pushed herself into him, feeling his hot breath through her skirts as he inhaled then exhaled deeply. When both were standing, she guided his hands to her waist. He moved closer. Through their clothing she could feel something she had nearly forgotten, as solid as the wooden arm of her rocking chair.

Her knees turned to jelly, but Peter held her up with powerful arms. He drew her still closer, then tilted his head to the side and brushed her lips with his. Hands still behind his head, she pulled tighter against him, kissing him with pressure—and desperation.

Locked in his embrace, Millie walked backwards, guiding him to the cabin door. She reached back with one hand. The door opened inward and once inside, they kissed with a hunger that left no room for rational thought.

He dropped his suspenders and she unbuttoned his shirt.

She unlaced the bonnet ties under her chin and dropped the headpiece to the floor, feeling soft hair spill onto her shoulders.

He stared for a moment, looking perplexed by her prairie dress. She began at the top of a long row of buttons and unfastened them quicker than he may have imagined possible. He watched as she pulled the dress down over her shoulders, then rotated her hips, wriggling out of it in deliberate, sensuous motions.

She stepped over her clothing, then reached out and stripped off Peter's shirt. He unbuttoned his trousers and they stood facing each other, an arm's length apart. Their clothing had been shed—except both still wore the one-piece Mormon undergarment. Peter's wide-eyed stare seemed directed at the erect nipples Millie felt straining against cotton fabric. He glanced down. Below the bottom ties, she sensed her underwear gaped open, perhaps revealing a tiny hint of treasure, gold to match the tresses resting on her shoulders. Where Peter's manhood bulged against the rough cotton, she saw a small but growing dot of wetness.

Neither spoke. The otherwise silent room was filled with the sound of heavy breathing.

Millie suddenly closed her eyes, cupped both hands over her garment-covered breasts and took a deep breath, releasing it in a long sigh. She recalled the covenants she—and Peter—had made to God to obey all his commandments—including "thou shalt not commit adultery."

Surely, Lord, you would not deny me a moment of happiness in such a bleak existence. From somewhere deep within, she heard her best friend's warning. "Ponder hard on the consequences—think about Clara."

Millie Gale pondered. The penalty for her sin would be expulsion from the community of saints, almost certainly without her daughter. She shook her head so violently the tears flowed sideways, then she bent down, gathered up her clothing, and—

"Aunt Millie!" She turned to see Quincy's oldest son, standing in the doorway. Before she could speak, the thunderstruck teen swiveled on one heel and stumbled across the porch.

Millie turned away from the second man she'd ever loved and followed the boy out the door, crumpled dress pressed to her bosom in a desperate attempt at modesty. "Sam! Wait! Nothing happened! You can't say aught to—"

The young man swung up onto his horse and galloped away through the stubble of freshly cut grain.

She hurried back inside. "Peter!" she said, pulling her dress on. "You've got to leave the mission, now!"

Peter stepped into his pants and spoke as he buttoned the fly. "They can excommunicate me if they want to. In all honesty, joining this church hasn't worked out particularly well thus far."

"Quincy won't care about excommunication. He's a proud man—he'll wreak his revenge." Millie's voice cracked. "They'll be looking to castrate you, or worse."

Peter froze in place. "Castrate? Surely they wouldn't—"

"I know him, Peter. You got to leave the territory, now."

"I will if you'll come with me. I have a horse and small wagon, even a bit of money set by. We can start a wonderful new life in California."

"If you go alone, they may give up once they know you've left the mission. If me and Clara travel with, they'll never stop hunting us down."

"We'll not take the route they expect," he said. "No one will find us. Please, Millicent. You must come with me."

She shook her head violently.

He pled, "If you don't trust me, Clara will be lost to you." Her shoulders slumped and her forehead crinkled in confusion as he continued. "Don't you see where this inevitably goes? They'll keep Clara. But you'll be cast out of the church, sent away from the Mission with naught but the clothes on your back. In a few years, when the poor child's fourteen or fifteen, your sweet daughter will become the second or third wife to someone just like Quincy—and you won't be there to prevent it."

The brutal truth of his words struck her like a felled tree. Millie's tears flowed freely, and her shoulders heaved with sobs. "There must be another way."

"Leave with Clara and me—or be driven out all alone—those are your only choices. I swear in the name of Israel's God I will keep you both safe. But we must leave now!"

A dozen *what-ifs* raced through Millie's mind, colliding, ricocheting off one another like runaway stones in a rockslide.

I hardly know the man, would life with Peter be as I imagine?

I'd be deserting dear Evie. Can I survive without my best friend? And she without me?

My sweet girl would not grow up with Tommy. Clara would never ever see him after today.

It also means breaking sacred promises. Would I be turning my back on God?

And resonating the loudest, *But what will Quincy do with me and my Clara if we stay?*

Millie released a frightened sigh, then fixed her eyes on Peter's. "Clara's due back in about an hour. If you're not here by then, I'll know you came to your senses."

"And if you're not here—"

She acknowledged with a silent nod, then watched Peter sprint to his horse and gallop away.

~22~

Clara stepped through the front door of the Gale cabin and into a kind of whirlwind. "Ma, I'm back." Ma did not seem to hear her, she was bustling about their tiny home in some crazy kind of hurry, jamming clothing into two burlap bags recovered from the root cellar.

Aunt Evie and Tommy followed Clara through the door. "What in blazes is this about?" Eva gasped.

Ma forced a heavy wool coat into the bag, then looked up. "What's it look like?" she said in a breathless bark. "You kids wait outside for a minute."

"No." Clara folded her arms across her chest. "I deserve to know." She didn't go out and neither did Tommy.

"You and me are leaving, Clara. With Peter."

"With Brother Wilton?" Clara stared at her mother, unable to make a grain of sense from what she'd just heard. "Leaving?"

"We're leaving Quincy, his evil sons and this godforsaken desert for good. But we got to hurry."

Fear and confusion fogged Clara's thoughts. "For good? Forever?"

"We're about to start a wonderful new life." But Ma didn't sound convinced.

"With Brother Wilton?" Clara gulped. Ma nodded yes. Clara looked at her mother with wide, unblinking eyes. *Has she gone mad?*

Nearby, Tommy's head sagged, tears rolling off his cheeks and onto the wooden floor.

Ma turned to Aunt Evie. "Come with us. Please. Come with us."

"Millicent Gale! Stop and think for a minute," Aunt Evie said. "Think about the risk. For you and Clara."

"Yes!" Clara said. "What about me?"

"You don't understand. Things have happened. The only choice worse for us now would be to stay."

Clara felt like the room was spinning around her. She was suddenly in a world where nothing made sense, a world where her wants held no sway.

"You're not leaving, Mil," Aunt Evie said. "Take a breath and gather your wits back about you."

"It's too late," Ma said again. She embraced her friend and sobbed, her tears wetting Evie's shoulder. "There's no other—"

"Whore!"

Pa Quincy filled the doorway. "Everyone out!" he roared.

The large man gave Aunt Evie a rough push toward the door, then he picked both children up by the backs of their clothing and tossed them. They landed hard, got up and scrambled to follow Tommy's mama outside.

From the front porch, Clara heard him bellow, "Not you, slattern!"

"Nothing happened." Ma was begging now. "I know what you're thinking, but we didn't—"

"You're lucky we don't still stone adulteresses. Maybe we should."

The words sounded to Clara like a foreign language, perhaps the one spoken in hell.

"Quincy, please," Ma sobbed. "You don't under—"

"Where is he?"

"Who?"

Clara got up and stepped to the door in time to see Pa Quincy backhand Ma across the mouth, splitting her upper lip in two places. "The English devil that frigged ya under my own roof!"

"Stop! Stop hurting my mother!" But Clara's scream seemed to go unheard.

"Quincy, please listen," Ma said. "We didn't—"

Pa cut her short with a closed-fisted punch to the side of her head. Clara felt the stunning blow as if she'd received it herself. Ma slumped to the floor, bleeding, unconscious. Clara tried to run to her, but one of the boys grabbed her from behind and wouldn't let go.

With strength that seemed to Clara beyond his old age, Pa Quincy picked Ma up and threw her over his shoulder. She was limp as a blanket, and her poor head banged against the door's edge when he carried her outside. Clara shrieked in horror as with each step, her mother's face bobbed against the old man's back, blood pouring from her mouth and soaking into his shirt and trousers.

Then he threw Ma into the bed of his waiting wagon, not so much as blinking when her head hit the floor with a loud thump. "Nephi, looks like two sacks of clothes inside. Fetch 'em."

"Have you killed her?" Aunt Evie screamed. "You will surely burn in hell."

Killed? Clara's legs failed, and she crumpled to the pine porch.

The evil man sneered. "She's my wife, and I'll do with her as I see fit—and I ain't the one's headed for hell. Now you get on out of here, Sister, before I start thinkin' you might have been part of this unholy trouble."

Clara managed to stand and scramble into the wagon. She lifted Ma's bleeding head into her little lap, her hand feeling the warm and slippery blood. Shaking so hard she could scarcely speak, the little girl managed the sincerest prayer of her life.

"Dear Father in Heaven, I can't live without my ma. Strike me dead where I sit, that we both may be—"

"Hush up, child." The murderer hauled his considerable weight onto the wagon's seat and flicked the reins, calling back over his shoulder, "Sam, you and the boys follow with the wheat. When we get home, I'll tell you what we'll be doin' to that Limey fornicator."

Ma let out a shuddering groan, the happiest sound Clara had heard in her whole entire life.

~23~

Peter's mind raced faster than his horse's legs. Everything had changed in an eye blink. Until today, his had been a simple life. He exchanged help around the farm for a vacant bedroom in the home of Gwinn and Sally Forzenant, an older couple with grown children back in Great Salt Lake City. He had not found steady work since the Deseret Iron Works closed, but Peter saved most of what money he earned from odd jobs and bought a horse and wagon—even put away some tools, extra clothing and food against the time he would leave Parowan. Until today, his plan had been to relocate after he secured a good job up north, probably Provo or Great Salt Lake City. He never calculated on leaving the area to run off with a married woman—until he met Millicent Gale.

She shan't be married to Quincy for long. I'll find a way for her to divorce the disgusting old man, then Millicent and I will marry. And he made himself a second promise. *The first time I make love to her will be as her lawful husband.*

As soon as he was home, Peter tossed the harness rigging over his horse's back, then cinched bit collar, girth and trace around the sweat-slicked body. He threw his things into the wagon as fast as he could, heart pounding with anticipation—and powerful dread. Last thing into the wagon was Peter's only firearm, a British Enfield, a potent long gun with rifled barrel.

He stepped back into the Forzenant home. At a small writing table, he found a quill and bit of paper, dipped the feather into the inkwell and wrote:

My Dear Brother and Sister Forzenant,

I have left the area to seek my fortunes elsewhere.
Thank you for a warm bed and for your pleasant companion-
ship. I shall think of you often.

May God bless you with continued health and happiness.
Your brother, Peter F. Wilton

He left the note on the dining table and walked out the door for the last time.

❧

The sun was just beginning to set as Peter approached Millicent's cabin. From a distance, it struck him as it hadn't before that the place was small and in generally poor repair. "She deserves better. I'll build her a proper home in California."

He had already decided they would make their new home in San Diego. San Bernardino was closer, of course. It had been a Mormon settlement until 1857, when Brigham Young called the California colonists back to Utah. *Some Church members must have stayed behind. Would they be sympathetic to our plight or label us apostates? Doesn't matter—we'll just be passing through.* Peter grinned. *We've plenty of travelling time to sort out Millicent's divorce and our marriage.*

When he was within a hundred yards of the home, Peter tugged the reins. "Whoa, girl." He carefully scanned the scene. *Something's amiss.* It was nearly dark, and no light shone from inside the cabin. No candle. No fire. Nothing. Peter's head drooped. "She changed her mind." He felt as if his soul had been ripped from his body.

Moving slowly, like a dream in which he dragged himself through the thick mud of an English bog, Peter got down and let the reins rest on the footboard. "Can't stay in the mission," he said to himself. "North is naught but Mormons for three hundred miles, so . . ."

He took one more glance around, then forced himself to climb back onto the wide seat and take up the straps. "Walk on, girl."

"Brother Wilton, wait!" His heart flooded with hope. It was a woman's voice.

"Whoa, girl."

Eva Dunning stepped through the door. "I have to talk to—"

"Where's Millicent?"

"With Quincy, but—" He flicked the reins and the horse moved ahead. "It was not her choice," Sister Dunning called out. "He thrashed her unconscious and took her away."

"Whoa, girl." Peter laid down the reins and jumped to the ground. He clenched both fists until thick forearms strained against his shirtsleeves. "I'll kill the man." His voice was a menacing growl, and for a moment poor Sister Dunning may have feared for her own safety.

"Right now, Quincy is getting up a posse," she said. "Friends and family, maybe even militia. What's more likely is they'll kill you."

Peter glowered. "Maybe one's as good as the other."

"Either way, you're of no use to Millie."

He kept silent.

"Good brother, if you care about Millicent Gale, you'll leave the mission tonight and not look back. No matter your wrath, one man alone is no match for them."

Peter punched a fist into his palm. "I can't just—"

"They'll be searching for you in the morning, maybe even tonight."

Peter stared into the distance, lost in thought. "And while they're hunting me, Millicent and Clara will be at the house alone," he muttered in a voice hoarse with anger.

Sister Dunning shook her head. "No, Brother Wilton. You can't succeed."

"I'll stalk the house until they leave—then collect Millicent and the girl, and we're off to California."

"You're more likely to get yourself—and Millie—killed."

Peter jumped back on the wagon.

"Maybe even Clara," she called after him.

He heard, but chose not to respond

"Peter Wilton, God help you do the right thing," Sister Dunning said, her voice fading behind him.

~24~

When the molten anger began to cool, Peter realized he couldn't risk a direct encounter with Quincy's men. He hid out until dark. Then, with only a slivered moon to light the way, he kept horse and tiny wagon off the thoroughfare, steering his rig through sagebrush flats in the general direction of the Gale place. He found a little hill overlooking the property from about fifty yards distant and tucked the wagon into a grove of scrub oak, low and densely gnarled. Peter retrieved his rifle from the wagon bed and ducked behind a bushy cluster to commence his watch.

The windows of the home glowed pale yellow, and it appeared none of Quincy's horses were missing. *Surely some, maybe all, of the Gales are home.* The door opened suddenly, leaking light. A moment later, a large figure appeared, silhouetted in a dull corona of lamp shine. *Is that Quincy?* A portly figure stepped out, then turned to close the door. *It's him.* Peter's heart jumped and his grip on the long gun tightened. *He's not on my track. Not just yet.*

Barely seen in the dim light, Quincy moved his bulk in a semi-waddle to the nearby necessary, then closed the privy door behind him.

Peter's racing mind now matched his runaway heart. He patted his rifle. *The Enfield is accurate at triple this range. I can shoot him through the door right now and be done with the whole business.* He raised the rifle and pressed its butt into his shoulder. With his right thumb, he adjusted the ladder sight to the estimated distance between the muzzle and the flimsy wooden door. Squinting his left eye closed, Peter sighted along the barrel with his right—but the gun bounced and jumped off target with every heartbeat that hammered through his chest and skull.

He finally lowered the rifle and shook his head, rebuking himself in a whisper. "Don't be a damned fool, Peter Wilton. Shooting Quincy would do naught but give the militia justification to hunt you down and kill you." He slumped to the ground, gun cradled in his lap. *What now, then?* He tumbled the question over and over in his mind while darkness crept toward dawn.

⁊◦⟨

Some hours had passed since Peter'd begun the watch, and his bladder was painfully full. He stood, stepped a few feet away from his makeshift nest and unbuttoned his trousers. Holding the flaccid flesh in his right hand to direct the stream, he recalled how rigid the member had recently been. So much had transpired in the short time since the almost-adultery. He closed his eyes and relaxed. With a small sigh of relief, Peter drained away the discomfort, rolling the knots out of his neck while he finished up.

Outlining the mountains to the east, a thin stripe of purple was beginning to bleed into blue.

A distant shout: "Come on, boys. Let's go find us that son of Satan and separate him from them tiny British balls."

Peter pushed a branch aside. In the predawn gloom, three boys followed their father out the door, all carrying old style muzzle-loading rifles. He took his eyes off the house long enough to assess his own situation. The lightening sky revealed a problem: The hiding place he'd selected in the dark of night would soon leave him and his wagon exposed. As night gave way to sunrise, he would stand out more and more. Nothing but low sagebrush surrounded his little thicket—moving to another spot without being detected would soon be impossible. He could probably drop to his belly and disappear in the underbrush, but some part of the horse and wagon would surely be visible above the crest of the hill. If the Gale posse did not leave soon—and if any one of them glanced his way—it was certain to touch off a deadly shootout.

"What are my possibilities?" Peter asked himself in a rasping whisper. The answer was inevitable. "None good. My Enfield's far superior to the Gales' old muskets, so I could kill at least two of them before I went down. But no matter how much blood I might shed, the outcome remains the same—my life, and any chance for happiness with Millicent—will be over." He crouched lower. While he watched the Gale family prepare to geld and likely leave him to bleed to death, he prayed no one at the house below took his eye off the task at hand.

Then his horse gave a whinny.

No! Peter dropped to his belly.

He raised his head enough to see that near the house below, a teenage boy stood frozen in place.

"Hush up!" the boy said, staring in the direction of the nearby hill. He seemed to listen as hard as he could but gave no sign he'd heard anything more. "Others of you hear somethin'?" he called.

The two younger boys shrugged and shook their heads.

"Whaddja say?" Quincy demanded.

"Might have heard somethin'," the boy said, pointing in Peter's direction. "Up there. Horse, maybe."

"Don't stand there like no wooden Injun, Sam," Quincy grumbled. "Get on up the hill and check." The young man leaned his gun against the house and started walking. "The matter with you, boy? Take your dang gun." Sam fetched the rifle and started back to the hill.

After two more seconds ticked by, Peter knew what he had to do. He'd wait in silence for the boy to get closer, then charge out of the brush, the Enfield aimed at Sam's head at point-blank range. But Peter would not touch the trigger.

How very strange that it should all end here. I so wish I'd had the time to make dear Millicent happy.

From somewhere, a different scenario popped into Peter's mind. He made his way to the wagon, guessing that the boy could not yet see him, but knowing every second brought them closer together—and the sky a bit brighter. As quiet as he could be and still make it fast, Peter unhitched the horse, slapped it hard on the left flank, then dropped to the dirt.

The animal ran downhill so fast the approaching boy had to jump out of the way to avoid being trampled. The poor horse had gone many hours without water, and while Sam stood and brushed himself off, the creature continued its mad dash for the trough where Quincy's livestock drank.

"Nothin' but a thirstin' runaway," Quincy yelled. "Get yourself back here."

Peter lay prone for a full ten minutes after he heard the Gale posse move out, then he rolled over and sat up. He carefully scanned the view over the sage, from his hiding place, he could see a distant puff of orange dust kicked up by the Gales' loping mounts. He turned his head and took a long look at the house. *Are Millicent and Clara inside? Did someone stay back to guard them? I'll have to take the risk, rap on the front door and see who answers. Well, perhaps not rap exactly.*

Rifle in hand, he approached the house at a run, hoping to minimize seconds exposed in the open. He reached the home and pressed his back against the outside wall just to the right of a front window. Slowly, he leaned over to peek in—but saw nothing. Like many settlers', the Gales' windows were not glass, but pale-colored cloth saturated with animal fat. Some light passed through the greased fabric, but there was no seeing in or out.

Looks like it's rapping after all. He stepped to the door, gave a couple of solid knocks, then ducked around the corner of the building and listened.

The door creaked open and someone called out in a tentative voice, "Hello? Who's there?"

Peter sighed with relief and stepped into sight. "Millicent!" he whispered loudly. "Over here."

It was a few seconds before she seemed able to talk. "Peter, no! It's too dangerous."

"You alone?"

"Yes, but—"

Peter hurried her inside and closed the door behind them. He looked at Millicent's face and cried out, "God in heaven! What did he do to you?" In the dim light, most of the left side of her face was a fresh, dark bruise that bore witness to the violence. Her lower jaw was swollen, the broken bottom lip caked thickly with dried blood. He reached out and touched the bruise with two gentle fingers.

She winced. "I'm well enough, Peter. Really."

He forced down his anger, shifting focus to the problem at hand. "My wagon is hidden nearby. I have everything we require to make it to California—but we'll have to leave now."

Her entire body sagged.

"What's wrong?"

"Clara's not here."

"Where is she? We'll go collect her."

Millicent gave a sad, slow shake of her head. "Quincy took her with—in case you showed up here."

Peter averted his eyes for a few seconds of thought, then, "You must come with me. Now."

She shook her head violently. "Not without my daughter."

"I'll return for her. I swear it by all that is sacred." He saw the agony of indecision in Millicent's countenance and pled, "They've already taken you for an adulteress, you'll surely be cast out from among the saints. Clara will be forever lost to you."

Millicent's tears flowed freely, her shoulders heaving with sobs. "There must be another way."

"Leave with Clara and me or be driven out all alone, those are your only choices. I swear in the name of Israel's God I will bring her to you. But we must leave now!"

She nodded. "It'll take me but a moment to fetch the sacks I packed earlier." Peter hurried out to retrieve his horse.

She soon stepped out the front door and sighed, "Always wanted to soak my toes in the sea."

Millicent Gale did not look back.

~25~

A single day had passed since Peter spirited Millicent away. Near the Gale cabin, Ginger stood, head down, nibbling on a patch of low grass. At the sound of another horse approaching, the old mare swiveled her head for a lazy look. The oncoming animal bore Peter Wilton—a fact that held no apparent interest for Ginger. She returned to the task at hand, tearing off a green tuft, her lower jaw moving back and forth, chewing with age-worn teeth.

Peter used his knock-and-hide method, and Tom came to the door speaking matter-of-factly, "Hello, Brother Wilton."

Peter signaled for silence with a finger to his closed lips and beckoned the child to his side. "Tom, my boy, who else is here?"

"Just me and Mama."

"Very well. I need to talk to your mum."

They went inside where Eva glanced up from folding clothes to see what must have looked like a different Peter. He knew his hair was disheveled, his face a patchwork of thin, strawberry blond whiskers, clothes dusted with dirt.

Eva gasped, "Brother Wilton! You mustn't be—"

"It's all right."

"No! Quincy's out looking for you."

"That I already knew," he said with a crooked half smile.

"Why in heaven's name would you risk your life to come back here?"

Peter glanced over to the boy. "Be a good lad, will you, Tom? Step outside and fetch my mount a bit of water. Need to talk to your mum alone." Tom shrugged and hopped out the door.

"I need your help. Millicent needs your help."

Eva looked stunned. "Stop right there," she said. "Where's my Millie?"

"Safe."

"You kidnapped Millie? You terrible—"

Peter gave his head a sad shake. "Why would you even say such a thing."

"She'd not have left on her own, not without Clara."

Peter looked at the floor and sighed. "She did—and I swore on my life I'd bring her daughter to her. But I can't accomplish it without your help."

Eva's eyes grew wide. "Do you think I'm mad? The bishop would cast *me* out. He'd give my Thomas back to—" She stopped herself midsentence.

Peter was confused by a single word. "Back?"

Eva continued as if Peter hadn't asked about her son. "You've already put Millie's life in danger."

"She's well," he protested. "On her way to California with the Clayworths."

"Clayworths?"

"Big emigrant train, probably the last one until next summer. Passed west of here yesterday."

He read Eva's hopelessness in her face. "Clara's back at Quincy's main house," she said, "while he and the militia are combing the mission for you."

"Is the child alone?"

"Of course not. Clara's under constant watch by Quincy's wife Jezzie and guarded by the boys—with guns," she said. "There's no way to get her out of there without a lot of lead flying—and if you get that little girl hurt, I'll kill you myself."

163

"All I have to do is bring her to the wagons," Peter said. "When Dan Clayworth heard our story, he swore to protect us. His train is well armed, I don't think Colonel Dame'll chance taking big casualties for an apostate and a single child."

Eva's expression hardened. "You can't know that to any certainty." Before Peter could respond, she continued, "But first you'd have to collect Clara. And I can affirm that is an impossible task."

Peter's sunburned lips formed a thin smile. "It is possible, with your help."

"Brother Wilton, you know I can't get involved."

"Then I'll find another way." He sighed deeply. "But some of Quincy's family may have to perish."

Eva shook her head in frustration. "There's no talking you out of it?"

"None."

"Then, before God and His angels, make me a single promise, Peter Wilton."

He hiked an eyebrow. "Anything."

"If Quincy or the militia get to you, you'll surrender without a fight."

Peter stiffened. "I'm not afraid to die."

"It's not *your* life I fear for," Eva said. "Now tell me the plan."

~26~

September 20, 1860

The Parowan Ward's weekday prayer meeting had just ended, and Eva and the other women along with numerous children stood outside the Rock Chapel. As usual, the brethren lingered inside, deep in man talk. It was late afternoon. Mothers pulled collars up against an unseasonably chilly wind while Thomas sat on a large rock, watching the children warm themselves with a spirited game of tag.

Eva walked up behind Jezzie. "Good evening, Sister Gale."

Jezzie turned to the voice. Her face registered surprise, probably that Eva Dunning was smiling at her.

Head down, poor Clara slouched at Jezzie's side.

"I trust you are well?" Eva said. *I expect no warmth from the woman, but she can't ignore the bishop's daughter-in-law.*

"Uh, yes, good enough."

Eva nodded, forcing her smile to widen. "And Brother Gale?"

"Satisfactory, I guess. So then, I'll wish you a blessed week, and we'll—"

"Clara!" With a few swinging steps, Thomas was at his best friend's side. Clara tried to pull away to greet him, but Jezzie gripped her hand all the tighter. Likely unsure what to do, Thomas just leaned on his crutch and smiled at his best friend.

Eva gave Jezzie a pat on the shoulder. "I'm making prickly pear jelly tomorrow." She seemed to have Jezzie's full attention,

165

the tart-sweet delicacy was certainly a rare treat in the Gale household. "May I bring some by later in the week?"

"Of course. I mean, if you'd like to." Jezzie paused for a moment. "Best come afore Saturday, though."

"Saturday?"

"Quincy'll be back."

Eva glanced in the direction of the chapel door. "Oh, I hadn't noticed you were alone," she lied.

"You coming by when he's to home, it might be kind of, you know."

"I understand." Eva feigned a sad look. "I wish it were different between us."

Jezzie responded with an ambiguous grunt.

"I could use some help," Eva said.

"Huh?"

"Gathering the pear pods."

Jezzie was obviously surprised. "I couldn't really—"

"Clara and Thomas usually do it," Eva said.

The faces of the listening children beamed with hope. Clara tugged her stepmother's hand. "Please, Aunt Jezzie. I promise I'll be well behaved."

"I'm not so sure, girl."

Clara got louder and whinier. "I'll do double drudgeries when I get back."

"You mean when you get *home*." Jezzie squeezed the girl's hand harder.

"Yes, ma'am. *Home*."

"She could come with us right now," Eva proposed. "I'll bring her and the jelly on Friday."

"I don't know—"

"Bennet'll keep her safe. You might even enjoy a bit of time to yourself."

Jezzie squinted her left eye in concentration. "All right," she said. "But the girl's got to be home afore Saturday. And best not to make mention of this to Quincy."

Eva gave her a wink and a reassuring pat on the thick arm. "Just between us girls, Sister Gale."

Jezzie released Clara, and the girl gave Thomas a happy hug.

❦

"Who decided to name this cow path a road?" Eva laughed. The track was scarcely more than a dirt ribbon where animals and wagon traffic had beaten down some of the sagebrush and weeds. Ginger plodded along the center where loose dirt had been churned into dust by myriad hooves. The wheels of Eva's little buggy were narrow-set, not wide enough to stay in the ruts cut by bigger wagons, so Eva and the children laughed when their rig dropped in and out of the deep grooves, rocking them side-to-side.

"Aunt Evie," Clara said.

"Yes, dear?"

"Could we please stop by my house?"

Eva was surprised. "I'm afraid if we do, Jezzie might change her—"

"I mean our cabin. I think there's an old frock still there. Don't want to gather pricklies in my church clothes."

❦

"Whoa, girl." Eva pulled back the reins and the wagon stopped. From a quarter mile away, she could see smoke wafting from the chimney of the little cabin that she knew had been recently abandoned.

"Ma's back home!" Clara hooted.

"Not possible," Eva muttered, mostly to herself.

"She is, I know it! Everything's gonna be back to what it was. Make Ginger hurry up."

Eva got the horse moving again, but there was no hurry-up left in the aging mare. While they approached the house, Eva ran potential accounts through her mind, none of which made sense. *Something's well off the beam. Best turn the wagon about and flee, right?* But propelled by curiosity and perhaps a bit of misplaced hope, she kept the horse moving toward the small log home.

When they got within ten yards, the cabin door opened a crack. Eva stopped the horse. She watched and waited, ready to turn Ginger and somehow coax her into a sprint if need be.

The door opened wide, and a woman stepped out. "Hello and welcome," she called out. It was not Millie, not anyone Eva had encountered before. The woman on the pine porch was tall and slender. She wore a prairie dress and apron like nearly every woman in the Mission, but without a bonnet, her smooth brown hair fell to her shoulders.

"Just now baked biscuits. Will you have some with me?"

Eva stared without blinking. "Who are you?"

The stranger approached the wagon, and Eva could see she was probably in her mid-thirties. "I'm Sister Warnock."

Sister Warnock stepped to the side of the wagon and extended a hand of greeting, but Eva made no move to shake it. "Who are you?" she repeated.

The woman responded with a warm smile. "Still Sister Warnock. But I'd be delighted if you'd call me Katherine."

Eva's thoughts were spinning like a desert dust devil. "What are you— Did you marry Quincy?"

For just a moment the question seemed to confuse Katherine. Then she laughed. "I see. This is his cabin, so naturally you thought— Actually, I'm still to meet the good Brother Gale."

"Yet you're living in his home?"

"Arrived earlier this week from Great Salt Lake City. President Dame suggested I stay here until . . ." Her voice trailed off.

Eva thought this might make a bit of sense after all. "On your way to California, Sister?"

The woman shook her head. "No. I plan to make Parowan my home."

Eva was stunned that anyone would banish herself to this rugged existence, but she could not think of a polite way to ask Sister Warnock if she were "crazy as a pet coon under a red wagon," as Granny Eadie liked to say. She just inclined her head to the right where Clara sat. "The girl lived here before. Needs to fetch a few things."

"Of course. Come in, all of you."

Eva preferred not to go inside, but the thought of Clara alone with this stranger caused her deep discomfort. "I'll go with her. You wait here, Thomas."

Within a few minutes, Clara had gathered her things and they were on their way to the Dunning home.

∞∽

The wagon made the turn and headed through the fruit orchard. "Another surprise?" Tommy blurted. He spotted an unfamiliar rig in front of the Dunning house. "Mama, who is that?"

Clara began to tremble. "N . . . nobody should be here, right?"

"No cause for alarm," Mama said in a calm voice.

Ginger picked up her pace and they were soon at the house. Mama stopped the wagon and they climbed down and went inside to find—Brother Wilton.

"You!" Clara ran over and commenced pummeling the man with tight little fists. "What have you done with my ma?" she screamed.

Mama grabbed Clara from behind, holding her arms to her sides. "Clara, wait. Let me explain."

"He stole my ma away!" Her cheeks were wet and angry hot. "Aunt Jezzie said I'll never see her again."

Mama took Clara by the shoulders and turned the girl to face her. "You'll be with your mother very soon," she said.

Tommy felt as confused as Clara looked. "What?" the two children said at the same time.

Brother Wilton knelt and looked into Clara's tear-filled eyes. "I promised your mother I'd bring you to her."

"Where is she?" the little girl sobbed. Tommy joined in with his own tears.

"Safe."

"Brother Wilton will take you to her," Mama said. "You must leave soon."

"B . . . but," Tommy blubbered. "When can Clara come see us again?"

Mama looked at him in silence, and the sadness in her face told him he was losing his best friend forever. Tommy felt like bees filled his head, stinging and buzzing and stinging and—
"That's not fair!" he screamed. "She can't just leave."

Mama knelt and took his hand. He yanked it out and turned his back to the liar.

He felt hands on his heaving shoulders. "I know how painful this must be, Thomas. But please, listen to me."

"No!" he yelled. "Clara's not staying. We're not making jelly. You told a lie." The bees were still there, and now his chest was achy, heavy with anger and sadness.

"Please try and understand, Son. I had to, I—"

"You told me lying was a sin. But you're a liar, Mama! And you're not even my real mother."

"Tommy." Clara stepped to his side and held his hand. "I have to go."

He couldn't believe, would not accept, what she said. "I don't want you to," Tommy sniffled.

"If I don't go with Brother Wilton, it'll be just like my ma died. I won't see her again till heaven." She gave his hand a squeeze. "I miss her so bad, Tommy."

His chin quivered, but he could not speak. The memory his most horrible day returned—the day he almost went to heaven from a rattlesnake bite. How hard he'd prayed not to be taken from his mama. Tommy took a deep breath and said the hardest words he'd ever spoken: "Go to your ma, Clara." He pulled his best friend into a big hug, sniffed twice, then whispered into her ear. "I'll find you in heaven someday. I promise." The bees stopped, but his tears did not.

৵৵

On Friday, Eva delivered prickly pear jelly and another lie to Jezzie: that Brother Wilton had showed up unexpectedly and ripped Clara from her arms.

"Now you've gone and did it to me, Eva Dunning," Jezzie wailed. "Quincy's gonna be madder than—" Jezzie's last words were lost in quavering fear.

৵৵

Saturday morning dawned, waking Jezzie from a fitful sleep. Instead of getting out of bed and tending to the day's chores, she pulled the blankets tighter around her. But the heavy covers could not protect against the fear that coursed like ice-melt through her veins. *My husband will be home afore dinner—and he's gonna blame me.*

About eleven o'clock, Quincy came through the door to find her still bundled in bed. He hurried to her side and said, "Jezzie, what's ailin' you? Been taken by the fevers?"

"No, Quincy," she muttered. "I done somethin' bad wrong." Jezzie went on to deliver the news of the abduction.

He raised his fist above his head.

"Please, no," she begged. "It's not my doin'."

He hesitated, then opened the fist and delivered a head-snapping slap to her left cheek and ear.

"It sure enough is your doin'. How foolish you gotta be to believe a single word comin' out of that Dunning woman's mouth?" He paused for an angry breath. "If Bennet won't chasten her, I'll ride over there and do it myself—soon as this business with the Englishman's concluded."

"Quincy, you have to forgive me. I—"

"Hush up! I'll hear no more from you." He stood and turned his back to the sobbing woman. Moments later he issued a thoughtful sigh. "Ah, let her go to her whore mother," he mumbled to himself. "One less damnable mouth to feed."

෨ඏ

On the following Sunday, Warren Dunning found an envelope addressed to President Dame on the steps of the Rock Church. Warren sought out the president, and the two men retreated to a quiet corner of the chapel where Dame read the missive out loud:

> *Common Law Bill of Divorcement*
> *William H. Dame, President*
> *Parowan Utah Stake of the Church of Jesus Christ of Latter Day Saints*
>
> *Dear President Dame,*
>
> *I, Millicent Parkinson Felder Gale, do hereby declare myself divorced from Quincy Nebbus Gale effective September 22, 1860. Having never entered into a marriage with*

Mr. Gale which was recognized under the laws of the United States of America, it is my legal right to unilaterally effect this common-law divorcement.

Signed: Millicent Parkinson Felder Gale, September 22, 1860
Witnessed: Daniel Jedds Clayworth, September 22, 1860

~27~

Fort Parowan - September 25, 1860

"Time to cease your lightmindedness, Sisters." The nattering stopped immediately. When Lavinnia Dame, local Relief Society President and First Lady of the Parowan Stake, spoke, people listened—and obeyed. She was a serious woman in her mid-fifties who knew there was a local legend she had smiled on one occasion—but not a soul'd yet dared come forward with a claim to have seen it.

The dozen or so women were wives of the most prominent local church leaders, the earlier cheery buzz no doubt a manifestation of the sisters' delight at the rare chance to enjoy the beautifully appointed domicile.

They were met in the home Lavinnia proudly shared with husband, William H. Dame. It was located in Fort Parowan, at the center of Old Town. That the residence was the earliest and finest in the entire area was only right, Stake President Dame was the Mormon equivalent of a Catholic bishop—except for his four wives. He was also Regimental Commander of the Iron Military District, four battalions of citizen soldiers armed and sworn to protect the Mormon theocracy at all costs.

This was President and Commander Dame's main home. His three younger wives shared a small farmhouse in New Town, well outside the walls of the fort. Lavinnia took pride in the fact that she was the only wife in residence at the primary home and that William seldom visited Virginia or Lydia nor even the youngest and prettiest, Sarah Ann. She sometimes smiled to herself when she thought that therein lay a possible explanation for a surprising fact: The head polygamist was childless.

"As president, I call to order the meeting of the Iron Mission Chapter of the Relief Society of the Church of Jesus Christ of Latter-day Saints," Lavinnia declared. "First order of business, may I introduce someone new to our stake, Sister Katherine Warnock. President Dame asked me to invite her here on account of her considerable experience as a seamstress." The long-limbed woman stood and smiled. The sisterhood returned the smile, but with an evident air of uncertainty.

Lavinnia continued, "I remind you that when the Society was created, our beloved prophet Joseph Smith charged us 'that the Society of Sisters shall provoke the brethren to good works in looking to the wants of the poor—searching after objects of charity, and in administering to their wants.'"

"Amen," the sisters spoke in unison.

"William, er, President Dame, is concerned that some in our midst have naught but rags to keep out the cold." Lavinnia went on to explain that her husband had assigned the group to sew a few basic items for the poorest of the mission's families.

She did not tell them that he shared with her a second, hidden motive: "Ascertain as much as possible about the new sister. Something may be rotten in the state of Denmark." She had not a clue where Denmark was, nor even what that had to do with the mysterious woman, but Lavinnia always did as her priesthood head instructed.

Over the next three hours, the ladies completed three little girls' dresses, half dozen boys' shirts and four woolen nightgowns for young babies. Lavinnia noted that Sister Warnock demonstrated only the most basic sewing aptitude. *Skilled seamstress? I think not.*

She also observed that the woman who called herself Katherine was a charming conversationalist with an uncanny ability to draw information from others while revealing little about herself.

∂๛

Two days later, Detective Kate Warne's elbow was steadied by Daniel, a teenager who knew her as only as Sister Katherine Warnock. A growth spurt was likely upon the lanky boy—his denim trousers reached only to his ankles and the shirt cuffs stopped well short of the lad's wrists.

She stepped up to the wagon seat and slipped a small stack of newly made children's clothing under the lap blanket resting on the seat between her and the older woman. "Pleasure to see you, Sister Dame," Katherine said. *A pleasure not yet to have been found out, of a certain. Perhaps today will yield some bit of information pointing to the captured child.*

She deigned a nod. "While we are out here, it would be acceptable to use our given names, Katherine."

"Very well, Lavinnia." Katherine patted the pile of clothes. "How many visits will we be making?"

"Just three," Lavinnia said. "But they're some ways apart."

∂๛

The wagon stopped in front of a dwelling that made Katherine's drafty cabin seem like a castle. The home was little more than a cave dug into the side of a steep hill. Katherine stopped a gasp. Back in Chicago she had heard that many Mormons, especially outside of the Great Salt Lake City, lived in privation. But nothing had prepared her for this. In front of a tattered blanket that served as a door, a frail woman squatted next to a cook fire.

"Good day, Sister Jens," Lavinnia called out.

"Hello, Sister Dame." The woman stood to greet them, and Katherine stared into hollow eyes, deeply set above pale, sunken cheeks. Her age could have been anywhere from twenty to fifty.

Daniel helped the ladies down. After handing Lavinnia some of the clothing, he retook his place on the driver's seat, then picked up a Book of Mormon and commenced reading.

Katherine watched three grimy children, ages approximately four to seven, approach. The urchins' movements were sluggish, and she wondered if they were afraid of the strangers or simply malnourished . . . or perhaps their blood had been thickened by the early autumn chill.

"May we come in?" Lavinnia said.

"Uh, yes, of course."

Sister Jens pulled the blanket door to one side and they entered the windowless cavern. Except for slivers of light that leaked in past the hem of the blanket, the dwelling was dark. When Katherine's eyes adjusted, she squinted to see the furniture—one narrow bed, a three-legged table and two rickety chairs.

Without waiting to be invited, Lavinnia took one of the chairs. Sister Jens motioned to Katherine to take the other. The mother stood while the listless children who had followed her inside dropped onto the floor, the only padding between their bony bottoms and the dirt a layer of wheat straw darkened with use and smelling vaguely of molding fruit.

"Sister Jens," Lavinnia began. "President Dame is concerned that you and the children have not been attending sacrament meeting."

"Since Oscar died, we've only been able to—"

"We've sewn special clothing for the tiny ones," Lavinnia interrupted. "If we leave it here, can we think to see you in Sunday services?"

"We have no horse nor—"

"I'll send Daniel to fetch you. Have them lined up by nine." She held up plain dresses for the two girls and a blousy shirt for the youngest, a boy. The children jumped to their feet and reached for something they had likely never seen before, an article of clothing that had not already been worn thin by another child.

"Tut, tut," Lavinnia warned. She handed the clothing to Sister Jens, then addressed the children, "These here are church clothes. You wear them now, they'll be soiled for Sunday. Also, Daniel placed a crate of victuals just outside."

With tears in her eyes, the grateful mother hugged the items to her chest. "Thank you, Sister Dame and Sister—" She seemed to draw a blank.

"Warne," Katherine said.

Lavinnia looked confused. "Warne?"

". . . ock. Katherine Warnock."

෩

The Jens family now behind them, the women rocked in gentle rhythm to the horse's gait. "Thank you for including me in this errand of mercy," Katherine said. "My heart is hurting for poor widow Jens. The sister has such a sad lot in life."

"True enough," Lavinnia said. "My husband seeks a good brother to marry her, take her and the little ones to his hearth. Until that day, I'll see they're clothed and fed." She turned away, perhaps to hide a tear or two.

"Your kindness is an example to every sister in the church, Lavinnia." *The woman is an unlikely angel. In spite of the dour exterior and haughty manner, I can't help but find her oddly dear.*

"So, Katherine, it's as yet unclear to me how a single woman such as you finds herself in the Iron Mission."

Katherine was cornered. She had hoped not to reveal her fictional past so soon, but having rehearsed the story many times, she answered without hesitation. "In 1859, my husband and I traveled with a wagon train bound from Fort Leavenworth to Cherry Creek."

"Cherry Creek?"

"Pikes Peak, Kansas Territory near the Utah border," Katherine said. "We hied ourselves out on news of a big gold strike."

"You're a long way from Pikes Peak."

"My husband perished in an Indian attack eight days after we crossed into Kansas. Cheyenne tribe."

"How did you—"

"After burying Franklin, I journeyed on with the emigrants for a way. I held no interest to remarry, and knew I wasn't cut out for a gold miner, so when the wagons passed through Great Salt Lake City, I just stayed."

Sister Dame looked surprised. "And you embraced the Restored Gospel?"

Katherine offered a silent prayer her pounding heart would not be heard. *This is the big one, Kate. Just tell it like you practiced.* "Zina Young took me in."

"One of President Young's wives?"

"Yes," she said, struggling to keep her voice even.

Lavinnia's interest seemed to surge. "Zina Diantha Huntington Jacobs Smith Young? That woman must have some stories."

"She is an angel on this earth." Kate willed a tear. "Because of that dear sister, my heart inclined toward the Saints."

"So why not stay?"

Katherine lowered her voice to a whisper to prevent Daniel from hearing. "May I speak to you as a friend and confidante?"

"Of course, my dear."

"Brother Brigham seemed to take an interest in me. I was recently widowed, and more recently baptized. It was all such a blur, that I—" Katherine's head sank.

"Decided to get yourself as far south as possible?"

"Not precisely," she said. "When President Young knew I wasn't to be his, he determined I should come here."

Lavinnia looked away, likely considering the new information at some length. Then she gave Katherine an almost-smile and a friendly elbow nudge.

"Another of Brother Brigham's wives or banishment to the Iron Mission? Hmm. Not sure which is the worse." She nudged Katherine again. "If I may speak as a friend and confidante."

"Of course." Katherine tittered a nervous little laugh. *Why has it just this moment struck me this is the worst alibi possible? Dame can easily check its verity. The hourglass just turned, and I've got no more than a week before he reaches church authorities in Great Salt Lake City and lays bare my deceit.*

಄

When they arrived at their next stop, Katherine and Lavinnia learned that Sister Crowther was out with the older children, gleaning barley from a neighbor's field. So they left the new clothes with seven-year-old Daphne who had charge of the three youngest.

Daniel helped the sisters back in the wagon. They settled in, and Lavinnia called out, "Daniel, do you know the way to the Hopkins place?"

"I do, Sister Dame."

"That'll be our last stop before home."

"Yes, ma'am." Daniel flicked the reins, and they lurched underway.

"How many children in the Hopkins family?" Katherine asked.

"Just one. Lottie had a baby boy a few months ago, but I fear she suffers mightily."

"Baby melancholy?"

"Not in the way you're likely thinking," Lavinnia said. "She lost a young girl—been two years now—but even with the new one, she can't get beyond it."

Katherine spoke without looking at her traveling companion. "The poor, poor woman. Two years ago, you say? How old was her daughter?"

"About three, if I'm not mistaken."

Katherine did some quick arithmetic. *That's the year the orphans were recovered.*

托托

From the wagon Katherine noted the home was small, a porchless log cabin with sod roof, all in apparent good repair. Nearby stood a well-made corral with two healthy horses. She smiled at a large vegetable garden, the rock-wall perimeter patrolled by three fat chickens that seemed hopeful a peapod or two might try to escape.

"Whoa, now." Daniel pulled on the reins and the horse made a smooth stop. "Here we are, Sisters."

After their young squire helped them down, the two women slapped road dust from their skirts and presented themselves at the only door. Lavinnia knocked and called out, "Hello, Sister Hopkins. Relief Society's here. Are you to home?"

Katherine heard the cry of a baby, at first faint, then louder. The door opened, and the mother appeared—her shrieking child wrinkled and altogether too small for the racket it was raising. The woman was gaunt, impossibly frail for someone Katherine guessed to be no more than thirty. The mother's tawny hair was likely quite lovely when cared for. Today it hung in limp, oily twines.

"Uh, hello, Sister Dame," she said with obvious surprise.

"Good day, Sister Hopkins. May we come in?"

"Yes, of course." Lottie stepped back and they entered.

Katherine had to force herself not to gasp—the inside of the home did not match its neat exterior. The only light struggled in through grease-soaked cloth that covered two window-sized openings. In the near darkness, she could see the home's single room was no more than twenty feet long by twelve feet wide, albeit the tiny space seemed larger because it held so few belongings.

"Lottie, this is Sister Katherine Warnock. She's recently arrived here from Great Salt Lake City."

"Welcome. Please sit down, Sisters." Lottie motioned to two chairs next to a small wooden table.

Katherine saw at a glance there was not a third place to sit. "Thank you, Sister Hopkins, but I'm a bit tender from that hard wagon seat. I prefer to stand."

Lottie was hesitant, but she sat down and immediately began to fuss with her clothing. She undid three buttons then a knot of strings underneath, baring a tiny, flaccid breast. The child latched on and the crying stopped.

"We've brought a few things for the baby," Lavinnia said. "Remind me of her name."

"Jacob."

"Of course—a boy. How old is he now?"

"Jacob's just past eight months."

Eight months? Katherine thought. *I'd have guessed not more than half that.*

"Is he well, dear?" Lavinnia asked.

"Suffering from the catarrh, I fear." As if to confirm his mother's diagnosis, the baby boy issued a wet sneeze that misted the front of his mother's dress. "I'm much concerned now the weather's turning colder."

Lavinnia held up a heavy woolen nightshirt, too big for Jacob by at least half. "Here's just the thing to keep the wee one warm on bitter nights."

Lottie took the garment and her face lit up. "Thank you. I . . . I just— Words fail me."

Lavinnia and Katherine responded with kind looks.

With her free hand, the mother held it up for her uninterested child. "Look, Jakey, a warm nightgown for you, my baby boy."

"He's so beautiful," Katherine effused. "Sister Dame said you lost a child. A girl?"

"Three years old," she said. "Rosie was a cripple."

"So sad," Katherine said. "What happened to the poor girl?"

"Well, she—"

A seething, warning look from Sister Dame seemed to stop Lottie mid-sentence. "We'd best be going," Lavinnia said, then she slid her chair back and stood. "Can we look forward to seeing you and Charles and young Jacob on Sunday, Lottie?"

"Yes, of course."

"Till then." Lavinnia guided Katherine out the door with a hand at the small of her back.

Katherine allowed herself the tiniest of smiles. *There's something about the Hopkins family that Lavinnia is hiding. I must find it out.*

૨∽જ

"She told you Zina Young took her in?" From behind the desk in his study, William Dame scrutinized Lavinnia over the tops of narrow reading glasses, feeling his forehead crease with equal parts confusion and concern.

"She did, William. And she said when she spurned President Young's affections, he sent her here—a banishment of sorts."

William rubbed his brow with two fingertips. *This made no sense.* "Someone should have sent me word she was coming."

"Perhaps. Or maybe the whole thing was a bit, uh, awkward for the Prophet."

"Tread lightly, wife."

Her facial expression softened. "The Brethren know how harried you are, William. Probably chose not to trouble you with such a trifling matter."

Dame tilted his head in thought, his sunken cheek propped up by a knuckle. "Easy enough to ascertain."

Parowan's sovereign leader picked up his quill and dipped it in the nearby inkwell. "Dear President Young," he began.

~28~

September 27, 1860

On an old horse borrowed from Lavinnia Dame, Detective Kate Warne was on her way back to the little Hopkins home. The day was pleasant, but she shivered at thoughts of the upcoming encounter. *Not at all certain how I'll be received. And if word gets back to Dame that I've been snooping about, there'll be none but hell to pay.*

At length, she reached the cabin and tied off the swayback nag. "Courage, Kate," she whispered, then took the five steps to the door. She offered her warmest smile when Lottie opened up. "I know I was just by here yesterday, but I wanted to talk a bit more," she said. "Hope I'm not intruding."

"Sister Warnock, what a, uh, pleasant surprise." The look on Lottie's face suggested it was more *surprise* than *pleasant.* "Uh, come in." She nodded in the direction of a small cradle. "Jakey's fast asleep. Please sit down. What was it you wanted to talk about?"

"Rosie."

The name of her child seemed to strike Lottie speechless.

"You didn't give birth to Rosie, did you, Lottie?" Kate was fishing.

There was long pause, then Lottie spoke with a quiver. "I did. She was my little girl."

Kate used her least threatening voice. "Rosie was three when you lost her, right?"

Lottie nodded but did not speak.

"Crippled?"

The mother gasped. "How did you—"

I may have just gotten a bite. "Right forearm—from a gunshot." It was not a question.

Lottie's face lost what bit of color it had. "I really shouldn't talk about—"

"Army men came and took her away, didn't they?" Kate said in slow, deliberate syllables. Lottie kept her silence. "Have you ever puzzled on what's become of Rosie since the soldiers collected her? How she's faring now?"

Lottie lowered her gaze. Fat tears rolled down her cheeks and onto the floor. "But how would you—"

"What in blazes is going on here?" someone yelled from the doorway.

Kate's body stiffened and her heart missed a beat. She whipped her head around to see an angry man, wiry thin, of medium height with light brown hair worn unusually short. *Keep your wits about you, Kate.* The nervous, twitching look on his face suggested he may well be inclined to violence.

"You must be Charles," Kate said, fighting to keep her tone even.

"Who in blazes are you?" he growled. "And what you doing talking about our little girl?"

In the desperate hope they would return her trust, Kate made a split-second decision to confide in the Hopkins family. "My name is Kate Warne," she said. "I work for Pinkerton's in Chicago."

Charles and Lottie stared open-mouthed—Kate realized the introduction was no more enlightening than if she'd announced her recent arrival from the moon.

Charles approached Kate with open aggression. "Best tell me right now how it is you're talking about our Rosie."

Kate flashed a smile intended to be disarming. "She's well, Charles. Poor arm's never going to heal, of course, but she's in Arkansas, in the care of a loving aunt and uncle."

Lottie managed a weak smile. She appeared to have given up the ruse that the girl was their own.

"Sarah Elizabeth Dunlap."

"What?" Charles blurted.

"That's the name Jessie and Mary Dunlap, her mother and father, gave her. Of course, they didn't survive the attack. But the orphaned Sarah—your Rosie—is back home, along with two older sisters."

Lottie's eyes grew large with surprise. "She had no sisters."

"She had nine siblings, Lottie. The army found two of them at Jacob Hamblin's ranch."

"Two? You said nine." Lottie's face contorted in apparent confusion.

"The oldest seven . . ." Kate took a deep breath and blew it out, ". . . were killed out there on the Mountain Meadows, alongside their mother and father, Sarah's—Rosie's—mother and father."

Lottie began to shake uncontrollably. "Seven dead children," she mumbled.

Charles pulled her into a tight embrace and spoke over his wife's shoulder. "This's the last time I'll ask it. What's your business here?"

"There's still one more."

Charles and Lottie shared a confused look, but neither spoke.

"A boy who was never returned to his family—the last orphan," Kate said. "And I think you may know where he is." She was fishing again. *It's not at all certain there is an eighteenth survivor. And even if he exists, I've naught beyond a feeling these people know a thing about him.*

Lottie gasped. "Charles, I think we should—"

"Kate, right?" Charles Hopkins stared at the rough pine floor.

"Yes. Kate Warne. From the Pinkerton's Detective Agency."

"What I'm about to tell you could get us all killed."

"I can protect your family, Charles."

He responded in a voice thick with cynicism. "Not from around here, are you, Kate? We're yet to see how you'll handle Dame's militia."

Charles and wife shared another look. Lottie gave him an almost imperceptible nod.

"I got a story if you want it," Charles said. "But you've been cautioned. Just hearing it could cost your life."

"I'm listening."

Lottie spoke first. "She was not more than a year when they brought her."

"Picture it, Kate," Charles said. "An innocent child with her arm half shot off. Who does that to a baby?"

Lottie began to sob. Kate gave her a sympathetic look, then turned her gaze to Charles and said, "I think I—" He averted his eyes. "Sorry, Lottie," Kate said. "Please go on."

Lottie calmed herself enough to continue. "They said Paiutes killed her parents. Attacked a passing wagon train west of here."

"They?" Kate pressed.

"President Dame and another brother I didn't recognize," Lottie said. "My first question was 'what's her name?' but of course there was no way of knowing that. Next, I asked how long we'd be caring for the poor little—" The racking sobs returned.

Charles rubbed his wife's back, then picked up the story. "President Dame told us she was ours, to raise her up as a God-fearing Latter-day Saint. And he made us take an oath to say naught but that the child was our own flesh and blood."

"But of an instant you went from childless to having a one-year-old with a bullet wound. How could anyone—"

"Not saying folks believed she was ours," Charles said, "but you can be certain no one dared speak it."

"And there were other children," Kate said.

Lottie nodded. "We knew there were a few. Never sure how many nor where they all got to."

"How about a boy, would have been three when Mormons murdered his parents." Kate enunciated *Mormons* with deliberate emphasis. "Redhead, six toes on his right foot."

The color drained from Lottie's face, and she stared at Kate, finally mumbling, "Our people didn't kill them. It was Injuns."

Kate clenched her jaw and pressed on. "The older children, the few that survived, said they saw white men—some dressed as Indians, others not—kill their families."

"That's unthinkable!" Charles yelled.

"Fear and anger have often driven men to do unthinkable things."

Lottie began to weep. "I'll not believe that a friend, a neighbor might have shot my Rosie."

Baby Jacob issued a little moan, and Kate lowered her voice to just above a whisper. "The important thing is that the last boy is alive and somewhere nearby, isn't he?"

"Thomas, he—"

"Lottie," Charles interjected. "Think hard before you say another—"

Lottie silenced her husband with a look of raw defiance. "Bishop Dunning let them keep him. Then they cut off his leg and—"

Charles finished the thought. "Chopped off the poor boy's leg. One with the extra toe, of course."

"Oh, no," Kate said in low growl. *Someone took the leg of a poor child to preserve their awful secret?* For a couple of seconds, she felt strength drain from her like water through a half-cupped hand. Then she inhaled deeply, air filling her lungs and rage flooding her very being.

"Yes," Lottie said.

"Is he still alive?"

"He is," Charles said. "And I know right where to find him."

Fueled by righteous anger and tender sympathy, Kate made her decision: *Were Mr. Pinkerton here at this moment, he'd surely conclude the child's wellbeing outweighs earlier instruction not to try and retrieve him.* "Tell me his name and where I can find this child."

Lottie and Charles shared a look. "You'll need help gathering him up," he said.

"What are you saying?"

"I'll help—for a price," Charles said.

"What price?"

He glanced at his wife, and she gave him another subtle nod. "Get us out of this godforsaken place and stake us to a new life in California."

Kate looked in his eyes, then into Lottie's. "You're sure?"

"Surer than sure," she said.

Kate nodded. "Then let's contrive a plan."

~29~

October 10, 1860

"Whoa now." The messenger pulled back the reins, and his galloping horse slowed to a trot then a walk, then stopped at the hitching post in front of Parowan's finest home. He jumped off and whipped the leather straps around the bar, glancing at the animal and at himself. Sweat had turned the trail dust into a reddish paste that covered horse and rider. "No matter," he spoke out loud, then reached into a well-worn saddlebag and retrieved a letter addressed to:

> *William H. Dame, President*
> *Parowan Stake of Zion*
> *ALL POSSIBLE HASTE*

The rider sprinted to the front door and pounded with urgency until Sister Dame opened it. "You look a fright. What's the fuss, young man?"

"Sorry, Sister. President Young directed me to deliver this letter without delay."

He held out the envelope and she took it. "The president isn't here just now. You'll have some hot food and cool water."

"Yes ma'am. Thank you, ma'am." He took a single step before she stopped him with her upraised palm.

"We'll meet 'round back."

❧

Eva called to her son, "Finish packing your things, Thomas. Get a wiggle on. Your father will be here any minute."

"Mama," Thomas whined, "why can't I just stay here by myself?"

His mother patted him on the shoulder. "Because you're six years old, that's why."

In truth, Eva was as unhappy as her son at the prospect of spending two days and nights at the home her husband shared with another woman. But Bennet was taking Naomi—now his favorite wife—to Santa Clara for her niece's wedding, and it was Eva's duty to help. "Someone has to care for the young'uns," Bennet had said. "And you're family. Remember?"

"But they're real mean," Thomas said.

"I won't allow the Shand children to torment you."

He folded arms across his little chest and frowned. "You can't stop 'em."

Eva knelt next to her son and looked him in the eyes. "I'll take a switch to anyone who even speaks cross to you."

Her boy shook his head. "You can't."

"I can and I will."

Thomas turned and walked away, mumbling, "You can't, and you won't."

Seconds later, Thomas said, "Sorry for sassing, Mama. I just feel like, kind of sad anymore." The little boy's eyes welled.

"Missing Clara?"

He nodded. "I can always talk to Woobydog, but she doesn't answer too good, uh, too *well*. 'Course I miss Aunt Millie, too. It's kind of like—" Shoulder-heaving sobs overcame her boy.

Eva knelt and embraced him, whispering in his ear, "Thomas—" They hugged each other tighter, and she and her son wept without words.

❧

Hiding behind a spreading apple tree near the corner of the orchard, Detective Kate Warne watched the front door of the Dunning house through opera glasses. Done in mother-of-pearl and bright brass, the dainty lorgnettes looked out of place, bordering on comical but suited to the task at hand. She would have preferred a seaman's spyglass, but such an instrument was far too unwieldy and conspicuous.

At the sound of horse's hooves behind her, Kate lowered the tiny binoculars and sidestepped left, keeping the tree between herself and the path that ran through the center of the grove.

Kate watched a man fitting the Hopkins's description of Bennet Dunning park the one-horse rig in front of the house and climb down from the seat. When he'd disappeared inside the front door, she took the opportunity to move to a spot where she was still well concealed but close enough, she hoped, to hear normal conversation.

Bennet emerged from the door with the red-haired child. Just behind them was a woman Kate assumed was the one who called herself "mother."

"It'll not be a problem," the man said. "If the boys bedevil you, they'll be answering to me."

Sure enough, the foot that could positively identify him is gone. How far will these dreadful people go?

The image through the lenses was jittery, but Kate thought she saw a sardonic eyeroll from the wife.

"But I really, really don't want to go to Shand's house, Papa."

Shand's house. Kate made a mental note.

"We'll be gone just two days," Bennet said. "And don't be calling it Shand's house."

"But it—"

"That's enough." Bennet hoisted the little boy up to the wagon seat.

"Don't forget Woobydog," the child said. The man lifted a three-legged animal to the child's side.

Kate waited till the wagon was well on its way, then hiked back to a thicket of scrub oak where her horse nosed the ground for acorns. "Hmm." She spoke out loud now there was no one to hear but the animal. "That rag-wrapped *whatever* she laid in the wagon bed looked to be about the size of a rifle."

⃟⃟

An hour later, Kate tied off her ride to a creosote bush and stepped to the Hopkins home.

Inside the cabin, Lottie stood and bounced the baby while Charles and Kate took the two small chairs. "Learn anything?" Lottie asked.

"They were heading for the Shand house. What's that?"

"Bennet spends most of his time with his second wife," Charles said. "Naomi Shand Dunning."

"Know where the place is?"

"Of course," Charles said.

"Best I could tell," Kate said, "Eva and the boy are staying there for a couple of days while he and—her name's Naomi, right?" Lottie nodded. "While they're off to a wedding."

Charles scratched his chin. "So, it'll just be Eva and Tom and the other children?"

Kate signaled affirmative with a little dip of her head.

"This could be our chance," Charles said.

"I think so. You both still right with the plan?"

Husband and wife replied with vigorous nods. "As long as you get us out of here," Charles said.

"Good. A big herd of cattle are nearby, running late on their way to California. I promised the drovers a lot of money to let us join them."

~30~

The first day at the Shand house was not so foul as Tommy had feared. Bess, the oldest and orneriest of the Shand-Dunning children, had gone with her folks. Aunt Naomi wanted the girl to attend the marriage of her Aunt Nettie. "After all," she'd said, "my girl's fifteen. Could be getting her own proposal any time now."

The minute she and Tommy arrived, Mama called a sit-down with Karl and Kyle. She told the bullies exactly what would happen to them if they tried something mean. Karl, the thirteen-year-old, blustered a bit, but both boys ultimately agreed they'd "not so much as look cross" at their stepbrother. Seeing their auntie-mother lean her old musket up against the wall just inside the door may have helped focus their attention.

The Shand boys' strategy was to make themselves scarce except at mealtimes. That was fine with Tommy. He was happy to do their chores while they were busy with whatever they did. And he was more than happy to help with Aunt Naomi's new baby, Sophronia Elizabeth. Pudgy and happy, his six-month-old half-sister—or whatever she was to him—was an amazement and delight. Tommy had seen the baby only a few times before, at church and from a distance. But now he felt so grownup and proud that Mama trusted him to help. Here he was, only six years old, holding Sophie all by himself and even feeding her little sips of milk from a narrow-neck bottle. And the baby helped him not to think so much about how he missed Clara, who would always be his best friend.

Sophie closed her tiny lips, probably to let Tommy know she'd had enough to drink. She squirmed and grimaced, then began to cry, surprising and upsetting big brother. "Mama, did I do something wrong?"

"No." Mama smiled. "She just needs a little burp."

"But how do I—"

"Let me take her. You go for a bucket of water."

৵৹৶

"How come you move along so good, Woobydog?" Tommy said. Fetching water was no easy task for a boy with a missing leg.

The dog responded with a look that might have meant, "I'd help you if I could."

He sought clear water with the least of sandy grit, so Tommy walked upstream till he found a spot where the creek ran slow and deep. Woobydog got there first, soon lapping the cool water with her long speckly tongue. Tommy squatted down on the bank next to her, laying the crutch aside and balancing on his right hand and left knee. He struggled but was finally proud—and relieved— to have filled and lifted the tin bucket without falling headfirst into the water.

The walk back to the house was even more challenging. Left arm extended for balance, Tommy held the bucket handle in his right, pinching the top of the crutch in his armpit and swinging it forward with twists of his body. It was slow going, but he and Woobydog finally made it back to the house with most of the water.

And without noticing someone was watching every labored step.

৵৹৶

Full, burped and drowsy, Sophie lay swaddled in her crib. Tommy sat nearby, rocking the cradle slowly while Woobydog slept at his feet. When Sophie's eyes finally closed, he smiled and spoke to her in a soft whisper, "Such a beautiful little thing. I can't believe you're my—"

A loud cracking, like a boot against the front door.

In his fear and confusion, Tommy perceived what happened next as a single violent, perplexing moment:

The waking baby shrieking in my ear strangers bursting through the door Mama running for the musket screaming "You will not take the child!"

Sharp-edged terror tore through Tommy deeper than anything he'd experienced in his whole life. He was so scared, he couldn't see or hear everything right. But his mother's cry echoed in his ears. "You will not take the child!"

Tommy reached into the cradle and grabbed Sophie, planning to hop out the back door with her and just keep running. But he stumbled over his dog.

He held tight to the baby, softening her fall by keeping his own body between Sophie and the floor. He landed hard, head snapping back and hitting the wood with a dizzying thump. But his tiny sister was unharmed.

Groggy from the fear and the fall, Tommy lay on his back, still holding the baby girl.

Someone grabbed Sophie from his arms.

A man bent over him.

Woobydog growled.

He heard a deafening boom.

The man's body jerked halfway around, then dropped to the floor.

Someone—a woman?—dragged the man out the door.

He saw a long red smear on the floor.

Then Tommy saw nothing.

Something damp and cool on his forehead.

The sound of his mother's voice.

Tommy opened his eyes to brightness that made the sides of his head hurt real bad. "Mama. What did— Sophie! Where's Sophie?" Yelling made the hurt even worse.

"She's fine, thanks to you," Mama said.

"I don't understand."

"Bad folks came. But we're safe now."

"Why would anyone want to steal a little baby?"

There was a long pause, then Mama said the words that made him think he still might be confused from the fall. "They weren't here for Sophie, Thomas. They came for you."

∽⌖∽

The next afternoon, Eva heard hoof beats and creaking wagon springs. She opened the door and looked out to see Bennet stop the buggy. Naomi and her daughter Bess climbed down, and Bennet guided the horse to the back of the house.

A few minutes later, Bennet stepped into the room, staring at the partially splintered door and a dark, red-brown stain in the porous pine below his feet. "Is Sophie alright?" he yelled.

"She's fine," Naomi called back. She was already holding her baby close to her full bosom.

"So, tell me—"

Eva interrupted Bennet. "Bess, would you please go outside with Thomas."

"I don't have to do as you say," the teenager replied.

"She said please. Now you two get on out for a while." Bennet's tone brooked no more backsass.

Bess stepped out. Thomas followed in the step-swing gait that his crutch required. Eva closed the door behind them.

"What in all wrath took place here?" Bennet asked.

"They came for Thomas."

It seemed to take a few seconds for Bennet to absorb the information. "When?"

"Yesterday."

From the back of the room, Naomi's voice interjected. "Came for him? Who came?"

"Americans? Soldiers?" Bennet asked.

"Not soldiers," Eva mumbled, "Charles Hopkins."

Bennet looked stupefied. "Charles Hopkins?"

"Yes. And Sister Warnock, the tall woman who moved into Millie's cabin."

Bennet's face fell blank. "I'm not grasping it."

"Nor am I," Eva said.

Bennet headed to the door. "I'll ride to President Dame's right now. He can send some militia after them."

Eva stopped him with, "Wait. That could be a misstep."

"Misstep?"

"President Dame doesn't want trouble. He'll simply order Thomas gone."

Bennet was quiet for nearly a minute, then, "More than likely he will. Seems the mission's not secure with the boy here."

Still holding the baby, Naomi stepped closer. "What in the name of heaven's goin' on?"

"Not full certain," Bennet shrugged.

Eva looked into her husband's eyes. "For just right now, I think we'd be safer if you stayed with Thomas and me for a bit."

Naomi flushed red. "You listen up. My husband's not going nowhere."

"He's *our* husband," Eva said. "And his first duty's protecting his family."

"That's as may be, but he ain't sharin' a bed with, with—"

"With his wife?" Eva said, her voice getting louder. "Who do you think—"

"Stop it, both of you," Bennet said. Then he turned to Eva. "Buggy's still hitched. The three of us are heading out right now."

"Oh, no you won't!" Naomi shrieked.

"For once, just let me finish," Bennet grumbled. "I'm going to make a report to President Dame, that's all. But I daren't leave Eva and the boy alone. We'll be back." He turned to his first wife and said, "You'll be staying with us a spell. And there'll be no more discussing it."

Eva despised the idea of sharing the house with Naomi and her vile children, but not as much as she feared for Thomas and left alone and vulnerable. "All right," she said.

Bennet patted her shoulder and said, "Good girl."

Eva bristled at the condescension, but Bennet seemed not to notice. He put on his sweat-stained hat and stepped out the door. She and Thomas followed close behind.

☙•❧

"I knew it!" William Dame stormed out of his study and into the kitchen where his wife kneaded dough on a board of smooth yellow pine. He waved President Young's letter in front of her nose.

"Knew what, William?"

"The Warnock woman. Brother Brigham's never heard of her. She's a liar, most likely a spy."

Lavinnia shook her head. "Told you right off she was lying—but a spy?"

"Snooping around, asking all those questions. What could she be but a damned spy for the United States government? Should have had her arrested when first she showed up."

Dame changed into his uniform, strapped on his sidearm, and fetched a long gun. Then he kissed Lavinnia goodbye and headed to the door, intent on riding to the Gale cabin and bringing back Katherine Warnock—or whatever her real name was—dead or alive.

He stepped outside to see an approaching buggy. Bennet Dunning stopped the horse, jumped down to the ground, and rushed up to Colonel Dame. "Sir," he said, "they came, tried to take the boy."

Dame put a settling hand on the younger man's shoulder. "Take your time, Brother Bennet. Catch your breath, then let me know exactly what's transpired."

Bennet continued, "They came while I was gone, tried to seize the boy away from my wife."

"The boy? The orphan boy?"

"Yes sir. They—"

"Americans?"

"No, sir. Charles Hopkins." Dame was staggered, but he let Bennet continue. "And the new woman that's been staying out to the Gale cabin."

"Katherine Warnock." Dame spat it out like a moldy strawberry.

"Yes, sir."

"When?"

"Yesterday, sir. Afraid they got a big head start on us."

Dame responded with a thoughtful nod, and Bennet continued. "I'll go with you right now, if you got an extra mount. Eva can take the wagon and get on home."

The colonel thought for a moment. "Now's no time to be leaving the boy with naught but a woman. Get them to safety, and if you pass anyone along the way, tell them I'm gathering men to the fort."

કે⊸ક

Kate had already galloped the wagon well out into the desert when she pulled back on the reins. "Whoa. Hold up." *I'm loath to take the time, but there's no avoiding it. Charles's injury needs attention. And I'm answerable, after all.*

She climbed back to where the bleeding man and his family lay. "Look after the baby, Lottie, while I tend to Charles."

His bloody shirt and underclothing concealed the damage, so Kate tore away the reddest, stickiest patch. In her law enforcement career, she had witnessed some nasty gunshot damage. Each one had been a veritable fountain of blood, so she was surprised to see Charles's wound had nearly stopped bleeding. The relative lack of gore allowed her a clear view of it. Eight inches below his armpit, the ball had torn a shallow gash through skin, muscle and a thin layer of fat. The wound gaped open on one end, jagged shards of one rib protruding.

"Tell me," Lottie groaned, averting her gaze.

"Not gut shot," Kate said. "Should heal up in time—if he doesn't get the fevers."

"Thanks be to our Lord," Lottie said. "What're we gonna do now?"

"We're moving a herd of longhorns to California."

~31~

Tommy watched Kyle approach. Mama was off to a neighbor to trade for some eggs, but Woobydog was at his side. She issued a low growl, and he calmed her with, "It's all right, girl. For now."

"Boring around here, ain't it?" Kyle said.

"Kind of."

"Me and Karl's gonna have some fun pretty soon here. He said you could play, too."

Tommy was not convinced. "Doing what?"

"Riding Daddles."

"Daddles?"

"The calf," Kyle laughed.

"I don't think I—"

"Don't be so offish, Tommy." Kyle patted Tommy's shoulder. "It's just a calf. Follow me."

Tommy picked up his crutch. *Can't be worse than just sitting around here. And anyway, I always did want to go cowboyin'.* He fell in behind Kyle, Woobydog at his heels, and they walked about a minute. Older brother Karl waited outside a big pine corral that held some longhorns and a big Jersey milker, probably Daddles's mama. The thirteen-year-old held one end of a thick rope, the other end tied around the neck of a real big weaner, reddish brown to match his mama cow. It had a light underbelly, white outlines around its eyes and a shiny black nose.

"Tommy, meet Daddles."

His papa ran a small herd, so Tommy knew a bit about cattle. He tried to hide a surprised gulp when he saw Daddles. *This is Daddles? He's got to be 600 pounds—way too big for a boy like me to ride.* "That's not a calf, he's a weaner."

"Weaned, but he's still a baby, only eight months old."

This "baby's" twice the size I was expecting. Got to get out of here lest I get hurt. "Too big. I can't even get my legs around him—uh, leg."

"Sure you can. Just watch Kyle," Karl said. The younger boy hopped up on the beast's back, and his brother led Daddles around by the rope. The animal's walk was so slow and calm that Karl had to yank the line up a few times to get Daddles to lurch just enough to keep the rider interested. Karl took a step closer. The rope went limp and Daddles stopped.

Kyle tossed a leg off and slid down the fat brown flank. "Nothing to it. Now it's your turn."

Tommy had reason enough not to trust the Shand boys, but Daddles was obviously a sweetheart, and Kyle's easy ride looked enjoyable. Kyle interlaced his fingers and turned his hands palms up. With a small hop, Tommy stepped in the makeshift stirrup, and the other boy boosted him onto Daddles's back. The calf was wide, and Tommy was right, his one-and-a-half legs were not enough to straddle it. The boy leaned far forward and caught a grip on the rope harness. He knew he looked kind of silly, so when the Shand boys started laughing, he just joined in. *This is already a bit of fun.*

"Ready to ride?" Karl asked.

Tommy touched his forehead as if it was a cowboy's hat. "Shore 'nuff."

Instead of guiding Daddles by the rope, Karl stepped to the animal's side. He whipped the lead under the body, just in front of the hind legs—the rope slapped the poor animal directly in the testicles, and Daddles leapt forward.

Kyle laughed till his shoulders shook. "Another time in the twiddle-diddles!" he called out. His older brother gave the privates one more solid whack then dropped the rope.

Daddles charged off in a lurching run. Thomas held tight to the rope collar, but the beast began to buck. Unable to keep his grip on the rope, Tommy flew off the animal, landing hard on his only foot.

Karl and Kyle laughed till tears ran down.

Tommy raised his head from the dirt. Daddles was no danger, the weaner was running away as fast as his hooves would take him. So Tommy decided to simply get up and hop the thirty yards back to his crutch. He bent his knee and placed his foot flat on the ground, but when he put weight on it, hot pain seared the ankle and he dropped back to the dirt. The anger and embarrassment hurt even worse than his foot, so he lay there for a spell, turned away so the evil boys would not see him cry. *Laugh all you want, Shand brothers. Someday, some way, I'll have my revenge.*

❧

A few hours later, Eva stepped into the far bedroom in Shand's left wing, hers and Tommy's chamber. She set a tan leather coaster and a cup of Brigham tea on top of an elaborately carved walnut dresser. The piece was dark and heavy, held up by curved Victorian-style legs—and somehow smelled of lavender. Thomas sat on a matching four-poster bed. The home was beautiful, the imported furnishings exquisite beyond anything Eva had seen in The Mission, or anywhere, for that matter. Jealousy gave her a little prick, but she ignored it. *My Thomas is more to me than all the riches of Europe—but it seems I failed him today.*

She handed her son the cup, and he drank in small sips. "I'm so sorry, Thomas," she said. "Ankle feeling any better?"

It was evening. She was alone with Tommy, the nasty Shand-Dunning boys had wisely found somewhere else to be.

"Hurts dreadful," Thomas said. "Mama, please." His voice was pleading, but not whining. "Can't we just go home?"

"I must be sure you are safe."

He looked up at her through rust-colored eyebrows. "But I'm not safe."

"At least your papa is—"

"He's never even here. You're the one who took care of those bad people before."

Eva nodded and almost smiled. "I guess I did."

"But you broke your promise about the mean boys. Let's go home. Please."

Eva sat silent for a moment. She had no answer other than, "I'll talk to your father about it."

"That means 'no, we're not going.'" Thomas threw up his arms in mock surrender.

Eva nodded. "Not just now. Sorry."

Thomas thought for a moment. "I got a idea. Been thinking about it all day."

He told his mother the plan in detail, then asked, "So you'll help me?"

"Hmm. Not such a grand plan, perhaps."

"It's my turn," Thomas said. "You made me come here, now you have to help."

ॐ

Eva gazed into the steam rising from a skillet where a dark red mixture boiled. Staring into the rising cloud, she thought about yesterday's bull riding incident and felt sadness from not keeping a pledge to her son.

"You all right, Mama?" Thomas asked.

"Yes." She broke from her reverie and ladled some of the fruity-smelling brew into a nearby tin cup, then looked up and offered her son a wry smile. "There, that should do it. Fetch me the honey, Honey." A grin stretched across his blocky face, and Thomas found the china cup that Naomi Shand used as a honey jar.

"If you ever make chokecherry jelly," she said, taking a handful of light brown seeds from a small bowl, "be sure every pip is out—there's something in those kernels'll give you the backdoor quickstep as surely as a belly full of green apples." She dropped the tiny cherry stones into what remained of the boiling juice and winked as she gave it a stir. "You find what you were looking for, Thomas?"

His wide smile revealed the gap where he'd lost a tooth the week before. "Gophie's in a bag out back."

☙❧

The next day, Eva made dinner, the heavier, mid-day meal of farm folk. She first took a dish to the bedroom for the pregnant Naomi, then cooked for the youngsters. A thick slab of bacon sizzled in the skillet, and she used a hand-carved wooden spoon to push it around, coating the blackened pan with hot grease. "How's that smell, boys?" she asked.

"Mighty good, Aunt Evie," Kyle answered. Karl and Thomas nodded their agreement.

"There's just the one piece of bacon, so you'll have to share. But I have eggs enough for all. And a surprise."

The Shand-Dunning brothers smiled like they could hardly believe their luck. *Guess Naomi doesn't cook much*, Eva thought. She tapped the now-crisp bacon with the spoon, breaking it into small bits, then Eva cracked six fresh eggs into the pan and scrambled the delicious mixture until it was firm, but still golden.

"Dinner's ready," Eva announced. Wooden bowl in hand, Karl elbowed his way to the front of the line. Kyle gave Thomas a forceful nudge and moved in to claim the second spot. Her boy voiced no complaint, but the smallest of smiles danced across his face. She hoped the other boys hadn't noticed.

After she dished the steaming eggs into their bowls, the children returned to the table where Karl and Kyle commenced shoveling down the food. "Boys," Eva said. Only Thomas looked up. "Don't you think we should thank the Lord for His bounty?"

The brothers did not slow their eating. Karl shrugged indifference and mumbled around a mouthful of eggs, "Too late now."

Eva smiled. *Perhaps it's just as well.*

Minutes later, she assessed the situation: Thomas had left a bit of scrambled egg uneaten, but his stepbrothers had already licked their bowls clean. Time for the surprise. "Fresh bread and chokecherry jelly sound good?"

"Hell, yeah," Karl said. She shot him a stern look, and he revised his answer to, "Er, yes, ma'am, Aunt Eva."

Eva set out a plate loaded with thick slices of warm bread that gave off a rich, yeasty aroma. Alongside the bread platter, she placed a wooden bowl filled with dark red jelly. Each of the brothers seemed intent on loading his piece of bread with as much sweet as it could carry. Neither seemed to notice that the slice Aunt Eva served her son was already spread.

❧❧

Tommy ate kind of slow. His thoughts went back to what was the saddest time of his whole life. For months after the bad leg problem, he mostly sulked about the house. He needed time to get better, of course. But he was also really scared, kind of thinking there was a snake or a scorpion or something behind every bush and under every rock. Sometimes he was so frightened he would not even walk outside to the privy.

Mama never complained, but Tommy knew dealing with the stinky chamber pot made life a bit worse for everyone. Papa had tried to convince him that there was nothing out there to hurt him—probably.

Clara was the one who finally coaxed him back outside, a few more steps each day. After a couple weeks, she brought along a burlap sack with something mysterious. When they found a good sitting rock, Clara said, "Wait here and just watch." She walked a ways, turned the bag upside down and shook out what looked to Tommy like a baby rattlesnake.

When she bent over and reached for the serpent, Tommy screamed, "Clara, don't!"

"Just a little gopher snake." She took a few cautious steps in Tommy's direction. "You trust me, Tommy?"

"Yes, but—"

Real, real scared, Tommy watched Clara and the snake approach. What he saw was a light brown body and dark marks, a lot like that rattler.

Twenty feet out, she stopped. "You all right?"

He finally took a breath and said. "If you don't come any closer."

"It's just a gopher snake, Tommy. You've seen them before—can't hurt anybody," Clara said. Her voice was calm.

Gopher snakes were in the foothills near home. He had spotted lots more of them than rattlers, but Tommy still found them scary. Clara once explained that a gopher snake kept itself safe by looking and acting like a rattlesnake—and a rattler had cost him his leg. Tommy squinted hard at the snake—no rattles, no triangle-shaped head—a gopher snake, sure enough. But still—

After Clara put the snake back in the bag, she stepped to Tommy's side and said, "We'll get you used to Gophie a bit at a time, all right?"

"Maybe. But no way I'm calling it *Gophie.*"

It had taken a real long time, but Tommy eventually lost his fear. He even came to call their new pet Gophie.

Tommy's attention came back to the doings at hand. Karl, the older brother, was first. He doubled over, stomach rumbling so bad Tommy could hear it. Karl bolted out the door like a scalded cat, younger brother Kyle close behind.

The boys raced each other for the only outhouse, the smaller Kyle soon taking the lead. He threw the old wooden door open, raised his foot to step inside, then froze in place—right where his step would have landed, a small snake was coiled, head raised, tongue licking the air. The boy spun around and ran.

Tommy had followed them outside. Leaned against the back wall of the home, he watched the funny scene. "Hey, dolt," he called to Kyle. "It's just a gopher snake. Can't hurt you."

It seemed Karl hadn't heard, He did a kind of dance, dropping his trousers and fast-waddling the rest of the way to the privy, then stepped inside and closed the door behind him. A single second later, the older boy burst out the door screaming, "Help! Rattler!" His pants hobbled him at the ankles, and he fell face-first into the dirt, bawling and crawling away as fast as his bare knees would carry him.

"By golly," Tommy whispered. "Mama was right about those chokecherries." He tossed his head back and laughed harder than he ever had before.

☙❧

Hours later, Eva stood outside the front door, staring west and shifting her weight from foot to foot. *He should have been back by now.* Dawn to dark, Bennet roamed the nearby foothills, leading his cattle to the few meadows that had not surrendered their green to the yellow-brown of fall. Eva knew her husband longed to be hunting for the evil woman who had tried to hurt his family, but he remained obedient—more or less—to Dame's order to stay home and guard his charges.

The setting sun pierced the Parowan Gap, a narrow split in the low-lying western mountains. It would soon be dark, but still no sign of Bennet. She made her decision—*can't stay here after today's shenanigans*—but had to admit to some doubts. *Am I protecting Thomas or just putting my son at greater risk? The Hopkinses and that woman must have an escape plan, must be on their way south, never to come back, unless— Was it possible? Could President Dame have furtively sent them to spirit Thomas away?* She shuddered. *No. He would have been more—* Her thoughts were interrupted by approaching hoofbeats.

Eva waited inside while Bennet finished hanging the tack and combing out the horse. It was completely dark when he finally opened the front door. She watched him enter from her spot near the cookstove "Everything all right?" she asked. "You're later than usual."

"I'm fine." Bennet stepped in and took his place at the table. "Ran into a couple of militia boys and we talked awhile."

"Have they found the Hopkinses?"

Bennet waggled his head. "Not really looking, far's I can tell. Colonel Dame's thinking is they put in with men driving stock through."

"Cattle don't travel all that fast. Couldn't they've caught up to the drovers by now?"

"The colonel doesn't want that kind of trouble, so they just—"

"Gave up?"

"Doesn't matter, Eva. There'll be no more mischief from Charles and Lottie and what's-her-name."

"It's certainly not Katherine," she said. "Don't suppose we'll ever know her real name nor learn who set her up to the mischief."

"Likely not," Bennet said. "But as I said, she's—they're gone now."

"Doesn't mean she, or someone, won't be back."

"They're gone, Eva. Don't go borrowin' trouble."

She folded defiant arms. "Either way, Thomas and I are going home tomorrow."

"And I'll be more'n happy to deliver you," Bennet said with a sigh.

❧❦

That night, some thirty miles southwest of Parowan, Kate sat surrounded by darkness and the lowing of two hundred cattle. Nearby, half-a-dozen drovers huddled around a big campfire, backs to the cold night, mostly swapping lies about sexual conquests. Kate was no stranger to how some men jawed—she had spent most of her life around rough characters but had no stomach for it this night. So she found a sitting stone well back from the circle.

When she'd wrapped herself in a blanket and settled, Kate bit down on a belt-tough chunk of jerked beef, grinding her teeth and yanking her head sideways to tear off a stringy bit. *Maybe that's why they call it jerky.* From a dented tin cup, she took a sip of coffee and swirled it around in her mouth, hoping to soften the gristly morsel. The thick black liquid matched her mood, "bitter as wormwood," the Good Book called it. *I bungled this one up pretty bad. Disobeyed a direct order from my superior—and there's naught to show for it but a good man shot.*

She glimpsed the Hopkins family in the nearby wagon. Lottie and the baby huddled together under heavy quilts. Her husband lay nearby, twitching in sporadic bouts of pain. Kate was grateful to have made it to the safety of the cattle camp ahead of Dame or whoever he might have sent. She'd done a good job of patching up the man's wounds and was almost certain he would heal—eventually. In the meantime, back in Parowan, the orphan's she-bear "mother" and God-knew-who-else were surely on high alert. *What now?* She stared into the blackness that filled her cup. *Deliver the Hopkinses to safety, of course. And then? Then worry about how to get myself back to Chicago to face the music.* The strategy was simple, but oh, so far from easy.

~32~

Chicago, Illinois - February 15, 1861

S he pulled her coat collar tighter around her neck, but the wind off Lake Michigan still stabbed like a ragged icicle. Kate had spent nearly four miserable months making her way back to Chicago, all the while fearing this moment more than death itself. Staring at the door directly ahead, she was racked by sudden shuddering brought on not by biting cold but borne of dread. She swallowed hard and reached for the knob under the familiar insignia: "Pinkerton's National Detective Agency."

Ruby Seddon had made the return trip to Chicago, anxious to hear Kate's news firsthand. She and Allan Pinkerton listened in rapt silence while Warne, eyes cast downward, gave her a report of events in the Utah Territory. "My error was grave, that I surely know," she concluded.

The Scotsman fixed his fiery gaze on her. "Detective Warne," he said, "can ye think of a single reason I should not sack ye on the spot?"

Kate signaled *no* with a shake of her head.

"Maybe even report ye for—"

"Hold up them horses, Mr. Pinkerton," Ruby said. "She was sent to find my grandson." She turned her head, addressed Kate, "And you found him, right?"

Kate nodded. "I did."

"You're sure?"

"He was red-headed, six or seven years old—and had an extra toe on his right foot. That is, before—" Kate's voice faltered.

"May God curse them Mormons that cut it off." Ruby was desperate to wipe away any doubt that this was her Levi. "Guess there's not the chance of a snowman in San Antone the boy had a dog."

"He did, actually—a three-legged mutt."

Ruby stood. "Praise the Lord! He's still got—"

"Woobydog, of course!" Kate said. "Brought all the way from Arkansas—named after you, no doubt."

Ruby leaned down and hugged poor Kate as best she could. "Bless your heart. The whole thing went total cattywampus, no denying that." When Ruby released the awkward embrace, Kate raised her tear-wet face. Ruby graced her with a forgiving smile. "But your heart was right, and you found him. So now we can—"

"We?" Mr. Pinkerton shook his head vigorously. "I cannot in good conscience send Kate back there."

Ruby leveled her gaze on the man. "Of course not. I'm the one's going."

Pinkerton shook his head. "No! Not after all that's—"

"I'm Levi's blood kin. If—when—I bring him back with me, by the law it ain't kidnapping. You're the one told me that part."

"I know how you must feel, Ruby," Kate said. "But the only law these people recognize is what comes down from Brigham Young himself. The game is up—you can't just waltz in out of nowhere and take your grandson now. Local militia will be waiting and watching. They'd kill you in an instant and not think twice about it."

"And I'd not think twice about dying for Levi, blood of my blood." Ruby looked away for a moment, then, "But best I live to care for him. You was there, Kate. How'm I going to do it?"

Before his detective could reply, Allan Pinkerton drew in a deep breath and exhaled a sigh. "There's no dissuadin' you, Ruby?"

"If that means talking me out of it, answer's no."

"All right, then," Mr. Pinkerton said. "We'll want a plan—a right crafty one." He pushed quill, inkwell and two sheets of foolscap folio across his desk to Kate. At the top of the page, Kate wrote *UNITE MRS. SEDDON WITH HER GRANDSON.* Pinkerton insisted that the next line read *WITHOUT BLOOD-SHED.*

"The list should begin with 'An armed guard must accompany Mrs. Seddon at all times,'" Kate said.

"I can't spare a single man," Mr. Pinkerton said. "Every last one of them's contracted to the U.S. government, preparing for the inevitableness of war."

"And my husband can't go," Ruby said. "Harold's with his militia battalion, making them same preparations."

Pinkerton thought for a moment, then his aspect brightened. "Not to worry. I know of just the man."

"Excellent," Kate responded. "Which brings us to number two: *STEALTH.*" She took a quick breath and continued, "But the most important point is the third, *DO NOT UNDER-ESTIMATE WILLIAM DAME.* He is the religious and military leader of Southern Utah, with a built-in network of spies and trained soldiers willing to die—and no doubt kill—for him."

Pinkerton tapped the page with two fingers. "Which is precisely why you're not going back, Kate."

She gave it one more try. "But I can disguise—"

"There'll be no changing my mind on this. If Dame's as sharp-witted as you say, he'll be onto you quicker'n an Irishman on a whiskey-soaked potato."

Kate stood. She placed both palms flat on the table and leaned in toward Mr. Pinkerton. "I know how fraught with danger this is. You cannot allow Ruby to attempt this alone."

Mr. Pinkerton smiled. "Not alone, just without you, my dear Kate." He turned. "Ruby, one last chance. Can I talk you out of this fool's errand?"

"I'm going," Ruby said, "with or without y'all's helping."

Soon the two-page plan was complete, and Pinkerton handed Ruby the papers covered in Kate's careful handwriting. "You'll learn it by heart. This can under no circumstances be found on your person." Pinkerton waited while she nodded her agreement, then he continued, "We'll make travel arrangements. Send me word the minute you get to San Francisco."

"A Pony Express letter?" Ruby asked.

"Time you get there, Pony Express'll be out of business," he said. "Western Union will have our country connected shore to shore."

❧

Three days after the planning meeting, Ruby Seddon stood staring. She blinked twice and stared again. She'd heard stories, descriptions of the ocean, but nothing had prepared Ruby for the scene spread before her. "It's just so durn big!" she exclaimed.

"It is quite a spectacle," Kate said.

Boston Harbor dwarfed the largest lake Ruby had ever seen. And beyond the huge chunk of land protecting the bay, the open ocean reached forever, or at least to a distant fog bank that hid the horizon. Rowers shuttled tenders back and forth from a dozen tall-masted ships spaced across the anchorage. There were also a few sleek clippers tied up directly along the wooden wharf, swarmed by sweaty men muscling up and down narrow gangplanks with heaping carts and barrows.

Between piled bags and stacked crates, crowds of confused-looking folks milled about the dock area. Some appeared to be arriving, passengers wearing strange clothing soiled from months at sea. More presentable groups herded children and dragged wooden steamer trunks, about to embark, Ruby reckoned.

An especially well-dressed gentleman passed nearby. "Beg pardon, sir," Ruby said to the lanky man. "Mind if I ask you a question?"

Her companion blanched. "Ruby, I told you not to speak!" Kate said in an urgent whisper.

For a moment, the man glanced around in apparent confusion, then focused on Ruby. "You're a Southerner!" he blurted.

"I am, sir, but—"

"So, you're what the enemy looks like."

Kate intervened. "Not the enemy, sir. Just two frightened women escaping the trouble that's so soon to be upon us."

"Soon, indeed," the man said. "Word is rebel traitors have taken a certain Fort Sumter in South Carolina. An act of war, if ever there . . ." The man's voice seemed to Ruby to just fade to nothing.

Feeling as if her very breath had been stolen from her, Ruby turned away without explanation. *War? If it's war, Harold'll be called out with the rest of his brigade. Oh, sweet Lord in Heaven, please keep him safe. You know how I love the old man. And we two are the only family poor Levi has left.*

ॐॐ

"It will be a fine adventure," Kate said without conviction. She and her wide-eyed companion stood before the *Gull Atlantica*, a square-rigged brigantine with masts that stabbed seventy-five feet into the sky. Following the women, a teenaged boy pushed a wooden barrow holding a suitcase packed with her Bible and the few other items Ruby had deemed essential for the long passage.

When the ship's tender tied off at the pier, Kate shuddered. Her last journey was an all-too-recent memory. Parowan to California with a wounded man, his family and a pack of ill-bred cowboys. San Francisco to Panama via ship, through the steaming jungles of the isthmus, then four weeks aboard a Bermuda-rigged schooner before landing in Boston. The expedition had consumed months of Kate's life, and the much older Ruby was about to undertake the same grueling route in reverse.

A little shiver buzzed along Kate's spine, guilt and relief washing over her at once. In truth, she was thrilled not to be boarding the ship. But she wasn't distressed by the dangers and depredations that surely waited. What she detested, even feared, were the months of inescapable, unrelenting, soul-crushing boredom. *Perhaps Ruby will handle it better.*

~33~

Parowan, Utah Territory - July 15, 1861

L eaves hid the first of their plump red tomatoes, but Tommy was determined to find them. Surrounded by the sharp smell of vines, he crawled on his hands and knees, nudging the bushy branches aside as he went. He stopped and frowned at a morning-glory weed that wound itself around two tomato plants, determined, it seemed, to choke the life out of his favorite food. He untangled the wicked vine, followed it to the spot where it grew from the ground, then gripped the bottom of the stalk and tugged with just the right amount of hard. "Gotcha," he said when the dirty roots came up without breaking. Then he crawled a few more feet down the row and harvested three red prizes, all fat and firm.

Mama stood at the edge of the garden, holding his crutch. Since the incident with the Hopkinses and that woman, she had not let him out of her sight. "Dinner time, Thomas," she called. "Find any Tommy-toes?"

The nickname never failed to give him a laugh. "Found five, right at the end of my foot. Oh, and three nice 'maters."

Once inside, Mama cut the tomatoes, fanned the slices out on a large plate and set them on the table next to thick slices of brown bread. "Thomas," she said, "would you please return thanks?"

He said a quick grace, making sure to thank the Good Lord for their wonderful garden and fruit orchard. Then he and

Mama laid on the slices, sweet red juice soaking into the bread. It was probably the best thing about summer.

Without rap or warning, the door latch turned.

"Under the table!" Mama yelled, leaping up and grabbing the loaded rifle she still kept just inside the door. In less than a wink, she pulled the butt tight to her shoulder and aimed the weapon.

From outside, someone threw the door open.

Tommy gasped. His mother was pointing a gun at the center of his father's chest.

"Hades' sakes, woman—just need to talk to you," Papa growled.

Still shaking, Mama set the old gun back in its place, then gave Papa an odd stare. He had not stood in their doorway even once since bringing Mama and him back from the Shand house last year. "Bennet, I, uh— You're just in time for tomato bread."

"Let's step outside, Eva."

∂~∽

Eva followed him onto the porch. When Bennet had closed the door behind them, he spoke. "President Dame just received news from Great Salt Lake City: The war's begun."

"The Americans are marching on Utah?"

Bennet shook his head as if to say, *silly woman*. "War between the states, North against South. Point is, there won't be soldiers around here for a mighty long time. They got more than enough to do for now."

Eva's face brightened. "So Thomas is safe?"

"No army'll be coming. And whoever that Katherine woman was, Dame's standing order is to capture her on sight."

Eva relaxed a bit. "Bennet."

"Yes?"

"Thank you for coming here to tell me," she said. "The news is such a relief."

"Now unload that musket and put it somewhere other than by the door," he grumbled. "Somebody's bound to be shot."

કર્

The light of two little candles danced about Tommy's room, softening edges and turning the all the colors a pale yellow. The space was small, with just one chair and a boy-sized bed. It was perfect.

Already in his nightshirt, Tommy was perched on quilts he'd bunched up in a pile. Sat in the room's only chair, Mama's smiling face looked like flickering gold. "Are you extra happy, Mama?"

"I am," she laughed.

"How come?"

"'Cause I'm here with you."

"You're always with me."

"Yes, but now we can cease worrying about people coming."

"Does that mean my bad dreams will stop?"

"When you say your prayers tonight, thank Heavenly Father that we don't have to fear any more. And ask him for only happy dreams, if that's His will."

Tommy smiled till his cheeks hurt, then gave Mama his biggest hug. "Sure hope that's His will," he whispered.

~34~

San Francisco, California - July 15, 1861

R uby Seddon leaned on the ship's rail, watching San Francisco loom ever larger. Unlike the endless flat of her Arkansas, this place was a jumble of steep hills dotted to their tops with red-roofed buildings. It was mid-morning, and brilliant sunshine glinted off San Francisco's broad bay. The conditions were ideal. A gentle offshore breeze filled the sails of the *Young America*. The three-masted clipper was built and rigged for speed—they'd made passage from the western shore of Panama to San Francisco in less than two weeks. "An astonishing feat," the captain claimed.

All told, Ruby had traveled just over three months and she felt as worn out as the few items of clothing she'd brought along. She inhaled the briny air and blew a kiss toward the east. "Wish you was with me, Harold," she said to the breeze. "Tonight, I'm sleeping in a real bed." A smile filled her face. "After I eat strawberries and cream till I'm full as a tick on a Carroll County coon hound."

The wooden pier looked to be a half-mile from where the ship was anchored. Small tenders pushed off in Ruby's direction, and it was not long until rowers arrived in eight leaky boats which they quickly tied off to *Young America*. Then confusion set in.

Dragging travel cases and steamer trunks, passengers pressed into tight clumps, unbathed bodies elbowing and shoving, desperate, it seemed, to finally set foot on the golden streets they had so long dreamed of.

At last Ruby stood on dry ground, though her legs were not at all convinced they'd left the pitching ship behind. *Disembarking*, as the crew called it, had taken nearly three hours, but she'd made it. *I'm finally in the Californee. So far away from Arkansas, may's well be a million miles 'twixt me and my Harold.*

Dragging her heavy suitcase, Ruby took in the scene. The mad bustle of San Francisco overwhelmed her. In contrast to the orderly canyons of Chicago's lofty buildings, this place was a bewilderment of shanties, hotels, shacks, and barrooms scattered about, no sign of thought nor plan. Without apparent concern for the poorer folk under foot, noble men and women rode in gleaming hansom cabs. Crowded about the carriages was the oddest mix of human beings Ruby had ever seen. Long-bearded men caked with dirt, painted ladies in gaudy dresses and all manner of workmen filled the street. And there were other, darker folks, the likes of which she never imagined.

Ruby soon ducked into a small café. The establishment had no strawberries, so she ordered a small steak, well done, and a wedge of cake spread thick with peach jam. She relished each bite, and when she'd scraped the plates clean, Ruby sat back, staring at nothing in particular and planning next steps in her mind. At length, she broke into a determined smile, pushed her chair back across the rough wood floor and stood. "How much I owe you?" she called to the proprietor, a slight woman in a once-white apron.

"Fifty cent," was the curt answer.

"Half a dollar? Can't be right."

"Welcome to California, Sweetie. If you ain't got the cash, kindly return the merchandise."

Ruby's brow wrinkled with confusion. "Sakes alive, don't think you want that."

The woman stepped over, hand outstretched. "Then cough up the four bits."

Reluctantly, Ruby parted with a precious half-dollar, then asked, "The telegraph here yet?"

"It is." The woman gave directions and Ruby and her case headed out.

০⊷৩

The cost to send a telegram was also disgraceful, ten cents for each word. So Ruby kept her report as short as possible.

Mr. Pinkerton STOP
Arrived SF STOP
All well STOP
Advise FULL STOP

"No way of knowing when he'll get back to you," the operator said from under his eyeshades. "Maybe check tomorrow."

Ruby smiled and nodded. "Thanks to you. Know where I might find a cut-price hotel, preferably also a house of ill repute?"

The man's mouth and eyes opened wide. "Well . . . I . . . uh . . . guess the El Diablo would fill that bill."

Months before, Pinkerton had told Ruby the man she sought would likely be in the roughest part of San Francisco, the Barbary Coast, sailors called the district. So she made her way to Pacific Street, the reputed center of local debauchery, and stopped at Number Forty-Nine, a place designated by a single red lantern and crooked sign as the El Diablo Hotel.

Fear and disgust washed over her, and Ruby hesitated for a moment, wishing there was another way. But Mr. Pinkerton's instructions had been clear, so she shrugged and stepped through the door. Seated behind a small writing desk was a plump woman Ruby guessed to be in her forties. *That gal's wearing enough face paint to whitewash a barn. And she could be hiding a punkin in that cleavage—or maybe a six-shooter.*

"Help you?" the woman asked.

"Sure enough," Ruby replied. "Need a room."

"How long?"

"One night, maybe more."

The hefty woman laughed, her ample bosom heaving up and down. "We rent by the hour, Darlin'."

Sounds like I'm in the right place. "Let's start with seven hours—with a bath and clean sheets. And I could use a bit of help finding a man."

The clerk broke into another full-body laugh. "Find a man? Now you're speaking my tongue. I'm Cassie, by the way."

Ruby stuck out a hand and Cassie shook it. "Ruby Seddon," she said. "Looking for a rough-edge gunslinger name of Niall Gallagher. Know of the man?"

"Met plenty of ruffians in my day," Cassie said, "but not this particular gent. A lot of men such as you've described can be found at The Coast."

"The Coast?"

"Saloon not far from here. Wouldn't send you there at night, but I'll provide directions in the morning, if you like."

"I would. Also, can I ask you a different question?"

"Of course."

"Saw some folks today confused me," Ruby said. "Skin's a bit like an Injun's in color. The men—least I reckon they was men—wore strange clothes and some of them had a single braid of black hair running down the back. And their eyes was peculiar, maybe like when a white man squints into the sun."

Cassie shook with another laugh. "You've never seen a Chinaman?"

"Say that again?"

"Chinamen. The railroad brought them over to lay track through the mountains."

Ruby shook her head in wonder. "Not so many Chinamen back to Carroll County."

❧

Ruby came down the stairs from the second-floor room. Her sleep had been mostly unaffected by the constant noise of bedsprings creaking and voices moaning and arguing—the El Diablo was quiet as Jesus's tomb compared to the crowded ship—and it didn't lurch and rock about. In fact, six-hours of uninterrupted sleep was the most she'd had in three months.

Cassie greeted her with a friendly, "Morning. You able to get some rest?"

"Your place here's heaven on earth," Ruby said.

"And all this time, I thought it naught but a tumble-down whorehouse," Cassie said, shaking with laughter.

Ruby soon joined her laughing, and the mirth felt nearly as healing as the long sleep. When they'd both settled down, Cassie asked, "Where's that Carroll County you spoke of, Ruby?"

"Arkansas. Most beautiful spot on God's green earth."

"This your first big city?"

"Afore coming here, I spent a bit of time up to Chicago, a right fearsome place."

Cassie's face turned serious. "Chicago, eh? That burg's a Sunday School compared to Frisco. Promise me you'll be careful."

"That I shall."

After Ruby arranged for another forty-eight hours' lodging, she said, "No more time to dawdle, I got a duty. As for finding this Coast saloon, which way should I be heading?"

Armed with Cassie's instructions, Ruby stepped out into light fog that put her in mind of misty morning in a child's fairytale.

First stop was the telegraph office. There was no word yet from Mr. Pinkerton, so she set off to find the establishment Cassie recommended.

๛

I'm thinking Cassie's right. This here city might just be the vilest spot on the face of the earth. In no more'n twenty minutes of walking, I passed seven drinking dens, all of them open for business at such an hour. She'd also stepped around two unmoving louts, senseless from drink, she hoped. Then she spied what she was looking for, a huge sign carved to read, "The Coast."

Ruby walked through swinging doors and into a space much larger than she expected. For a short bit, she gawked at something that simply didn't exist in her Southern Baptist world. "Well, I'm plumb stonnied," she whispered. "This here's a dancing hall." Perhaps thirty tables surrounded an open area the size and shape of a four-horse corral, its floor worn smooth and dark from use. There was nobody dancing at this hour. At least she didn't have to witness that—yet.

Looking dusty and depressed, a few men were scattered around the large establishment, each staring into a glass of what she assumed to be some form of alcohol. Ruby shook her head in disgust. *Not yet nine in the morning, and these ne'er-do-wells's already giving in to the demon. Wish to Heaven I could just turn around and light out for Arkansas, back to my Harold.*

She made her way between tables to the far wall where a man was wiping a bar with a surprisingly clean towel. He was tall and thin, wearing a bowtie and a boiled white shirt, dark vest protected by an apron. Behind him was a gigantic mirror with frilly writing: *The Coast. Where blear-eyed men and faded women drink vile liquor.*

"Help you, ma'am?"

"Hope you can," Ruby said. "I'm looking for a man."

"Any man?" The barkeep stroked the ends of his mustaches, a hint of mockery—or maybe hope—in his aging voice. "Name's Jonathan, I'm the proprietor."

Ruby couldn't help a tiny smile. *Must not be many women the likes of me darken them saloon doors.* "Pleased to meet you, Jonathan. Looking for a feller name of Gallagher, Niall Gallagher. Heard of him?"

The barman leaned over and rested his elbows on the polished wood. His voice was low and serious. "Might know of a man by that name."

"Young man, small in stature?" Ruby pressed.

"That's him, all right. But Gallagher's a mighty rough customer—I'd steer well clear of him, I was you."

"Him and me's got business."

"He aware of this business you speak of?"

Ruby ignored the question. "Been told I'd likely find Mr. Gallagher in your establishment."

Jonathan offered a shallow nod. "Chances are about halves he'll be drinking here tonight. If he does show, it'll be around eight."

"And you'll make acquaintances?"

The lanky bartender gave a quick shake of his head. "I'll point him out—rest'll have to be up to you."

Ruby was struck by the mix of fear and respect the man seemed to have for Gallagher. *Looks like Mr. Pinkerton steered me to the right feller.*

⧉

Just after seven that evening, Ruby Seddon pushed through the doors and back into The Coast. It was filled with lively music from a small orchestra consisting of a piano, trumpet, and a hefty woman playing a squeeze box that threatened to crush her bubs with each pump of the bellows. The dance floor was crowded with all manner of men, from ragged oafs to well-dressed gents with gold chains looping from their watch pockets. There was not so much variety among their dance partners. Most all the women wore scant dresses that showed their bloomers when the men gave them a spin. *Bet them gals is ugly as dung hills without their war paint and fancy clothes. Don't know if I should, but I kinda feel sorry for them.*

Most of the tables and chairs were full, many of them with trollops sitting on men's laps, giggling and whispering in their ears. The air in the saloon hung thick with curses, the smell of workmen's sweat, and the smoke of dog-cheap cigars. Ruby fought back a disgusted gag and wound her way toward the bar, unable to avoid puddles of what she hoped was spilled beer. Looking weary and harried, the man she met earlier was still on duty. But tonight, he had three helpers, all busy passing alcohol to fallen angels—for delivery to their recent acquaintances, no doubt.

Ruby stepped to the bar and Jonathan said something difficult to hear over the music and merriment. Ruby inclined her head in his direction, and he leaned over. "Not here—yet."

She hollered back, "I'll wait."

"Not here, you can't."

"Meaning?"

"A woman sitting alone in my place? That'd never do."

"So, what am I—"

"There's a few seats up the stairs." He gestured to the side wall and a narrow staircase.

Ruby climbed the steps to a balcony the length of the hall below. To her left were closed doors with sounds of sin behind them, on the right, a simple railing. She pulled a chair over and sat, elbows resting on the long wooden banister, eyes on the swinging doors at the front.

Four hours later, Ruby sighed and stood. She descended the stairs and headed for the doors, no closer to meeting—let alone striking a deal with—the infamous Mr. Gallagher.

❧❧

Whether due to a second full night's sleep, the rare sun-drenched morning or the workings of the Holy Spirit, Ruby woke up full of hope. *Surely Mr. Pinkerton's telegram will arrive today. And surely Niall Gallagher will show his face at the Coast.*

The sun reflected off the crinkled bay in endless sparkles, its rays warming Ruby's face and her very soul as she walked the few blocks to the Western Union office. Once inside, she offered the telegrapher a friendly, "Good morning, sir." He nodded but did not look up from translating rapid clicks into scribbled words.

In less than a minute he finished and stood, the just-written message in his hand. "I believe this is what you've been waiting for," he mumbled. He handed the page to Ruby without making eye contact, a grave look on his pinched face.

Mrs. Seddon STOP
Glad you are safe in California STOP
Harold Seddon killed battle Wilson's Creek Missouri STOP
Deepest condolences STOP
Allan Pinkerton FULL STOP

"Oh, no," Ruby muttered. *My darling, my Harold? My rock, the strongest man I ever knew taken from me after forty-three years yoked together like the finest team of oxen.* "Dear Lord, I hope he didn't suffer." Her legs failed her, and she sagged against the counter.

❧❧

Hours later, Ruby shuffled into The Coast and ascended the stairs, eyes still blurred with tears and thoughts as scattered as magnolia leaves in an autumn zephyr. She found her chair and commenced watching the doors, when memories of her beloved Harold arose. Ruby somehow forced them down, but other, odder thoughts popped up to take their places. The phrase "like a whore in church" came to her from nowhere. She remembered a time or two when she'd heard the rougher men back in Carroll County refer to someone in an uneasy situation with those crude words. Now, sitting alone in the loathsome room, Ruby mused, Guess I'm kind of the opposite of that—but no less out of place.

Ruby watched and wondered each time a man walked through the swinging saloon doors if this was Mr. Gallagher. She spoke out loud, no one near enough to hear—or care. "I was a widow them other nights, too," she said. "Only difference is, this night I know it." She wiped her eyes and blew out a deep, sad sigh. "What in all nature made me reckon a country gal could travel to the big city all by herself and—"

From down below, the bartender caught her eye with a little wave, then tilted his head toward the front where a hatless man, heavy revolvers on both hips, strode through the front doors. He moved with a swagger, like he owned the place and everyone in it. As best she could tell from a distance, the fellow was young, maybe twenty-five. He sported a thick but well managed mustache, an upside-down horseshoe that reached his chin on both sides. He was also fancily dressed in a tan shirt, frontier style with the buttons arranged in a U shape. In contrast to his light shirt, the trousers were dark, supported by a tooled leather gun belt studded with what looked to be silver coins. Unlike the drunken sailors and filthy failed prospectors that mostly crowded the barroom below, this man's clothing seemed clean and in good repair.

"Man's reputation as a desperado don't seem right for such a dandy," she told herself. "Especially considering he can't be more'n five-foot-six and skinny as a stalk of Loosiana sugarcane."

Ruby kept her eyes on Niall Gallagher. He sat himself at a small table, and Jonathan scurried over. They spoke briefly and the barkeep hustled to produce his order—not beer, but a clean glass half full of honey-colored liquid that looked like the Kentucky whiskey Harold sometimes—

Her eyes began to well up. She gritted her teeth, told herself, commanded herself, *This ain't the time to mourn poor Harold—that's gonna have to wait. Now get up off your hind-quarters and go down and talk to the man.* She fortified herself with a deep breath, then stood.

☙❧

"May I set myself?" Ruby nodded to the single empty chair at Gallagher's table.

"Not looking for a pretty waiter girl," he replied without taking eyes off his drink.

Ruby couldn't help but laugh. "Ain't one of them fancies, if that's what you're thinking."

The man raised his head, likely surprised to see a tall, sturdy matron in plain clothing. "Don't reckon you are," he said, with his own little chuckle. "Sit if you like."

Ruby noted with interest that, unlike other men she'd known who were small in figure, this man's voice was deep and full. "Thanks to you, sir," she said and slid her chair closer to be heard over the hubbub. "Would you be Niall Gallagher?"

The man's countenance hardened. "Who's asking?" His raspy challenge seemed to give voice to endless miles on dusty desert trails.

"Name's Mrs. Ruby Seddon, out of Carroll County, Arkansas. Allan Pinkerton sent me looking for a man name of Gallagher."

"Pinkerton, eh?" He used a thumb and forefinger to push the mustache away from his lips, then took another sip of liquor while studying Ruby. After a long silence, he said, "Forgive my inquiring, Mrs. Seddon, but are you a God-fearing woman?"

"I am sir—born again of my Lord and Savior. But why would you ask such a thing?"

"Because it puzzles me to see a godly woman in this den of drunkenness and debauchery."

"I'm here for the sole utility of finding you."

"To what end, Mrs. Seddon?"

"I'll soon be heading to the Utah territory to find my orphaned grandson. The journey will be fraught with danger, and I'll need a man with a stiff backbone to accompany me. Mr. Pinkerton says you are that man."

"I am such a man." He looked deep into Ruby's eyes. "I may or may not be *that* man. But if you're telling, I'll hear more."

It took half an hour—and two more glasses of whiskey—for Ruby to explain her objective and offer to engage Mr. Gallagher as a sworn deputy of the Pinkerton's Agency. There was no need to list the likely perils, they were obvious to both parties.

"Me, a Pinkerton's detective?" Gallagher leaned back in his chair and gave a smirk. "Never thought I'd see that day." He paused for a moment, then added, "Of course this is a task best left to me and me alone, Mrs. Seddon. You'll tarry here in San Francisco, and I'll deliver the boy to you, in exchange, of course, for a fee we've yet to discuss."

"That ain't possible," she said. Gallagher seemed confused, so Ruby went on. "Without me as his blood kin, you'd be a common kidnapper, unacceptable for a Pinkerton's man—or anybody else."

Gallagher rubbed his clean-shaven chin with the backs of two fingers. "I do want to be a Pinkerton and would relish the chance to tangle with the Mormons again, that's sure as a gun."

A few minutes later they stood. "Agreed," Gallagher said. "One thousand dollars in gold to be paid by Allan Pinkerton's banking agent upon delivering the child to San Francisco."

Ruby ignored the proffered hand and said, "The child and myself, both alive and without serious harm."

"Of course," he said, and they shared a vigorous handshake.

Ruby left the saloon, glancing back at Gallagher and wondering, *What did the man mean by 'the chance to tangle with the Mormons again?'*

~35~

Parowan - July 30, 1861

Tommy dangled his foot over the edge of the wooden porch and scratched his dog behind her ears, trying hard not to think about Clara. "Today's supposed to be a happy day, Woobydog." He and his mother had moved back to the Shand house, "for good this time," Mama said. At least Karl and Kyle had not bothered him. They avoided Tommy completely. Their older sister Bess, however, had more than made up for the boys' inattention, taking every opportunity to bully and belittle "Pegleg."

"Today Bess got married and she's moving out." Woobydog responded with a contented sigh, more likely brought on by the gentle ear strokes than news of the cruel girl leaving. "Not so much gaiety as other weddings. Guess that's to be 'spected—been just a month since Aunt Naomi died. Pumonia, Mama said."

He heard the front door open. "Thomas, you out here?" Mama called.

"Yes, ma'am. Me and Woobydog."

Mama stepped out. "Woobydog and I," she corrected.

"Yes. Now you're out here, too."

His mother grinned and tousled his hair. "Aren't you the little smarty britches." She sat down next to him on the smooth, unfinished pine. "Everything all right?"

Tommy replied with a little shrug, then lowered his head and stared at the boards beneath him.

"What is it, Thomas?"

"Maybe I'm not such a good person."

Mama put an arm around his shoulder and pulled him closer. "Why's that, Son?"

He spoke without looking up. "It's kind of a secret."

Mama placed a hand beneath his chin and raised his head. "Look at me, Thomas. You don't have to tell me. But if you do, I promise to hold it," she said, and kissed the top of his head.

Tommy took a deep breath and exhaled. "I'm not sad like I'm s'posed to be." He saw that Mama looked puzzled. "About Aunt Naomi dying, I mean. I'm not happy she died, just not, you know, real sad."

"Can you keep a secret, Thomas?"

Mama has a secret, too? He paused a little, then said, "Sure."

She gave him a gentle elbow to the ribs. "Me neither."

~36~

San Francisco - August 9, 1861

With hopes of calming her growing nerves, Ruby struggled to take a few deep breaths. She stood on the same pier where she first set foot in San Francisco just a week before, and the thought of getting back on a ship so soon left her nearly frozen with unease.

"Feeling poorly?" Niall asked.

"Nah. It's just I've come to a mighty disliking for boats."

"Think you'll find the riverboat more to your preference," he said. "It's smoky, and the big paddle wheel's loud, but there's not so much tossing back and forth. In any event, it'll take us no more than two days to steam across the bay and up the river."

"Still not sure why we're boating to Sacramento—'stead of heading for San Diego."

"Southern trail's shorter, yes," Niall said. "But for a full 200 miles, the desert's drier than Ezekiel's bones. And once in the Utah Territory, we'd have to deal with Mormon spies and Indians turned against travelers by old Brig. Remember, there's no U.S. army to turn to—they're all out east fighting Rebs."

Ruby's head sank. "Don't I know that," she muttered.

Niall continued, "We'll take the Pony Express route to Camp Floyd, just short of the Great Salt Lake City. There we'll buy a team and wagon and take the cutoff to the south stretch of the Mormon Trail. A little longer, a whole lot safer. And the Overland Stage will convey us all the way to Floyd."

Ruby nodded. "Makes sense. I guess."

"By the way," Niall said. "To avoid unwanted attention, from now on you must refer to yourself as my wife, Mrs. John Pemberton."

"Ain't no way you're gonna—"

Niall broke into a grin. "Got no designs regarding husbandly prerogatives."

"That ain't what I'm talking about," Ruby chuckled. "You'll never pass as my husband—I'm just too durn timeworn for you."

Niall thought for a moment. "You may be right," he shrugged. "John Seddon it is, Mother dear."

Mother. Ruby rolled her eyes. *Hope I picked me the right feller,* she thought. *This one's awful polite for a ruffian—and kind of small. And what's he done such that he can't call hisself by his rightful name?*

As promised, Ruby found the big-wheel steamer smoky and loud, so she avoided the back of the boat—the stern, the crew called it—where the paddle beat the water and the coal smoke swirled down from a jagged crown atop the ship's stack. Her favorite spot was near the bow, from there Ruby watched the captain grip the hand pegs and spin the round helm. The vessel gradually made a quarter-turn until the broad bay lay directly behind, the ocean view partially hidden by gritty black billows. She assumed they were about to enter the mouth of the river, but the delta spread out like an unknowable maze of creeks, estuaries and likely deadends. *Hope the driver knows what he's doing. I sure as heck can't tell which one's the river.*

❧⚘

"That's a right purty sight," Ruby said to herself. In less than an hour, the delta had disappeared behind them, and they were steaming up the meandering Sacramento River, a broad ribbon of green bounded by rolling yellow hills.

"Yes, it is."

Ruby startled at the sound of Niall's voice. She hadn't realized anyone was near enough to hear her over the throbbing of the engine and the splashing of the wheel.

Niall stepped closer and held up a dark brown tube as if it was England's crown jewels. "Beauty, isn't she?"

"Beauty it ain't—what in tarnation is it?"

"Telescope," he said.

Ruby was no more enlightened. "Tell-a-what?"

"A seafarer's glass. Try it." Niall handed her the contraption and helped her sight through it to the distant hills. "What do you think?"

"Don't that beat all of 'em," Ruby said. "I'm seeing stuff I couldn't see afore."

"Might prove useful in our endeavor, mightn't it?"

"Well," Ruby drawled. "Guessing it might—"

"Two dollars and it's ours," Niall said, his hand outstretched and open.

Useful? Perhaps. Costly? Sure as eggs ain't chickens. Ruby handed over the precious two dollars.

~37~

Sacramento, California - August 12, 1861

Ruby and "her son John" paused inside the hand-carved double doors of the Clarendon House, a grand hotel just half a block from the Sacramento River where they'd left the steamboat behind. She turned and took a last look at the lobby. Upholstered in dark green and gold, six stuffed chairs and two sofas rested on a white floor Ruby guessed to be marble. In the center, a round polished oak table held a huge glass vase that overflowed with enough yellow roses to softly scent the entire space. But there was no time to linger. Niall held the door and she stepped out.

"Place's even more high-priced than where I was staying back to San Francisco," she said.

Niall grinned. "Not really a fair comparison."

"A bed's a bed," she joked.

"Your Frisco bed was in a bordello," he said. "The Clarendon House, on the other hand, is the finest hotel in Sacramento. Hell, the beds have springs, and someone changes the sheets every two, three days. And you're not paying by the hour."

"Reckon there's something to what you say."

"Enjoy civilization while you can. After Carson City, you'll be sleeping on the ground for near a month."

"Thought you said the Overland stopped at a way station most every night."

"Ever seen a way station out west?" Niall had himself a bit of a laugh. "Anyhow, what do you think, Mother?" He made a sweeping gesture with his outstretched hand. "Sacramento what you expected?"

Ruby gave her shoulders an indifferent hike. "So when we gonna leave this great state of Californee behind?"

"Stage leaves in . . ." Niall pulled out and checked his pocket watch. ". . . just over an hour."

☙❧

One hour later, Ruby watched Niall struggle to hoist a hefty travel duffel into the rear trunk of the stagecoach. "He is pretty tough for a small feller," she muttered.

A bulky man in dust-covered clothing stepped down from the driver's perch. "Never thought I'd spy you on this trail again, Niall," the man said.

"Name's John, John Seddon. Not acquainted with anyone named Niall."

"Uh, if you say so." A look of concern clouded the driver's face. "There gonna be unrest on this trip, Niall?"

The smaller man gave him a friendly clap on the shoulder. "No, Mick. Not so long as you call me John."

Ruby stepped over to where the two men stood. "That there's mighty fine coachwork," she said. The tall, enclosed carriage was dark red, wheels and spokes done in contrasting yellow. A sun-gold "O" covered most of the door, and running the length of the coach, just below the roof: OVERLAND * STAGE * LINES. Ruby smiled. "A joy to behold."

"Indeed she is," the coachman said.

"And them horses is beauties." Hitched to the wagon stood three matched pairs of handsome grays, tall but not too thick. "Near seventeen hands, looks to me," she said.

"Percherons," Mick said. He pulled down the cargo area door and buckled it shut with two wide leather belt straps.

"Percherons? Never seen the breed afore."

"Sturdy as a draft horse," Mick said, "but faster, more nimble." He climbed up to his seat and took the reins.

After she and Niall settled in, Ruby poked her head out the open window. "What's the dilly-dally, Son?" she yelled to the driver. "We gotta hie ourselves to the Utah."

❧

It was summer, but Ruby wore a wool sweater against the cool air in the hotel's dining room. Four days of difficult uphill travel had brought them near the peaks of the Sierra Nevada— Carson City just south of Lake Tahoe. Niall must have noticed her discomfort. He offered, "From here, it's all downhill—to the Humboldt, anyway."

"You sure?" Ruby asked.

"Been a while since I was east of the mountains. But I still know these routes like the lines in my palm."

"How long since you was a pony rider?" she asked.

"Shut the P.E. down just a couple months ago. Telegraph reaches all the way to San Francisco now."

There was a long pause as the word telegraph turned Ruby's thoughts back to the worst day of her life.

Harold Seddon killed Wilson's Creek Missouri STOP
Deepest condolences STOP

Ruby stared absently at Niall scraping egg yolk from his china plate with a bit of ham fat. "That hitting your spot?" she asked.

"It is, Mother,"

"See you changed your look a bit, my boy."

"Like it?" Niall ran three fingertips over the bare skin where his thick mustache had been.

Ruby couldn't help but smile. The lip whiskers had been replaced by a horseshoe outline, white against the rest of his sun-browned face. "Guess so. But why in tarnation would you—"

"Thought I'd make myself more presentable in case Brigham Young shows up to welcome us to the territory."

"That don't seem too likely," Ruby said. *Now the boy's laughing. Guess I was to take it as a joke.*

"Well," he said, "always pays to be prepared." He pushed himself back from the table. "Shall we press on?"

~38~

Great Salt Lake City - August 27, 1861

L orena Eadie lived in a clapboard house at the eastern edge
of Great Salt Lake City. It had been months since her
husband, or anyone else, visited, so she startled at the urgent
rapping on her door. "Who in all creation might that be?" she
mumbled. Lorena was in the middle of slicing summer squash
for stew, so she gave slick hands a wipe, then moved in the
direction of the door. Fourteen years earlier, her left ankle had
been pinned when a wagon tipped onto its side during a failed
attempt to cross the Sweetwater near Devil's Gate. The
resulting break never properly healed, leaving Lorena with a
permanent, and painful, step-drag gait.

Another knock, louder than the first, failed to speed her
up. "Hold your ponies," she hollered. "Got a bit of a hitch in
my gitalong." It did not help that the floor of her little shanty
was rough and uneven.

She finally reached the door and opened it to see a teenage
boy. "Ethan?" she said. "What brings you all the way out to
Sugarhouse?"

He doffed his cap with a slight bow, then held up a brown
envelope. "It's a letter, Granny Eadie."

Lorena smiled at the word "Granny." It was a label usually
reserved for women well beyond her fifty years—but with a
pronounced limp, thin gray hair and several missing teeth,
Lorena was often assumed to be much older than she was.

Ten years prior, someone had started calling her Granny—now everyone, even her grown daughter, referred to her by that moniker.

"From my husband?"

"No, ma'am. Appears to be from California. San Diego."

"Not certain I know anyone there."

Ethan studied his feet. "Actually, it's for your daughter."

Granny broke into a grin. "From Evie!"

"Not *from* Sister Dunning, it's addressed *to* her."

She took the letter and inspected it closely. "So it is," she said. "Well, don't that take the rag off the bush."

Ethan smiled. "Guess so, ma'am." He turned to leave, then suddenly swiveled back. "Got chores I can do while I'm here, Granny?"

"Such a good boy. I'd be obliged if you'd fetch me some water," she said. "Bucket's by the well."

Ethan closed the door behind him and Lorena dropped into a nearby chair. She studied the letter, turning it over in vein-laced hands. The letter had no return address, but was clearly postmarked "San Diego, California." *Who would possibly be writing to Eva from California?* She thought for a moment. When it it hit her, she laughed out loud. "Millie! God bless, you made it—soakin' your toes in the Pacific Ocean!" Then Granny Eadie busied herself finding an envelope and a quill.

A few minutes later, the boy delivered the water to Granny's kitchen. "That should do it. God bless, Granny, er, Sister Eadie."

"One moment, Ethan. Could you post this to Evie for me?" She handed him an envelope within an envelope. The return address read:

Mrs. Lorena Eadie
Route 14-Sugarhouse
Great Salt Lake City

According to what Granny gathered was Millie's intent, there was nothing on the outside to give away that the message inside had been penned by an apostate hundreds of miles away.

☙❧

A few days later, Lavinnia Dame answered a knock on her door. "Mail today?" she asked.

The teenager standing on her wooden porch with dusty hat in hand flashed a proud smile. "Yes, ma'am." He reached into a leather pouch worn shiny with use and pulled out a few letters bundled together with string. "This lot's for President Dame."

Lavinnia took the bundle. "Thank you, Brian."

He nodded, "Ma'am," and turned to leave.

"Brian."

The boy spun back around to face the woman. "Something else I can do for you, Sister Dame?"

"Is there other mail for the Mission?"

He responded without checking. "Yes'm. A letter for Sister Dunning."

"For Eva Dunning?"

"It is, ma'am."

"Who from?" she asked.

Brian pulled out the letter and looked closely. "Lorena Eadie."

"Sister Dunning's mother?"

Brian nodded.

"No need to ride all the way to New Town," Lavinnia said, reaching out a hand. "I'll be seeing her soon."

"Um, sure." Brian laid the envelope in her open palm.

☙❧

Later in the day, Bennet Dunning stood in President Dame's parlor, tearing open a letter the president had just handed him. He pulled out and opened a second envelope postmarked *San Diego, California*, then read the enclosed letter aloud:

> *Dearest Evie,*
>
> *Life in California is everthing I hoped. Me and Peters happily married and he's got a good job at the shipyard. Clara loves going to school every day but she still misses your Tommy something awful. Evie please. Do what I know you always wanted to. Leave Bennet and Naomi and all the Mormons forever. Stay with us long as you like while you make a fresh start. I promise you'll never regret it.*
>
> *Your my best friend, and I'll love you forever,*
> *Millie Wilton*
> *Post Box 741*
> *San Diego, California*
> *p.s. Peter will come fetch you. Just let me know.*

"She wouldn't actually go, would she?" President Dame asked.

Bennet tried in vain to read the expression on his leader's face. He was tempted to offer a simple *no*, hoping that would end the matter. Instead, he looked down at the paper for a few seconds, then angrily stuffed it in a pocket. "Being honest," he said, "there's no telling what she might do."

Dame stared off for a few seconds, then, "So, what if she did leave?"

Bennet was stunned. "I just lost Naomi, President Dame. Without Evie, there's not a one to care for the baby—and I'd be left a lone man."

The president rested a hand on Bennet's shoulder. "From what I'm hearing, your Eva's not been much of a wife for a long time."

248

Bennet acknowledged with a shrug.

"Isn't it time you took another?"

It struck Bennet more like a poorly timed order than a question, and he felt instantly dizzy and confused, like in a kind of fever dream.

President Dame continued, "The Fotheringham girl is near twenty—well past time she was given in marriage."

"B . . . but what about Evie?"

"Eva." The leader cocked his head to the left in a small, dismissive way. "If she stays, so be it. If she runs, we'll do naught to stop her. So, Brother Dunning, time to court the lovely Sister Fotheringham?"

President Dame had gone from reading the letter to planning to marry him off with such haste as to leave Bennet's emotions whipsawed.

"I'll take your silence as agreement. Now, about the boy. I think it's time he was given to a nice family in Great Salt Lake City. Plan on delivering him to me within the week."

Bennet finally managed, "Take Thomas from Eva?"

"We can't risk him running off with her," Dame said. "The boy's less danger to the Church if we know where he is. And remember, he's not her son—nor yours."

Bennet felt like someone or something had just pushed him down the steps at the Rock Chapel. "I . . . I know, President, but where would he end up?

A pause ensued, long enough for Bennet to imagine he'd hit the last step with a heavy thump to the head.

"Not your concern," President Dame said with finality. "Have the child to me no later than Wednesday noon."

Bennet bid a shaky farewell, then began the short ride to the home where his wife and children lived.

෨ඁ

Eva lowered the child until her pudgy feet touched the smooth pine floorboards. "That's a good girl, Sophie. Show your daddy what Thomas taught you." The toddler was unsteady as a sailor on leave, but she managed a bowlegged shuffle that got her to Thomas's waiting arms.

Bennet took his daughter from Thomas, hugged her tight to his chest, and whispered, "That's real good, Sophronia." Then he looked to Thomas and said, "Thanks, Tom—and Eva. For everything you've done for my baby girl."

Her son answered with a broad, beaming smile. Eva did not respond—she was conflicted, clouded. *I've never before heard him address our Thomas by his name. Are his eyes welling up a bit? Don't know if it's for the good or the bad, but something seems to have changed.*

Bennet addressed his wife, more emotional than the few baby steps warranted. "I, uh, I gotta leave about this time next week," he said.

The sudden announcement was a mild surprise. "Leave?"

"Bringing cattle out of the hills for the winter."

"For the winter? It's only August."

"Uh, President Young's predicting a real cold autumn."

First I've heard of that.

Bennet handed Sophie back to Eva. "Anyway, thought I'd bring young Tom along. Change'd be good for the boy."

She was astonished. "Take Thomas?"

"To help with the roundup."

"I . . . I don't know. He's, you know—"

"I've got but one foot, we all know that," Thomas said. "But please can I go? I can still fork a horse pretty good."

"Pretty *well*," Eva corrected. "And it's *may* I go."

Bennet gave Thomas a little wink. "Like I was saying, boy could use a bit of time with the menfolk. Leaving Wednesday morning, back after a week or so."

Thomas was fairly shaking with excitement. "Can I, *may* I please go on the roundup, Mama?"

Every day for the past four years I've prayed that Bennet would be a real father to Thomas. I should be naught but grateful for this moment. But the second she said yes, Eva felt a slow churning deep in her belly.

"Before I forget, this came for you, Eva." Bennet handed her an open letter that looked to have been badly crumpled, then smoothed out.

Bennet clapped Thomas on the shoulder. "Then it's settled. I'll fetch you about breakfast time on Wednesday." He looked to Eva, "Make sure he packs all his clothes."

"*All* his clothes?" The roiling in her stomach worsened.

"Of course, not all," Bennet said. "Just plenty enough for a week in the mountains. Oh, and one more thing."

"What's that?"

"Sister Fotheringham is coming by tomorrow. I asked her to take Sophie for a while."

"Nancy Fotheringham?"

"Yes," he said. "To give you a few days' rest. You surely deserve it."

Eva was stunned that Sophie was going somewhere else, even for just a few days. "Bennet, I don't think—" But he was already out the door.

~39~

R uby ducked and stepped out the door of a low, mud-colored hut. She groaned and rolled her head, neck creaking and sore from night after night sleeping on hard dirt floors. "Stagestop, my eye," she said to no one in particular. "Back to home, cows bed down in nicer'n these stalls."

It was nearly three weeks since Carson City, time marked by nothing but grinding exhaustion and unrelenting boredom. *But we're about to the end of the journey,* Ruby told herself. *Well, the end of this next-to-last cut.*

Niall emerged with the luggage and stowed it in the back of the coach. Before he and Ruby settled into the stage, he called up, "Forty miles or so to Camp Floyd, eh, Mick?"

"Camp Floyd, ya say?"

"Right you are."

For some reason Mick bellowed a hearty laugh. He hollered back between guffaws, "That's it, John. No . . . more'n . . . forty mile."

"We'll part ways there, my friend."

"You might find it rougher'n you're thinking to come by a team and wagon," Mick said. "There's been—"

"Shouldn't be a hinder," Ruby interrupted. "I got hard money. Now give 'em a taste of the whip."

Mick cracked the reins over the horses' backs and the coach lurched ahead.

"Tonight we'll sleep in real beds at the inn," Niall said. "Should be driving our own rig south by tomorrow."

Ruby responded with a smile seasoned with a measure of relief—and a pinch of fear.

ॐ

Hours later, the stagecoach rumbled to a stop, and Ruby stared over the door in disbelief. "Where's the people?"

Camp Floyd was nothing like the low huts that had sheltered them for the last few weeks. This was a town, and not a small one. A large cluster of adobe brick buildings glowed golden in the lateday sun, but there was not a citizen to be seen in Camp Floyd. No animals, no wagons, no immediate evidence that anyone called the place home.

Mick halted the horses in front of a narrow two-story structure fronted by a weathered sign: Stagecoach Inn. Niall climbed out and called up to the driver, "What in the name of heaven's God happened to Camp Floyd?"

"Gone," Mick said.

Niall's face showed disbelief. "Deserted maybe. But it's still here."

Mick laughed. "Camp Floyd's gone. You're standing in Fort Crittenden."

"The hell?"

"The place was first named after Secretary of War, John Floyd," Mick said.

"That I knew. So what?"

"Turned out Secretary Floyd was a goddamn Copperhead. When war broke out, he slithered outta Washington and headed south 'neath the sparrows. After that, Lincoln didn't reckon it right to keep his name on the place."

Ruby was puzzled. "But them folks didn't hightail it just 'cause the name changed."

Mick leaned back and let out a laugh. "'Course not. Abe needed all his troops fighting rebs. And without soldiers and the army's money, wasn't abundant reasons for anyone else to stay."

Ruby noticed a strange smile on Niall's face. *Relief?* "Inn still open?" he asked.

"Not fancy like it was," Mick said. "But even a saggy bed beats sleeping on the ground."

"The old store?"

"Open. Barely."

Niall squinted into the distance. "You sure?"

"Last I knew."

Ruby chimed in. "Can a body get a hot meal over to the hotel?"

৯৽৽৻

Twenty minutes later, Ruby paid for three rooms and signed the register for herself and her son. "You got an eatery in this place?" she asked the young woman behind the desk.

"Cafe's been closed for months. But you're welcome to join my man and me for supper."

Ruby hesitated. "Don't want to put y'all out."

"We'd actually enjoy some company for a change," the clerk said. "Got a big pot of chicken soup simmering in the back, and cornbread's in the oven."

"Caught a whiff just afore," Ruby said. "Smelled like heaven itself."

The hotel gal gave the back of Ruby's hand an affectionate pat. "Soup's on in thirty minutes."

Ruby nodded politely, then stepped back outside where Niall struggled with their luggage.

"John," she called.

"Yes, Mother?"

"Eatery's no more. But the proprietors'll have us at their table in half a hour."

❧

Next morning, Ruby joined Niall on the weathered wooden sidewalk outside the Stagecoach Inn. She raised her arms, enjoying a pleasant stretch and the just-up sun on her face.

"Let's you'n me get over to the mercantile and see if they got better'n stale bread and jerked beef," she said. "Gonna need provisions to get us to the Parowan."

Ruby gave his elbow a tug, but Niall recoiled. "No!"

She was puzzled by the urgency of the word. "But Mick said the store's open."

"I know, it's just— You go. I'll bring down the cases. Whatever you rustle up'll be fine."

"Sure enough." Ruby headed for the establishment thinking, *There's been some kinda burr under that boy's saddle all this way. Keep wondering just what it is.*

She stepped into the store, cleared her throat loudly, then called out, "Up and at 'em. Got yourself a customer."

An ancient, reed-thin man nearly tipped over the chair he'd been dozing in. He stood with some trouble, bent frame holding him in the form of a lazy question mark. "Um, yes, what you need?" he asked in a sleep-slurred voice.

"Mostly food. What you got?"

He scratched a matted beard. "Lots of apples and some dried apricots."

"Now we're talkin'," Ruby said. "What else?"

"Six loafs a bread."

"Fresh?" she asked.

"Baked just last week."

Ruby rolled her eyes toward the ceiling. "Of course."

"Oh, and plenty of hardtack and jerked beef."

Her head sagged. "Gimme the fruit and all the cow leather you got," she said. "And the bread, I guess."

With more than a bit of reluctance, Ruby paid what she figured was triple the fair price, then headed for the exit. She reached for the rusty doorlatch when something on the wall caught her eye. She stopped and stared at a yellowed poster:

WANTED FOR MURDER
Nial Gallager
Former P.E. rider, skinny, about five foot, five inches
big mustaches, dresses dandy
Known to pack matching Colt revolvers
$300 REWARD
DEAD OR ALIVE
Contact territorial militia GSLC

The writing on the wall slammed Ruby like an angry fist. It was nearly a minute before she could gather breath enough to speak. "So, storekeep—"

The old man cupped a hand to his right ear. "How's that?"

She tapped the poster and increased her volume. "Reckon this Gallagher feller must be quite the desperado."

"Bastard killed my brother. Hunt him down myself, had a few less winters on me."

"Of course," she said. "Bet he wouldn't have the sand to show himself anywhere in these parts, eh?"

"Don't suppose he would."

"Anyhow," Ruby said, "could folks even recognize the blackguard, seeing's there's no picture?"

"I'd know him anywhere," the frail old man said, reaching under the counter. "And if he ever does show his murderin' face around here, I'll be ready." He produced a rusty shotgun. Ruby guessed both eighteen-inch barrels were loaded.

☙❧

Just outside the corral where the team had spent the night, Ruby watched and listened carefully, forcing herself to stay out of the negotiations, at least for now.

"You got to sell me the horses, Mick," Niall insisted. "I found a decent wagon, but there's not a single animal in the whole wretched place."

The log rail bent where the large driver leaned back against it. He shook his head. "Can't do it, Johnny Boy. They're not mine to sell."

"I'm offering five times what they're worth." Niall gestured toward the Percherons. "And I'll take the weakest two."

"Won't make up for me losing my employment."

Niall laid a hand on his friend's shoulder and said, "Mick, think for a minute. Four horses will get you to the Salt Lake easy. When you arrive, buy another pair and profit the difference." Niall pulled five gold pieces from a pocket and thumbed them around his palm to reflect the sunlight. "All yours, Micky. Just say yes to five times what they're worth."

Mick stared at the glinting coins without speaking.

"Ten times," Ruby blurted. She stepped closer, then took the heavy disks from Niall and forced them into Mick's hand— along with five more she'd been holding. She fixed the big man with an intense stare and said, "There's your slugs. You got ten seconds to tell me we got us a deal, Son."

Mick opened his hands and smiled down at the gold. "Deal."

Ruby jerked her thumb in the direction of the nearby wagon, a small Conestoga. Its unpainted bed was badly weathered, but a nearly new canvas bonnet stretched nicely over the tensioned wood bows.

"Hook 'em up, boys," she said. "Time ta git gittin'."

It was just fifteen minutes or so since Ruby bought part of his team, but Mick and his four-horse coach were already gone. She smiled a little as she laid the last item, her quilt-wrapped

Bible, into the wagon bed. "That should do 'er," she said, and climbed up onto the wooden seat. "How long to Fort Parowan?"

Niall looked up from hitching the animals to the double-tree. "Three days, if we don't run into problems."

He finished with the horses, and Ruby scooted sideways to make room for him on the seat. Niall took his place, then bent low over the slanted footboard, reaching for the reins.

A deafening BOOM assaulted Ruby's ears, and a pie-sized chunk of the backrest exploded, blasting pine dust and wood shards into the air just above Niall's bent neck and head.

He stayed down. Slapped both hips. Came up empty-handed—the day he'd shaved his mustache, he'd hidden the Colts away.

"Niall, what is hap—"

"Get down!"

She dropped to the floorboards and cautiously peeked around where the corner of the backrest had been.

"The hell?" A figure carrying a stubby shotgun approached at an old man's pace. "He's taken his shot," Niall whispered to Ruby, handing her the reins. "I'll distract him and you—"

"Niall, no! It's a coach gun, double-barrelled!"

"He can't shoot both of us." Niall jumped from the wagon and hit the ground at a full run, headed for the protection of a nearby barn.

Another blast shattered the air.

Niall went down.

Ruby grabbed up the reins, but her eyes stayed on the crooked beanpole shuffling toward Niall and muttering, "Murderin' son of Satan." He dropped the spent shotgun into the dust and retrieved a revolver from the front of his trousers. "Finish you off, here and now."

Inside Ruby's head, thoughts buzzed and rattled like wasps trapped in a Mason jar: *If I don't act now, Niall is a dead man.*

Maybe he is a murderer deserves to die. But without him I may never see my Levi again.

She snapped the reins and turned the team at the pistol-toting man, fully determined to run him down. At the last second, the animals veered left, perhaps unwilling to trample a human. But the right rear wheel ran up the back of the man's leg. Ruby tried to ignore the sound of something snapping under the steel band, then she steered the wagon to where Niall lay.

"Whoa! Whoa, there." Ruby pulled back the reins and yanked the wheel brake. She jumped down and ran to her friend and companion, ignoring the old man's pained shrieks in the background. She knelt next to Niall. Blood issued from a cavern where the back of his left boot had been. He struggled to a sitting position. Ruby placed a supportive hand under his left elbow and asked, "Can you stand?"

The wounded man made a groaning attempt, but immediately crumpled back to the dirt.

She filled her lungs, then reached both arms underneath him and grunted, "Thank the good Lord for making you a little feller." But it took every ounce of her strength to heave the undersized man up and roll him over the edge and into the wagon bed.

Ruby hurried forward to the damaged seat, cracked the reins and yelled, "Gee up!" The big grays somehow sensed the urgency and lit out like their tails were on fire.

❧❦

Mick had driven his stage into Great Salt Lake City dozens of times, and each trip two things struck him: The streets were wide enough to turn his team completely around, and the city was noticeably bigger and busier than the time before. The newest addition to town was the Main Street Telegraph Office, "the exact spot where the lines from east and west were recently joined," the sign read. A few doors down, the Old Constitution Building was now the home of Zion's Cooperative Mercantile Institution, an ornately-fronted general store that was fairly bursting with everything from fresh butter to iron nails to woven rugs. ZCMI's facade bore the carved image of a beehive, the Mormon emblem of industry and hard work.

Mick smiled and nodded at the symbol. *Whatever else I might think of these Mormons, they're sure enough the hardest working people I've ever encountered.*

When he turned his eyes back to the roadway, he startled. "Whoa!" Mick yanked the reins and brought the team to a stop. A few yards ahead, two men stood blocking his side of Main Street. The one in a faded militia uniform seemed to be in charge. He was mostly unremarkable, average in every way except for his eyes, as close set and dark as a weasel's. Mick felt those eyes fixed on him even at a distance. The second man was large, wearing a fraying wool shirt and cotton overalls. *Probably here in case of trouble—shan't be any if I can help it.*

Big Man stayed planted in front of the horses while the other stepped to Mick's side.

"Let loose of the reins and step down," Weasel Face demanded.

"Can I help you, Mister—"

"Hazen, *Lieutenant* Hazen. Get down. Now."

Hot anger boiled up in Mick's chest, rising to his neck and ears. *Damnable Mormons.* He took long breath. *Don't do anything daft, Micky-boy. You're in their house now.* He stepped to the street.

"We understand you're looking for a pair of horses to make up your team," the lieutenant said, his tone more than a bit threatening.

Who the hell's "we?" Mick did not give voice to the question. He took his time, first looking at the man who now held the bridles of his lead horses. The outsized helper seemed nervous with the animals, but they were dog-tired, content to stand motionless.

"Got some for sale?" he said, trying hard not to convey concern.

"What happened, you're a pair short?"

Mick knew he had to tread carefully. He was not sure how, but apparently word of the horse sale had reached the city before him. He waited to see if the officer would reveal more.

"A good man got ran over by the horses you gave to that outlaw Gallagher and—"

"Hold on there, Lieutenant. I know naught about a man getting ran over. And I didn't give the animals to anyone. I sold them."

"To Gallagher, right?" the official insisted.

Mick faked a how-should-I-know shrug. "Told me his name was John. Last name was Sutton, or something like that."

"John Sutton, eh?" The officer's voice was edged with sarcasm. "Seems to me an Overland Stage man like yourself would know every single one of them Pony Express boys."

Mick was cornered. "He told me his name was Sutton. That's the God's-honest truth, Lieutenant. But I guess it could have been that Gallagher fella."

"Why's Gallagher in the territory? What's the rotter up to?"

"That the man never shared."

"This conversation's near over," the beady-eyed officer said. "You gonna tell me what Gallagher's up to—and ride outta here with your stage and a full team? Or does this end with us marching you to jail and confiscating the rig?"

Shit! Mick thought. *I haven't broken any laws, but this knob'll sure enough throw me behind bars if it suits him—and be more than happy to commandeer the coach and team.*

"Said he was headed for Fort Parowan," Mick said. "Never told me why."

"Parowan?"

"Bought a wagon and two of my horses, said he was planning to intersect with the south trail."

"If you're lyin', I'm gonna—"

"I'm not so doltish as to fib to you, Lieutenant. We both know you got me by the walnuts."

☙❧

Less than two hours later Lieutenant Hazen sat tall and proud at the head of a column of fifteen uniformed men galloping south out of Great Salt Lake City. In a small satchel strapped over his neck and shoulder, Hazen carried his orders: "Capture or kill Niall Gallagher."

~40~

Ruby ignored the horses' heaving ribs and the sweat steam rising from their backs. For some time, a single thought had filled her consciousness. *Get far enough from the fort, then give consideration to the wounded man behind me in the wagon bed—do what I can for Niall.* She glanced to her left at the splintery gap where the seatback's corner had been, and her current situation came into crisp relief: They were lost, and she'd pushed the poor animals without mercy for more than an hour. Ruby slowed the team to a walk and scoured the desert ahead for—anything.

After a bit, Ruby spotted something like a row of fence two hundred yards in the distance. "What's that sticking up yonder?" She steered the horses in that direction, and before long, the fence focused into a line of tall cottonwoods.

"Thank you, Jesus!" Ruby shouted. A little closer and she saw the branches had leaves—that meant shade. And the trees stood in a meandering row, likely following the course of a stream. "Gee up, nags," she called. "Gotta keep on for a just a few more minutes." Ruby prodded and the horses picked up the pace—a smidge.

When they reached a spot maybe fifty yards from the nearest of the trees, the animals bolted full gallop toward the grove. "Smelling water, ain'tcha? Run, boys, run!"

The wagon soon reached the treeline. Ruby shook her head in disappointment. "Not much more'n a piss dribble," she grumbled. The seasonal stream that nurtured the cottonwoods had likely stopped flowing months ago. What water remained was trapped in small, dark pools, but the horses bent and drank without hesitation. While the parched animals loud-slurped from the mossy puddles, Ruby moved back to the wagon bed where Niall was curled up among various items of blood-speckled baggage. She burst into tears.

He looked up and mumbled, "It's all right. I'm not in too much hurt."

"I'm not sobbing 'cause you went and got yourself shot," she fibbed. "It's just, I was counting on you to fetch my Levi. But now what am I gonna do?"

Niall managed a tiny grin. "You're nothing if not resourceful, Ruby. Anyway, I still got one good leg—and one more reason to hate those goddamn Mormons." Niall stifled a groan as he struggled to a sit. "Now pull this shot-ta-shit boot off my shot-ta-shit foot and let's get me patched up."

Ruby regarded the wounded man with judging eyes. "Maybe," she said.

For a moment, Niall seemed stunned beyond speech, then, "Maybe? The hell?"

"First off, I got to hear if you killed that old man's brother. Take your time."

"Man gave me no choice." Niall told the story between gasps he seemed unable to control. "Time I got to . . . Camp Floyd all my food . . . was gone." He continued through gritted teeth. "Just needed enough provisions to . . . to keep me alive."

"So his stores was gone?"

"He had plenty, salt pork, flour, apples."

So far, the tale was not making sense. "Then what? You stole his stuff?"

"He said . . . Brigham told him . . . all the people . . . to sell naught to gentiles."

"That there's complete skittles. Everybody's gentiles—can't be a sheeny within a thousand miles of here." She stared out at the endless sage, a pale gray sea, its surface broken only by the occasional dark of a juniper or a yellow patch of rabbitbrush. Ruby released a long, lonely sigh. "Not Jews nor any kind of anyone, way it looks from here."

"In these parts, gentiles . . . means everyone. Except Mormons." Niall paused for several seconds. He groaned, then his breathing calmed a bit. "Said I'd gladly pony up ten times the Mormon price, but the man stood firm."

"So you killed him?"

"No! I laid money on the counter, picked up a bag of flour, and walked for the door."

"And then?"

"Scattergun fired. Bastard tried to shoot me in the back, over nothing but four pounds of flour."

"Must have missed." Ruby was still unconvinced.

"Don't know how at that range, but I caught no more than a pellet or three. Anyway, I spun around to find myself looking down a second barrel. Drew my revolver and shot. It was him or me. Self defense, pure and simple."

"But you robbed him."

"No! The money I left was more than enough." He paused for a few seconds, then burst out with, "That goddamn flour was the only thing standing between me and slow death by starvation. Now will you tend to my foot?"

Ruby regarded him for a long, silent minute. *There's not really a way to know if he's lying, but giving the man benefit of the doubt seems best.* "I'll take your story as truth," she finally said.

"Take it for the truth? It's gospel, every word of it." A deep groan began in his chest and escaped through pursed lips. "Now help me. Please."

After three unsuccessful attempts to remove the bloody boot, Ruby laid Niall's foot back on the wagon floor as gently as she could, then said, "Give me that knife a yours. I'm cutting the thing off."

Niall blanched. "My foot?"

"Let's start with the gol durn boot, don'tcha reckon?"

"Of course." The fear on his face swapped back to agony. "I'm actually laying on it."

She rolled him halfway over, retrieved the hunting knife and handed Niall the thick leather scabbard. "You keep the edge keen?" He nodded. She sat down, raised his leg and rested the bloody-booted foot on the tops of her thighs. "Now you commence to biting on that knife case and I'll get to work on the shoe." *I know you fear the blood, gal—but you have to be strong. Poor man's got enough suffering without a hysterical woman scaring him half to heaven.*

Ruby set her teeth and began. The blade sliced easily through the gore-softened leather, and she soon exposed the wound. Ruby couldn't hold back a gasp. The shotgun blast had not destroyed the man's heel, as she'd expected. The buckshot load had struck higher, tearing a gash that ran low through the back of his calf. She squeezed her eyes tight shut for a few seconds then opened them. The grisly vision persisted. About half the muscle looked to be intact, and she saw no bone damage. *Stop gawkin' and get to work, woman.*

She used the slippery knife to cut a few strips from her long skirt, then tied them snug around Niall's wounded lower leg.

"Bleeding's mostly stopped," she said, hoping to reassure him by resting a red-stained hand on his shoulder. "Best I can do for now."

"How's it look?"

"You'll outlive it." She paused, then, "But I ain't gonna bluff you. For a while, maybe forever, that foot's gonna be useless as paps on a boar." Ruby commenced sobbing. "I'm sorry, Niall. I'm the one got you into this mess."

When Ruby composed herself, she raised Niall's head just enough for him to take two swallows of water from a drum-shaped canteen. "Can you drink a mite more?" He pulled his lips away and shook his head. "Later, then" she said, and lowered him back to the blanket-covered wagon bed, propping his foot on a leather satchel. "Heard it helps if you keep it higher than your head—or your heart—or something."

"We got to get going." Niall's voice was raspy as a saw.

"You and them horses need to rest."

"No time for that," Niall whispered.

"We can stay right here. Another day or two won't make no nevermind."

"Ruby, you don't understand. Brigham's militia will be looking for us by tomorrow morning."

"Militia?"

"Mormon soldiers—well trained and armed to the teeth," he said. "But for now, we have the advantage."

"Advantage? Not so sure about that."

"They've not a clue where we're headed. If we jump to it, we should be able to make Parowan before the posse knows we're even there—snatch your boy and get ourselves down to California."

Ruby sensed the urgency and her heart began to pound. "Then I guess we'd best git gittin'. But what we gonna do about your shot-up leg?"

"Pray to that Jesus of yours we live long enough to worry about it."

"Of course, but—"

"Just go. They catch us, my death is a certainty." Niall was whispering now, his eyelids drooping. "And likely yours."

Ruby placed a hand under his chin and raised his head. "Where?"

"Parowan, I already told— "

"But where in blazes is that from where we now set?"

The question seemed to confound the injured man. "I don't know where. I mean, I— Just head south for now."

"South? Can you be more?—"

But Niall was already twitching in restless slumber.

કે≫

Later, in the failing light of not-quite-sundown, Ruby spotted a structure, likely a small cabin. The nearer the wagon approached, the more orange sunset poured through gaps between the shack's ill-fitted sticks and logs. *Looks more like ribs of a skeleton than a house.* Just when Ruby got the two-horse team fully stopped, a woman appeared at the gap where a front door might have been. Ruby looked her up and down. *And this one's not much more than a skeleton herself.*

A dirty gray night shirt hung loose on the withered figure. Ruby had no guess as to the woman's age. Her face looked gaunt and drawn, but the hair was black as crow's feathers. She held an old pistol at her side, the heavy gun tilting her a tad to the right.

"Help you?" the thin woman asked. Ruby heard fear in the soft voice.

Niall remained hidden in the back, perhaps to keep from further worrying the woman.

The wraith shrank back a bit as Ruby laid down the reins. "Evening, ma'am. Name's Ruby Seddon, out of Arkansas."

"Arkansas? What you doin' way out here?"

"In the Utah Territory?"

"No," the woman said, stretching out a bony arm and pointing to the surrounding wilderness. "Out here."

"Actually," Ruby chuckled, "I'm mostly lost. Looking for the south stretch of the Mormon Trail."

"Headin' where?"

"Going to—"

"Our destination's not important," Niall interrupted in a hoarse croak. He sat up, and the dark-haired woman gasped at the sudden sound and sight of a man. "Do you or do you not know where we can pick up the road?"

Niall's abruptness seemed to turn the woman's surprise to anger. "You show up outta nowhere and commence to treatin' folks like that? Just go the hell back the way you come."

"I apologize for my son, ma'am," Ruby said. "John's a grump on account of his foot's hurting him bad. I'm just trying to hunt him a doctor."

The woman's face said she wasn't totally believing the story. "Closest sawbones's in Great Salt Lake City—southern route'll take you exact the wrong way."

"Uh-huh," Ruby nodded. "But there'd be someone in Parowan if we decided to—"

"There." The woman pointed a crooked finger. Thirty yards out, shallow grooves were just visible. "Follow the wagon tracks east. Sooner or later you'll meet up with a proper trail."

Ruby said, "How long you figure afore—"

"Not complete sure what you pair are up to." The woman spat and hefted the gun in two leathery hands. "But that's enough talkin'. Time for you and that ignorant boy of yours to skeedaddle." She raised the pistol in two hands, her right thumb going white as it struggled against the tight spring that tensioned the hammer. Before the mechanism could catch at full cock, her strength failed.

The bullet pierced nothing but sky, and the report alarmed the desert air like an unexpected clap of thunder. The Percherons lit out at full gallop like their tails were on fire—in the exact wrong direction.

It took some minutes, but eventually fatigue replaced the animals' terror. Ruby regained control and steered her horses in a sweeping turn, squinting through the dusk to line up with the narrow ruts.

Less than an hour later, she reined the horses to a stop in deep darkness. "Guess here's where we'll set till morning. How you holding, Niall?"

When he didn't answer, Ruby's heart fell. *Oh God most merciful, don't let the man be dead!* She scrambled to the wagon bed and knelt next to her travel companion, leaning into his face and saying, "Niall. Tell me you're still among the living."

A short but terrifying pause, then, "I am. Now leave me to sleep," he grumbled.

She breathed a relieved sigh, then climbed down from the wagon. For the first time in hours, her feet were on solid ground, her body was not bouncing and jostling from the craggy track. Trying to work the stiffness out of her neck, she leaned her head back, feeling an agreeable stretch from chin to chest. Ruby spotted a nearby break in the sage, a flat rock. She sat, then lay back, face to the sky. "Never seen the stars so bright," she whispered.

The Milky Way arched in a bright smear from northeast to south. The remainder of the firmament was a black velvet tablecloth littered with spilled chips of diamond.

"You up there, Harold?" she asked. "You was—you are— a good man, and I know you're with our sweet daughter, Samantha and her Frederick somewhere beyond them stars, all together with our loving Jesus." Tears streamed from the corners of her upturned eyes and down the sides of her face. "I miss all y'all so bad. I'll join you some blessed day, but right now I got a task I know you want me to complete. Find our Levi and bring him back to be reared by me, his last kin remaining on this earth."

She sat up, held silence for a few moments, then continued, "When you see the Lord, ask him to help your poor wife. I ain't doing too good on my own."

Ruby's head sank forward, and she wept till she'd drained herself of every tear banked since the day of the telegram.

~41~

R uby woke well before the sun brightened the canvas cover of the wagon box. She sat up, stretched, then looked over to Niall. He appeared to be asleep, so she laid a hand on his forehead without speaking. He gave a low groan then opened his eyes. "How'm I doing?"

"How you feel?"

"Hurts like hell itself, but I can tolerate it."

She removed her hand. "Forehead's cool and dry—that's real good."

"All right then," he said with a bad southern drawl. "Let's git gittin.'"

Ruby couldn't help but smile. "Took the words plumb out of my mouth." She clambered out and unhobbled the horses.

༚ঙ

Ruby rested the animals after urging them along for nearly six hours straight, probing the entire time for the perfect pace: somewhere between *gotta get there afore the Mormon army* and *can't risk injuring the critters.* "I know it's been a rough day. Sorry, boys," she said. "Wish I could unhitch you for a bit— but we just ain't got the time."

The big animals' powerful necks bent and stretched against the harness rigging. Rubbery lips skinned back to expose yellowed teeth as the horses tore up bunches of sweetgrass and slurped water that burbled from a small spring. Ruby gave an approving nod in the direction of her tired horses. "Seems you Percherons is as sound as they say."

From his seat on a quilt pile in the back, Niall called out, "Use what time it takes to make sure they get plenty of water."

"Thanks for that—I never would have figured," was Ruby's mocking reply. She climbed down and walked to the open back of the wagon, resting two hands on the wooden edge. Ruby regarded Niall for a moment. *Man don't look so bad as he might.* "How you feeling after that long old ride?" she asked.

"Not great. But it sure beats the option."

"Option?" The reply confused Ruby.

He raised an eyebrow. "You leaving me in the desert to die."

Ruby felt flustered and a bit hurt. "I didn't bring you this far to—"

"Relax, Ruby. Gallows humor, as they say."

She gave a resigned shrug. *Gallows humor? That don't make a lick of sense to this old lady—but I got neither time nor the inclination to hear the man expound.*

"Help me out of the wagon?" Niall said.

"Climb out? You sure?"

"Got to tend to my necessaries."

"Oh, of course."

"Think I can hoist myself backwards over the gunnel. If you'll just guide my good foot to a spoke—and keep the shot one from thumping into anything."

Getting out was awkward and obviously painful, but eventually Niall stood on the ground, one-footed, holding tight to the big wagon wheel with both hands.

Ruby walked around to the other side of the wagon, close enough to help if needed, far enough away to afford Niall a bit of privacy. After a few minutes, he announced, "That's that."

Ruby walked back around the wagon. "So where you reckon we set right now?" she asked

He scanned the surrounding country. "We've been traveling more or less uphill all day. Most of the sage's given way to juniper, so—" He took a deep breath and let it out in a sigh. "We're two, maybe three days from catching the track somewhere close to Fillmore."

"That's pretty good, right?" Ruby asked.

"Depends."

"On what?"

"On where the militia is."

~42~

September 5, 1861

It was just after four in the afternoon when Lieutenant William Hazen and his posse turned onto the main street of Fillmore. Even with horses uniquely bred and conditioned for long distance travel, covering the stretch from Great Salt Lake City in just three days had been grueling for man and beast. Hazen held up an arm, halting his mounted contingent in front of a two-story building. The part-time soldiers, most of whom had never been further south than Provo, stared at the surprising edifice.

"That's it, men," Hazen called out. "The old territorial statehouse." It was small by Great Salt Lake City standards, but easily the biggest and most impressive structure in this nondescript town. Deserted but not neglected, the building's ornamental fascia and freshly washed domed windows sparkled in the late afternoon sun.

"Private Charles," Hazen called to the second man in the column.

"Yes, sir?"

"Livery's at the end of the street. See the horses are tended to. Tell the groom we require fresh animals within the hour— we're on the spoor of a killer." Hazen dug deep into his shoulderbag and retrieved a paper. "And round up food enough for three days." Hazen gave the note to Charles with a flourish.

"No hangin' fire, Private. We'll be in the saddle most of the night as it is."

❧

Ruby pulled the door closed behind her and glanced around the little store. The shelves were crowded with various implements and tools, all dulled with gray dust. *Must not be many folks in these parts what can afford to—* Oh, *Lord. They're here!*

Even with his back to her, it was clear the man wore some kind of military uniform. *Got to be that militia Niall was yammering about.* Her first instinct was to run. Instead, she turned to the wall and feigned interest in a rusting iron hook. *If I tarry for a moment, I'll maybe get me some bit of information.*

The soldier's voice was loud and proud. "There'll be no cash exchanged, *Brother*. Perhaps you're not so good with words." There was a brief rustle of paper and the man read out loud.

Dear Reader,

The bearer of this letter, Lieutenant William Hazen, is under orders to capture or kill a dangerous criminal and enemy to the Church. It is hereby commanded that you provide Lt. Hazen lodging, sustenance, horses fresh and strong and whatever else he requires to fulfill my orders.

Yours in Christ,
Brigham Young

Ruby set the hook back on the shelf and slipped outside.

Breathless from worry, Ruby reached the wagon parked in a narrow alley that ran behind the Main Street buildings.

"That didn't take long," Niall said. "Where's the—"

"Hush up!" Ruby demanded in a throaty whisper. "They're here! Grab onto something. We're gittin'." She jumped to the seat, took up the reins, and walked the team down the backstreet and out of town as quickly as she dared without arousing attention.

Focused on the animals, she ignored Niall's questions for a full fifteen minutes. Then she suddenly turned off the trail to the east, weaving her way between closely spaced junipers. When the Conestoga was back in the trees far enough not to be seen from the established track, she reined the rig to a stop and said, "Military's in that little town we was just—"

"Mormons?"

"To a certainty," she said.

"How many?"

"Dozen, maybe more."

"Did you hear any talk of—"

"They're tasked by Brigham Young to find and kill you," Ruby said. "And there ain't no way we're outrunning them."

"So we hang back awhile," Niall said.

Ruby felt a stab of fear. "But when they catch up to us—"

"We'll hide till they pass by. Those boys can search every nook and cranny from here to the Santa Clara—they won't find us if we're not there yet."

"But if they get to Parowan first and take my Levi—"

Niall appeared lost in thought for a moment or two. "The child's got nothing to do with this. Probably."

~43~

September 7, 1861

In full military regalia, Captain Warren Dunning, Colonel Dame, and Lieutenant Hazen stood on a raised parade stand build halfway up a twelve-foot walls built of adobe bricks Warren had help fire a few years prior. Beneath the long roof below, the men from Great Salt Lake City. The posse had traveled for nearly a week on little sleep and short rations, so Colonel Dame insisted they take a hot meal and a well-deserved rest. They were finishing their meal, then one-by-one pushing away from the long pine table. Sister Dame and the other Relief Society sisters bustled about the Social Hall, clearing dishes and tidying up.

"Gallagher. That's the man's name, right?" Warren knew the answer, but hoped some small talk might take his mind off his son's sad assignment.

Dame nodded. "Mormon-hater and cold-blooded killer. And he might well be hiding right under our noses."

Warren was perplexed. "But Parowan? Why here, of all places?"

"Don't rightly know," the colonel said.

"Could it be some kind of dodge?" Warren asked.

Dame's forehead wrinkled. "Meaning?"

"Is somebody lying about where the man's truly off to? Maybe trying to throw us off his scent?"

"The story of him heading for Parowan might well be a ruse." Dame gave his chin whiskers a thoughtful stroke. "But President Young wants the man, and if Gallagher's anywhere within twenty miles of where we stand, I'll find him—with the help of the good Lord and fifty militia boys."

Over the next hour and a half, Warren watched the locals dribble in while the GSLC militia rested. Nearly all the newcomers were in uniform, the rumpled state of their clothing evidence that the part-time soldiers had been called up on short notice. Despite their ragtag appearance, there was a palpable atmosphere of bravado. And since the enemy was described as one wounded man with an elderly female companion, he guessed not one of the militiamen was wasting energy worrying about his own safety.

"Time to commence?" Dame asked Captain Dunning.

"I believe so, sir."

The colonel gave a stiff, officious nod, then addressed Dunning without looking at him. "Gather the troops at once."

"Sir!" The captain saluted, spun on his heel and stepped off to gather the men into an open square bounded by homes and barracks.

∽≪

"Ten-hut!" Warren yelled. More-or-less orderly rows of soldiers in more-or-less matching uniforms snapped to.

"Troops are assembled, sir," Dunning announced. He and Lieutenant Hazen stood facing the assembled men, each to one side of Colonel Dame.

"At ease, men," Colonel Dame thundered. "Our orders today are simple: Capture or kill a murderer name of Niall Gallagher. I said the task was clear-cut, but it may not be so easy as you're thinking." He paused. "This is a former Pony Express man and notorious gunslinger. He knows the territory—

also knows how to handle his revolvers—so take no chances. I'd sooner see Gallagher put down like a mad dog than any one of you take a bullet—or a scratch, for that matter."

The assembled men responded with loud hoots.

"At ease, soldiers!" Dame roared. "This is no laughing matter."

He gestured to Hazen and continued, "Lieutenant Hazen here has pursued the criminal for days. I'm turning time over to him to explain more about your object, his means of travel and such. After that, Captain Dunning will divide you into smaller squads and give orders as to where you'll be searching."

~44~

September 8, 1861

Ruby, Niall and their canvas-covered wagon settled in a mile east of Fort Parowan, just above the line where the cedar and scrub oak gave way to mountain forest. She leaned around a man-thick pine and raised the spyglass acquired from the riverboat captain. The sun was high in the desert sky, but the old telescope cast no reflection, its brass case tarnished to a dull brown. Yesterday they'd watched from their hiding spot while small teams spread out over the area, looking for a fugitive murderer, no doubt. She lowered the glass and spoke. "Curious. Today there's nary a soul to be seen."

"All in Mormon church," Niall said.

"Of course! Plumb forgot it was the Sabbath." She thought for a moment. "Guess it's time to hunt us up some vittles."

"But, Ruby," Niall teased, "you once told me you were a God-fearing woman."

"Sunday or not, ox's in the mire, my boy. And it's for sure you ain't up to it."

"Not speaking of Sabbath breaking. It's thieving I refer to."

"Hmm. Guess it is thieving after a fashion. But it's that or perish. So that there's another cow stuck in the mud."

"A bit like that flour I acquired some years ago in Camp Floyd, eh?"

Without another word, Ruby walked back to the wagon and commenced rummaging for the old burlap sack.

"Ruby," Niall called after her. "Don't dawdle. Services last just two hours."

ᘒᗕ

Tommy took the tiniest sip of grape juice then passed the heavy cup to Mama. A few tears started leaking from his eyes, and he lowered his head hoping no one would notice. *I know I'm supposed to think about Jesus when I take the sacrament, so how come everything just reminds me of Clara?*

It took *forever* till everyone got the sacrament, but finally President Dame was at the podium of the Rock Church. It was the first time Tommy had seen the man in his soldier clothes, and the sight of him wearing something other than his black suit and tie was ever so odd. Most of the brothers in the congregation, a lot of them strangers, also wore the army outfits.

"Brothers and Sisters," President Dame bellowed, "there'll be none of the usual preaching today. As many of you know, President Young has ordered me to hunt for a runaway murderer named Niall Gallagher. Militia searched most of yesterday to no avail. It pains me to continue the search on the Sabbath, but we'd best be about getting this ox from the mire. I'll now offer a benediction, then we'll conclude the sacrament meeting."

"Amen," he said when the short prayer was over. But before Tommy could stand, President Dame said one more thing. "The culprit is traveling with an elderly woman in a small wagon topped with hoops and bonnet. Send word if you spot them, but do not approach unarmed. Now travel to your homes in the love and safety of our Lord."

ᘒᗕ

With frequent stops to survey the surrounding area, it took Ruby half an hour to make the hike from the secret camp to within fifty yards of the nearest farm. She stopped and squinted hard. *Not seeing anything, but best go slow. Could be someone stayed home from services.* It was a clapboard home with a log outbuilding nearby. She approached with deliberate steps, keeping an apple tree heavy with fruit between her and the dwelling. The tree was only thirty feet from the house, and she made it without incident. Standing still as a post for a minute or more, Ruby watched and listened. Nothing. She twisted the nearest apple till the stem broke, then dropped it into her sack, plucked a dozen more and walked to the house.

Ruby opened the only door and stepped inside, leaving it ajar. When her eyes had accustomed to the lack of light, she saw the home's interior, a single room, crowded with bedding, clothing and a few sticks of furniture. She stepped around folded quilts to the corner where a blackened stove marked the cooking area. A nearby sideboard held heavy cotton bags which Ruby soon discovered held flour, dried corn and uncracked kernels of wheat. She whispered, "Oh, Lord, hope you can forgive me," then carefully untied each and poured about a third of its contents directly into her large sack. "And please make sure this poor family don't too soon notice some of their vittles's gone, nor go hungry for the lack of them." She hefted the sack of apples and mixed grains over a shoulder, then muttered, "Hope that's a smokehouse out back."

It was indeed a smokehouse, with four fat hams hanging from blackened iron spikes. Ruby freed one and added it to her heavy satchel. "Surely hate to do it," she said, "but soon we'll be feeding Levi as well." She reached for a second but froze before her hand got to it.

"Constance," a man's voice called out, "did you leave that door open again?"

❧

Ruby leaned on the wagon, breathing like a blacksmith's bellows.

"You look a fright," Niall said.

"Seems you was dead wrong about the length of Mormon services. Had to skitter like a squirrel half the way back here." Ruby hoisted a filthy, bulging sack into the wagon.

"Did anyone catch sight of you?"

"Not right certain."

~45~

September 10, 1861

You wanted to see me, sir?" Warren's Dunning's tone, always deferential to Commander Dame, was even more so today. The Dame home, specifically the president's study, was hallowed ground upon which he'd stood but once before.

Dame looked up from his paperwork, pulled off his wire-rimmed spectacles with one hand. "No sign of Gallagher, then?"

Warren turned both palms up. "No, sir, not a scent. Guessing he either took off to the west or skirted around Parowan and headed for Cedar City, or maybe straight to Santa Clara—if he even came this way. GSLC militia's gone, but as you ordered, I dispatched local riders to all surrounding areas."

"Very well. Thank you for the report, Captain."

"Yes, sir, whatever you—"

"Bishop," President Dame interupted, his voice softening. He stood, came around the writing table and placed an arm on Warren's shoulder.

"Sir?"

"Bennet on the plan to pick up the boy?"

Warren swallowed hard and prayed for courage. This was the moment he'd been fearing. "He and I been talking, President. With all that's, you know, been going on, maybe the boy staying with Eva for now's not the worst—"

The president turned and fixed sunken eyes on his subordinate. "Orders are orders, and these are straight from the Prophet."

From the Prophet? Brother Brigham knows of Thomas? Warren felt his legs go weak as willows, but he managed to remain upright and acknowledged his superior with a feeble nod.

"The child's the last link to what happened—out there." The president's voice lowered. "You surely understand that if the actuality came to light, it could mean the end of the Iron Mission, maybe even the Church."

"Yes, sir." Warren averted his gaze. "But Bennet sorely wishes he didn't have to speak a lie direct to his wife's ears."

"Easier this way, Bishop Dunning. And remember, he's lying for the Lord in the great cause of Zion. We all are."

A fearsome thought slammed Warren with force that nearly knocked his wind out. "B . . . but," he croaked, "no one's gonna hurt my grandson, right?"

President Dame squinted his eyes shut and pinched the bridge of his nose as if he were in some kind of pain. "In this, as in all things, only the Prophet knows the will of the great Jehovah." There was a long, terrifying pause, then he opened his eyes and added, "Never forget, the child is not your grandson, not the blood of Israel."

Warren felt his soul being torn asunder. *Not my flesh and blood, perhaps, but I've come to a grandfatherly fondness for Thomas. What now's to become of the poor boy? Surely The Brethren would not go so far as to sacrifice a child, even if they felt it necessary to protect God's Kingdom.*

"Bishop Dunning! Are you listening to me?"

Warren regarded the man before him with fear-dulled sight. "I, uh, I'll make certain Bennet delivers him, President."

President Dame laid a not-so-reassuring hand on his shoulder, and Warren's stomach rebelled. "There can be no kind of hitch," the president said. "You'll take a few men and follow him out to the Shand place. Early tomorrow."

"It shall be done, President." Warren somehow managed not to issue up the contents of his stomach until he was outside the home, beyond the leader's view.

❧❦

Tommy made his way to the rope clothesline with a series of smooth step-and-swing motions—after two years of practice, the crutch was second nature. He pulled a pair of britches and two shirts from the line, tucked them under one arm and started back to the house at his version of a run. "Mama," he hollered, "I gotta start packing for the roundup."

His mother met him at the front door and took the sun-dried clothes. "All right," she laughed. "But your papa's not coming till tomorrow."

"I know. I just want to make sure I'm all ready to go cowboyin'."

"*Cowboyin'* is it now?"

"Gotta round up them steers."

She rested a hand on her son's shoulder. "It's *those* steers, Thomas."

"I know, but cowboys—"

"You can be a cowboy and still speak proper English."

"Yes, ma'am," he replied. *But when we get up in them mountains, we're gonna talk the way cowboys talk when there's no womenfolk about—hell, might even do a little cussin'.*

"Looks like weather will be pleasant for the roundup," Mama said, breaking into Tommy's cowboy thoughts.

He looked around. The sun was bright in the big blue sky, but not so hot as just days before. "Shore 'nuff," he said.

"How about you and I take advantage of this nice morning? Maybe ride into the hills and gather a basket of pinenuts before the squirrels get them all."

"What about Sophie?" Tommy asked. "Oh, I forgot. Tell me again why she had to go with Sister Fotheringham."

Mama just shrugged.

"Can Woobydog come, too?"

"If she can keep up with Ginger."

Tommy rolled his eyes at such a silly joke.

"It's set, then. We'll harvest a big batch of seeds. I'll roast them up, and you can take a sack to share with the other cowboys."

He gave his mama a mischievous grin, then tried out his best cowboy drawl. "Can't hardly wait."

Mama's smile was so big it made the corners of her eyes crinkle. "Tomorrow will be here before you know it," she said.

❧

"Maybe this old thing was worth the two dollars after all." From the hiding place high in the pines, Ruby scanned the valley through the old spyglass. "Looks to me like them militias mighta gave up." Ruby lowered the metal tube. "Time to fetch the boy?"

"We have to be absolutely certain," Niall said. "Maybe give it one more day."

After a moment to consider, Ruby nodded. "Agreed. Tomorrow's the day we rescue my Levi."

~46~

September 11, 1861

S tep by stealthy step, Ruby eased the horses and wagon in the direction of what showed on Kate's map as *The Shand Farm*. "Whoa," she called out, reining back the Percherons and halting the wagon. Niall was at her side, his injured leg propped up on a blanket folded to pad the top edge of the footboard. Both squinted into the distance.

They were less than a quarter mile out, and Ruby could see the house was just as Kate described it, red adobe bricks, double front doors and wings running left and right. Smoke rose from three chimneys—one dead center, one at each end. Nearby stood a long stacked-stone barn and two corrals. The smaller was home to three fine horses, the larger held a half-dozen brindle brown calves, thick-chested, with horns so long and awkward their young heads seemed to slump with the burden.

"Shand home, of a certain." It was easily the largest house she'd seen since entering the Utah Territory. "You in there, my sweet boy?" she whispered to the breeze. Two fat tears escaped Ruby's eyes and rolled down weathered cheeks.

"We still on the plan?" Niall asked.

"My blood grandson a prisoner in a godless household. The so-called father sharing his evil seed 'twixt two women in different homes." She took a deep breath and exhaled. "Hell, yes, we're on the plan. Just gotta figure if my boy's in there right now."

"And figure it fast," Niall added. "Some militia may still be about."

"That bum leg of yours up to action?"

"So long as were not chasing nor fleeing on foot."

Ruby made the blunt announcement. "We're going in."

"Now?" Niall's tone suggested he was not convinced this was their best option.

Ruby set her jaw in firm determination. She gave a light wiggle of the reins, and the big horses began closing the 400 yards that separated them from the house.

"Best strap on them Colts," she warned.

❧❦

Eva saw a bucketful of water fly out of her son's hand as he stumbled and tripped through the doorway.

"Thomas! What the—"

"Strangers! Strangers with guns!" he screamed. His good leg flailed and slipped in the wet, and he scrambled unsuccessfully to right himself.

With strength beyond her own, Eva tipped the heavy table onto its side. She grabbed her son by an arm and dragged him behind the makeshift shield. "Stay!" she yelled.

In three steps, Eva reached the long gun that hung by iron hooks above the fireplace. She pointed it at the open door and pulled the curved butt tight to her shoulder. Working against a rusty spring, she trembled while thumbing back the hammer till the cockplate caught it.

Know I left it loaded. But did I— She looked down. "No!"

To avoid any accident, she'd removed the firing cap and stored it out of the reach of curious young hands. Pulling the trigger now would create no more than a sparkless snap. Eva's mother-mind quickly jumped from panic to plan. *I know the big muzzleloader's impotent, but whoever's about to come across that threshold has no way to—*

"Stand down, woman!"

The man in the doorway was only about Eva's height, but his deep voice was convincing. And both hands were filled with heavy pistols that from the muzzle end looked like cannons.

He kept one revolver trained on her, the other aimed at the tipped table that may—or may not—have been thick enough to stop a bullet from punching through and killing her son. Eva's thoughts of any kind of standoff were gone.

"Now!" he growled.

Without taking her eyes off the threat, Eva bent her knees and laid the weapon onto the wet floor.

"That's right." The man spoke evenly, calmly. "Now the boy comes out."

Eva hesitated, a dozen possible scenarios tumbling through her head.

"I assure you, ma'am, I intend to do no harm," the gunman said. "But how this plays out now rests with you and you alone."

Thomas remained in his hiding place, likely paralyzed by uncertainty.

"It's all right, Thomas," Eva finally said. She was trying without success not to infect the little boy with her own fear. "Come stand behind me."

"Not behind, to the side," a tall woman said as she stepped through the door. Eva's surprise was doubled by the fact that the stranger held Woobydog to her breast, stroking the contented animal.

Eva blurted, "Wh . . . who are you people and what do you?—"

"I'm Ruby Seddon. The boy's grandmother. Rightful. By blood."

It's here, the terrible day I prayed without ceasing would never come. The room began to spin, and Eva's legs wobbled. Had Thomas not been leaning on her, she might well have fainted to the floor.

࿔࿔

Bennet reined his horse to a halt and took in an unexpected sight: two large grays hitched to a Conestoga and tied off at the side of his home. "What in the dark dominion of Sheol is going on?" he muttered. "Wagon fits the description of the murderer's, but I can't think of a single reason Gallager would be here."

Adding to the strangeness, the front door stood wide open. Bennet called out softly, hesitantly, "Eva, Thomas? You in there?" From inside the house, he heard something. *Voices? Yes, but not in answer to my question.*

He slid down off the horse. *Surely something's off the beam.* From its saddle scabbard, he drew a short-barrelled musket. A glance confirmed the cap was in place, the gun muzzle-loaded and ready to fire.

~47~

"I hate her, "Tommy whispered to his mama. "She's not my gramma, she's a big liar."

"Shssh!" Mama warned.

He looked around, trying hard to understand. But his seven-year-old mind just could not make sense of the unfolding scene: a small man, drawn six-guns, Woobydog nuzzling into the chest of a strange woman. *Why'd she say she was my gramma?*

And behind the strangers, Tommy saw Papa slowly approaching the door with his stubby rifle in two hands, finger touching the trigger.

෭~෬

Ruby startled when her namesake dog squirmed in her arms and gave a high-pitched yelp directed behind her. She noticed her grandson's eyes shift to over her shoulder, seeming to focus on something beyond her and Niall. She flicked her head just far enough left to see the rifle's broad barrel, then Ruby called out, "Niall! Gun!"

Without moving his injured foot, Niall swiveled at the waist enough to spot the rifleman and train one of his big pistols on his face. "Best lay that blunderbuss down." he said.

The man hesitated.

"Now!" Niall yelled. "Don't make me shed the woman's blood in front of Levi." He leaned over and set down the rifle.

Ruby was impressed. *Seem's young Niall's been in the stew afore. Drawed down on the man without taking his second piece off the lady.*

"You. Step to the woman's side." Ruby pointed a finger at the now unarmed intruder. Niall tracked the newcomer with a gun barrel as he stepped around to the woman's left.

"Now move yourselves to them chairs." Ruby reached out and caught her grandson by the arm. "Not you, Levi." She gently set the dog on the floor. "You go out to the porch for a minute and play with your Woobydog." Almost as an afterthought, she added, "It's dreadful important to all of us that you don't wander off. Understand?"

"Please don't hurt him," the woman pled.

"I'm his grandmother!" Ruby hollered. "But hurting you growns? That's now up to all y'all."

The woman Levi called Mama said, "It's going to be all right, Son. Maybe use the time to feed Ginger a few of those wrinkly apples."

Ruby bristled at the word *Son*, but bit her lip to keep from speaking.

"Apples?" Levi said. "Do you mean—"

She cut him off with, "Fetch your crutch. I'll be along as soon as I can. Promise." He was shivering like the last oak leaf in a winter storm, but he did as he was told.

When the door was securely shut, Ruby spoke. "First off, you two have a sit while we get acquainted." Ruby nodded in the woman's direction. "Eva, right? Eva Dunning?"

"Yes," Eva mumbled.

"And you, sir, husband Bennet, I assume."

"How do you—"

"All right, then, Bennet and Eva. This here's the part you absolutely got to get the understanding of . . ."

☙◈❧

Outside the closed door, Tommy was bawling like he was still a baby. *Mama's in grave danger. I have to do something.* He looked around for something, anything. *A stick to hit the guns out of the mean man's hand? Big rocks to throw at his head?*

Then it struck him. "Mama said wrinkly apples. It's a secret message! I'm to hide in the cellar near Clara's— the cabin where Clara used to live. Don't know how that will set things aright, but I trust my mama."

☙❧

Stay strong, Ruby told herself. *It may not be that I'd really suffer them to die, but they got to believe I'd do it.* "At best, y'all're kidnappers," she said. "According to the law of the land and of the Lord, I'd be within my rights to have my man here shoot you dead where you set." Ruby paused to give the captives time to absorb the threat.

"Instead, I'm going to ask her . . ." She pointed to Eva. ". . . a few questions. If the answers ain't to my satisfaction," She tapped Bennet's forehead. "That one's going to die."

But instead of launching straight into her inquiry, Ruby paused. *Think maybe that's wrongways around. Got the feeling she'd be quick to sacrifice her man if it meant keeping the boy.*

"Plan's changing," she said. "*He's* speaking to the questions. *She's* the one taking a ball if he falters."

Niall moved his gun to the wife's head.

Ruby silently prayed, *Oh, God, don't let them put me to the test.*

"First off, did you really reckon taking poor Levi's foot would hoodwink a body? I got a eyewitness says this particular boy had an extra right toe."

Eva blurted, "I would never—"

"Quiet!" Ruby hollered. She gestured to Bennet. "He's the one I want to hear it from."

"I found the boy snakebit," Bennet said. "Leg got so rotten, Doc had to take it—surely saved him dying."

Ruby looked deep into the man's eyes, praying to discern truth from deception.

He held her gaze and continued, "That's the God's-honest truth, I swear it on my life."

"Ain't your life's at stake here," Ruby said. "How long's the boy been with y'all?"

"Four years now—ever since Injuns killed his—"

Ruby silenced him with her palm. "Injuns, huh? We'll get back to that real soon, Bennet. Meantime, you know for sure my Samantha was killed?"

"Samantha?"

"My daughter—and her husband—leaving poor Levi an orphan."

The husband looked down to the floor, his face flushed with shame, or rage, or—something. "I do." His voice got very small. "They were all killed."

"All?"

Bennet hesitated a few seconds, then, "Every last one of the growns, and most of the children."

"You seen 'em?" Ruby demanded.

He nodded. "Buried many with my own hands."

Bennet's testimony of the dead was not news, Ruby had known it for years. But to hear it from the lips of a man who had witnessed the horror firsthand felt like being caught up and washed away in a storm-swollen river.

Bennet disrupted her thoughts with, "I'll allow I've not been much of a father, but Eva is a mama any child would be plumb lucky to—"

The wife broke in. "For four years now—"

A hard look stopped Eva, then Ruby relented. "Go on," she said.

"For the first . . . two years," Eva said, "Thomas h . . . had terrible nightmares." The entirety of her body juddered with the weeping, and her voice trembled as if she were standing in a bank of snow. "Every n . . . night reliving the moment he was, was torn from his mother's arms. Please. Please don't . . . let that happen again."

"The woman the child was tore from was my daughter, Samantha Seddon Cantrell," Ruby said. "And his Christian name ain't Thomas."

"It's the only name he remembers," Eva pled. "And for more than half his life, I've been the only mother he's known."

Ruby felt suddenly sad and oddly jumbled—the triumphant moment was not unfolding the way she'd imagined it. *So what's the best thing for Levi? It's surely his wellbeing that matters, not this old lady's. But I can't allow him to be raised by bigamous heathens, never to know the saving grace of our Lord Jesus Christ.*

৵৵৻৸

"Mount up, men," Warren Dunning ordered. The four soldiers under his direct command swung into their saddles. "Our squad's to comb back over the southeast quadrant, the area of my son's place and thereabouts." *Of course while we're at it, Commander Dame would have me ensure that Bennet fetched up the boy, as ordered.*

Dunning took the point, and the small force rode through a gate set into the fort's walls and onto what was simply called the South Road, a well beaten track that connected Parowan to its nearest sibling, Cedar City.

৵৵৻৸

"Listen up," Ruby said, surprising herself with the calm in her voice. "Bennet here's going to tell us how my daughter and son-in law come to be murdered so nigh to this town of yours."

"Injuns attacked the wagon train," Bennet said. "I told you already."

"Lyin' son of Satan!" Ruby growled.

"It was Injuns," Bennet insisted.

She fixed his eyes with a stony glare. "Some of the children that survived was old enough to recall—and they spoke of white men, lots of them. If you value your woman's life, it's time to tell the truth—every last bit of it."

"And if you think for one second I won't pull the trigger," Niall interjected, "you are disastrously mistaken." He now had both menacing revolvers trained on Eva's chest.

Ruby braced herself for Bennet's response. *Last thing I want to hear is the particulars of my Samatha's murder. But I promised Senator Mitchell I'd find out for certain, once and for all.*

Bennet gave his head a violent shake. "No! You're asking me to break a promise, an oath I swore on my life."

The wife gasped, "An oath?"

"A blood oath. If I speak of it to anyone . . ." Bennet took a deep, trembling breath. ". . . my soul will perish. Don't ask me to betray it."

"I ain't *asking* nothing," Ruby said. "Speak now or your woman perishes—before your very eyes."

Bennet lowered his head and cleared his throat. "Word was some men on the wagon train had been bragging about being part of the mob that murdered Joseph." His voice was low and solemn.

Ruby gave her head a disgusted shake. "Meaning Joseph Smith?"

"Yes, the Prophet Joseph Smith. One of them even claimed to be in possession of the pistol that killed the Prophet."

"You hear these braggarts with your own ears?"

"No—just stories," he said. "There was also talk of them disrespecting Mormon women along the route with vulgar language and such. Neither did I witness that directly."

"So you Mormons just attacked the train," Ruby said, "and killed them all over some rumors?" Her breaths came quicker, now matching her racing heart. "Word is you took possession of their belongings, cattle, money—all of it."

Bennet did not respond—he just stared past Ruby with eyes as dull as dust.

"No more stalling," Ruby threatened. "Injuns? Or Mormons?"

Bennet's eyes rolled strangely upward, as if permission to speak might have been carved into the wooden ceiling. At length he continued, his words pouring out like the urgent current of a river at spring flood.

"We'd heard rumors of Injuns hitting that Arkansas train, but I'd no way to know if they were true till Colonel Dame assembled the militia. Said there'd been trouble with the Lamanites—"

"Who?" Ruby demanded.

"Indians," Eva said.

"Dame ordered me and a hundred or so men to go out to the Mountain Meadows and bury some dead." Bennet shook his head. "A hundred men—to bury a few bodies. How's that make any sense?" He took a few silent breaths, then went on. "But the strangeness of it all was that Dame ordered us to bring guns—not shovels, mind you—guns. Didn't take much to figure the killing wasn't over."

"You went anyway?" Ruby asked. "What manner of heathen are you?"

"My priesthood leader and my militia commander ordered me to go—and he's one and the same man." Bennet swallowed hard, then continued. "The sight when we got to the Meadows was a wretched one, wagons in a circle, under siege already five days. Outside the wagons, bodies of a few brave men laid where they were shot while trying to fetch water or go for help."

Bennet stopped, and a lightning flash of anger forked through Ruby's skull. "Every bit of it," she growled, "Now."

"When we first rode up, we could hear women and children inside the wagon fort crying, thanking God we'd come to save them. Poor folks had no way of knowing they were wronger than wrong. Anyway, we set up camp a ways out. After a bit of supper, Major John Higbee gathered us up and went over the plan. First thing he told us was—orders from President Dame and Isaac Haight, Stake President down to Cedar City—everyone in the train was to perish. He said, 'Any man not willing to do his priesthood duty can ride out now—and keep on riding till you're out of the territory and out of the Kingdom of God altogether.'"

Eva spoke through gulping sobs. "So why didn't you—"

Ruby silenced her with a glance, then turned back to Bennet. "What. Exactly. Happened?"

Bennet gave his head a sad shake. "Every man stayed. Next, Higbee told us God had shown him in a dream what to do."

Ruby heard herself blurt, "The Lord gives no dreams to men like—"

"And that plan was what?" Niall demanded, still covering Eva with his guns.

"Next morning, Brother Higbee sent John D. Lee to the wagon camp with torn cotton undergarments tied to a long stick."

"A white flag," Ruby whisper-gasped.

Bennet nodded. "Yes." A tiny, joyless laugh escaped his lips. "The symbol of peace."

"Go on," Ruby ordered.

"Train folks were suspicious, but they let him in. Once inside, Lee convinced them that if they'd forfeit their wagons, cattle, and other belongings, they could leave in safety that very day."

Ruby scowled. "And the wretched folk took him at his word?"

"Must have taken some talking—Brother Lee was in there more than an hour."

"So they surrendered?" Ruby asked.

"They were bone-dry out of water and nearly out of food. Wounded laying all about, babies dying for lack of mother's milk. They surely knew they had no other choice."

"They agreed to the terms!" Ruby screamed. "What in the name of all things holy could have went cattywampus?"

Bennet hung his head and began to weep. "Brother Lee lied."

"Demons from hell could not have laid a strategy more evil than that!" Ruby shrieked.

Niall ground his teeth, as if struggling not to wheel around and put a bullet into Bennet's face.

Eva sobbed openly.

Head still down, Bennet spoke just loud enough to be heard. "September 11, four years ago this very day. They came out, women first, some with babes in arms, then the older children. The youngest were in wagons, just behind."

He took a breath and continued, "Men were marched out last, paired up one militia to one migrant. Told them we were there to protect them from Injuns, make sure they got safe passage. I was next to a man, no more than twenty-two or three. They marched the women and young'uns off well ahead of us. When they were over a hill and out of sight, the leader of our group yelled something like, 'Brethren do your duty.' And . . ." Bennet was crying. ". . . we did."

All but Bennet held their collective breath. Through desperate tears, he continued, "I placed the muzzle of my carbine . . . against that poor man's breast . . . and pulled the trigger."

Ruby heard a gasp and turned to see poor Eva collapse in a loose heap onto the floor.

"You shot the unarmed man point blank?"

"No. The gun misfired." There was a long pause, then, "But I did, I did my duty. Clubbed him with the butt of the rifle till . . . till his head just—" Bennet dissolved into choking sobs.

"And others of your minions killed the women and children?" Ruby snarled.

"All but . . . the very smallest," the horrid man choked out. "The major said we were to . . . to spare the children younger than eight—on account of it's a sin to shed innocent blood." The man's tone revealed the dreadful irony of those words was not lost on him.

The room held stunned silence for nearly a minute, then Bennet continued, "Of course, the last orphan, the only one not conveyed back east, is poor Thomas." He turned to address his wife. "And I didn't come here to take him on a roundup."

Eva gripped the table's edge and struggled to her feet. "So why—"

Bennet seemed to revive a mite, wiping his tear-soaked face with a shirt cuff. "When President Young finally heard there was one child held back from the Americans, he was enraged, said the boy was a danger to the entire church. So Colonel Dame sent me to fetch him—for transport to Great Salt Lake City, he said." Bennet's head sank again. "Though I'm not at all certain the child was ever meant to arrive there."

Eva's and Ruby's tattered gasps came in near unison.

"I love the boy, my Thomas—I truly do." Bennet recommenced to weeping. "But I have never been able to look at him without remembering, without thinking of that poor man's blood on my hands. Without wondering, was it Thomas's father I murdered on that wretched, godless day?" He sniffed loudly, wiped his nose with a shirt sleeve. "Man was surely some child's papa."

Bennet's sobs stopped suddenly. He took in a deep breath, then raised his head. In spite of all the crying, his face was not red, but pale as a just-burst boll of cotton and strangely blank of expression.

He sprang toward Niall, taking him by surprise and knocking both guns from his grip. Loud thumps signaled the Colts hitting the pine floor. Niall dived for his weapons, but the injured foot slowed him down, and before he could reach either of them, Bennet kicked the guns to the wall and sprang for his foe.

The two women watched, stunned into inaction. Niall fought like a hissing bobcat, but the larger man soon gained control. He picked Niall up and slammed his head against the solid wood beneath them. The feisty little fighter lay still and silent.

"You killed him!" Ruby screeched

Bennet retrieved both guns from a nearby corner and pointed the one in his left hand at his adversary.

"Bennet, no!" his wife screamed.

The smallest of smiles graced Bennet Dunning's face. He dropped his left arm to his side, raised the gun in the other hand and pressed its muzzle hard against his own chest. "God forgive me," he whispered.

The blast of the .45 caliber pistol left Ruby temporarily deafened. For her, the man's death played out in silence, time seeming to slow. The point-blank blast slammed him over a chair, and he came to rest on his back, arms and legs splayed to unnatural angles, an expression on his lifeless face that looked strangely serene.

~48~

Mind muddled beyond thought, Eva stared down at her lifeless husband. A potent mix of competing sensations flooded her being. And for some unfathomable reason, the incongruous emotions offset one another, leaving her suddenly empty. "Is he—dead?" she asked in a voice as flat as her feelings.

"He is, ma'am," the other man affirmed in gentle tones. He had regained his senses and managed to stand up.

She nodded understanding—and a measure of forgiveness. "Rest in peace, Bennet Dunning," she said. "May God have mercy on your tortured soul."

"You somewhat right, Niall?" Ruby asked.

"Stunned, but still among the living, as you see."

"I'll fetch Levi. Niall, you stay here with Mrs. Dunning."

Within a few short moments, Ruby burst back into the house. "Where is he?" she screamed into Eva's face.

"You'll never find him," was her soft response.

In Ruby's eyes, Eva saw a dangerous mingling of anger, frustration and raw terror. "And just how do you reckon this story ends, woman?" Ruby growled through grinding teeth. "We're just gonna bid you a fond farewell and ride away?"

Niall drew one of his just-holstered pistols.

Eva's mind was racing, desperate to conceive of possible outcomes, likely answers to the question: 'Just how do you reckon this story ends?'

Unbidden, unexpected, the answer came, accompanied by a feeling akin to a warm quilt enrobing her very soul.

"How old are you, Grandma Ruby?"

Grandma. The older woman seemed astonished to be addressed by the title. "What?"

"Your age."

"Nearing sixty-two. But I ain't seeing what that's got to do with—"

"Your Levi is seven years old. That sound right?"

"He is, but—"

"There's a strong likelihood you'll not linger on this earth long enough to raise him to a man. Is your husband in good health?"

"I'm the child's last kin." Tears began to pool in Ruby's eyes.

"Take us with you. Both of us," Eva said.

Ruby stammered, "B . . . but—"

"Loving mother, devoted grandmother—doesn't he deserve both?" *Please, God, help her understand.* Eva watched the grandmother's expression soften. *She feels it too, this woman who risked everything for her Levi.*

"Mother and grandmother," Eva repeated. She looked long and hard at the woman who she hoped now pondered a course of action that would have been unthinkable just minutes before.

"Reckon maybe he does," Ruby whispered.

"I'll take you to him—then what?" Eva asked, her heart now hopeful as the first buds of spring.

"San Diego," Niall said

San Diego. Thoughts of Millie and Clara creased Eva's face into a soft smile. "Perfect," she said. "Always wanted to soak my toes in the sea."

"We ain't raising him no Mormon," Ruby said.

Eva averted her eyes, looking past Grandma Ruby in an unfocused gaze. *'Don't ever compel me to choose between my son and the Saints,' I once told Bennet. But in a strange way, he has.*

"No," Eva said. "I guess we ain't."

~49~

The ride was short, but for the entire twenty minutes, Warren Dunning agonized, argued with himself. What's the right thing to do? I'm obliged by covenant to obey President Dame—but he's the same man whose orders left young Thomas an orphan.

They were less than half a mile from his son's house when Warren called, "Halt!" He thought he'd caught the sound of something over the thudding of horses' hooves. He stopped the small company and asked, "Any of you hear anything?"

"Yes, sir," said a man near the front of the column. "Might have been a gunshot, sir. Well off in the distance." The three other men nodded.

The group fell silent, waiting and listening for a minute, maybe two. Nothing.

"Ride on, men," Warren said. "Keep your eyes wide and your ears keen."

❧❧

Hugging his knees and sobbing, Tommy sat on the old wood door atop Gale's root cellar. "Can't go in there. I just can't." He stood and scrambled thirty yards further up the hill, then squatted behind a thick juniper. "It's all right, no one can see me here."

He felt the rumble of hurrying hooves and peeked around the bush to see a covered wagon approaching fast—*the same wagon that brought the gun man and the mean lady who lied about being my gramma.* Trembling with fear, Tommy crouched lower.

The wagon stopped at the bottom of the hill, and the lady stepped to the ground, then ran up and yanked the old cellar door open. She leaned her head in and hollered with hurry in her voice, "Levi, you in there? Come on out, Son, We gotta git!"

She doesn't even know my name—how can she be my gramma? And where's Mama? Did the man with guns?—

White-hot terror overcame him. Tommy knew his life depended on coming up with a plan, and fast. *I could run up the hill, but even an old lady could catch a boy with one leg.* He flattened himself face-down against the dry dirt and prayed the woman who talked so peculiar would just give up and leave. And she did, sort of. She ran back to the wagon and yelled something Tommy couldn't quite hear to someone he couldn't see.

Now's my chance! On two hands and his only foot, he spidered up the steep hillside as fast as he could, fueled by fear for his very life.

Then a familiar sound froze him in place.

"Thomas! Wait, it's me!" Over the clattering rocks and his own heavy breathing, he recognized Mama's voice and stopped, then sat up and turned back to face the wagon. Happiness filled Tommy all up as he watched his mother jump down from the seat and run toward him, Woobydog at her side. He hurried down the little hill the best he could, and when they met, Tommy gave her the biggest—and dustiest—hug ever. "Mama, you're alive! You're really—" He stopped mid-sentence, then, "Tell me I can I stay with you forever! Please."

"Yes, my darling boy. We're going off with your grand-mother to find Clara and Aunt Millie. We will all be together forever and ever and ever." Then she nearly smothered him with kisses.

Tommy couldn't understand what Mama had just said, but he was too happy to care.

"Get in the wagon!" the old lady called. "Something's kicking up the dust back yonder."

~50~

G et 'em up, men," Warren Dunning yelled. "Don't spare the horseflesh!" No longer arranged in a neat column, his posse was on a dead run from the Shand home to the Gale cabin.

After discovering his son's bloody corpse among the tipped table and overturned chairs, Warren had accomplished the most difficult challenge of his life—he somehow forced himself to postpone grieving in order to focus on justice—and revenge. He'd said a quick prayer for the dead, then hurried outside, hoping for some clue, some sense of what to do next. Fresh horse and wagon tracks leading east had caught his gaze. Next stop in that direction was Quincy Gale's old cabin, former home of the adulteress, Millicent Gale.

Who could have done this to Bennet? Warren spurred his speeding horse, wind sweeping tears from the corners of his eyes to be lost in silver sideburns. *My flesh and blood brutally murdered in his own home.* He considered the possibilities. *Gallagher? But why in all creation would that scoundrel have been at the house? And what has he—or whoever—done with Eva and Thomas?*

"Wagon!" one of the men yelled.

Less than a quarter mile ahead, two big horses approached drawing a modest Conestoga. The driver stopped suddenly and whipped it into a sharp turnabout, the wagon coming close to tipping.

Warren focused on the rocking wagon. *Gallagher's reported to be travelling in a covered rig with a woman. Could this be the murdering culprits?*

He reached for the rifle in his scabbard, but quickly thought better of it. "Do not fire, men," he yelled, "till we know who's in the wagon."

Warren whipped the reins side to side. He and the other horsemen were closing fast.

☙❧

Heart hammering in rhythm with the eight galloping hooves just ahead, Eva gave her son a rough push below the box frame and screeched, "Stay down!"

Five mounted militia pursued the racing wagon, each man with the reins of his thundering horse in one hand, a raised pistol in the other. They were no more than twenty yards away and quickly narrowing the distance.

"Faster!" she yelled up to Ruby. "They're close enough to shoot us."

If the woman driving the wagon replied, Eva did not hear it over the rumble of the horses and the rattle-clatter din of wobbling wagon parts.

The militia quickly caught up to the panting animals. Two soldiers maneuvered their horses in front of the grays, and the team dug hooves into the dust to avoid colliding. Peering out the back, Eva saw the other men quickly surround the wagon.

Father Dunning dismounted. "Who all's in there?" he demanded.

"Eva Dunning," she called out. "And Thomas."

"Everyone out of the wagon, feet on the ground. Now!"

Ruby hesitated, perhaps considering a desperate run for it.

"Now, driver!"

Ruby climbed down to the dirt. At the same time, Eva scrambled over the rear board, then helped her one-footed son to the ground. Thomas leaned against her while they walked forward to take places alongside the older woman. As yet unseen behind the canvas, Niall flattened himself against the floor of the wagon bed, one revolver drawn and cocked.

Without warning, Dunning stepped to Ruby and pressed the muzzle of his pistol against her forehead. "Gallagher!" he yelled. "Come out with empty hands or your woman dies. Now, you murdering scoundrel!"

Eva held her breath. *Was their future now to end in more bloodshed?* A few tense seconds ticked by, then Niall crawled over the backboard and stood in the dust, hands and holsters empty.

"Eva," Warren said, "what are you doing with these lot?"

She took a deep breath, then: "Bishop, we—"

"She got kidnapped," Ruby blurted. Eva held her tongue. "Levi's my grandson. We come to fetch him."

Dunning seemed confused.

"The child y'all been calling Thomas, his name is Levi Cantrell, and he's going home with his family. We took the woman here hostage to secure safe passing."

"Eva," Warren said, gesturing to Gallagher with his gun barrel. "Did this man shoot my son?"

"No," she solemnly intoned. "Bennet died at his own hand—shot himself over something he could no longer live with." After a long silence, she continued, "I think you know what that was, Father Dunning."

His face paled and his shoulders sagged.

From the edge of her vision, Eva saw Niall's hand move to his back. Faster than any of the surrounding soldiers could react, Niall hopped behind the militia leader, one hand grabbing a hank of white hair, the other pressing the edge of a hunting knife against the loose skin of the older man's neck.

"Drop your weapons to the ground," he demanded. The armed men hesitated, and Niall barked, "Sure you want a showdown? I promise it will end badly for your man here."

Each let his gun fall.

"Now, back up ten steps, all of you."

One man made a slight feint in the direction of the captor. "Hold there, soldier," Niall snarled. A drop of blood appeared as he pressed the blade harder against Warren's throat. The would-be rescuer quickly took his backward steps.

"Ruby, you folks get back in the wagon and leave," Niall ordered. "I'll be along shortly."

"But—"

"Now, Ruby. Go!"

"Please," Warren croaked. "Leave the boy."

Eva took one step closer and said to her captive father-in-law, "Thomas and I are leaving together. You'll have to kill me to get him back." Warren seemed staggered at the pronouncement.

Eva helped Thomas into the wagon, then boosted herself up. On the front seat, her boy pulled Woobydog closer to his chest and squeezed himself between his mama and Grandma Ruby, all the family he had.

"Hiyaa!" Ruby cracked the reins and the team moved quickly up to a gallop.

෴

Warren Dunning wheezed, "You can't—"

"Quiet!" Niall warned. "Try anything and you're a dead man. Now walk forward till I tell you to stop."

Feeling the blade still at his throat, Warren took three obedient steps.

"Halt." In a single fluid motion, Niall took the knife from Dunning's neck, bent down and retrieved one of the discarded handguns. Warren felt the barrel jammed hard into his high back, forcing him to kneel. Gallagher headed for the nearest horse, but the wounded foot slowed him down.

A militiaman dived to the ground for a gun. From his knees, he got off a single shot that struck the outlaw between the shoulder blades. Niall Gallagher was likely dead before his body lay crumpled on the ground.

"Gotta go, Captain!" one of Warren's charges called out. "While we can still catch them."

He peered into the distance where a cloud of brown-orange dust marked the wagon's progress. Then he looked down to see that same rusty dirt soaking up Niall Gallagher's life's blood. "Mount up!" Warren commanded.

~51~

"**F**aster!" Eva screamed. "They're right behind us."
Ruby yelled at the poor animals, whipping the reins without mercy. But powerful as they were, the big grays could not pull fast enough to outrun men on horseback. In minutes, the wagon was stopped, again surrounded by uniformed men with drawn pistols.

Warren Dunning swung off his horse and stepped to the side nearest Eva, both his hands empty.

"Niall gone to meet his maker?" Ruby muttered.

Father Dunning nodded a solemn *yes*.

Tears drizzled down Ruby's cheeks.

The old man pulled himself up till he was awkwardly wedged between Eva and the vertical footboard. She held her boy tightly, but instead of grabbing for Thomas, Warren spread his arms wide. Tears streamed down both cheeks and onto his blood-smeared neck as he embraced his widowed daughter-in-law and grandson. Father Dunning held the hug, and after a few seconds, Eva released her grip on Thomas. Then she and the old man's grandson returned the tearful embrace.

"Go with God," he whispered.

Seconds later, Warren was back on the ground. He turned to his soldiers. "Holster your weapons. We got our man," he said with finality. "This time . . ." Father Warren leaned back his head and shouted to the skies, "This time—as God in Heaven is my witness—the women and children shall go in peace!"

He slapped one of Ruby's horses hard on the right haunch, and the big grays lit out like their tails were on fire.

THE END

THE END

Author's Note

An epiphany

On a brilliant southern Utah day in May 2013, I stood before a wave of polished granite set into the side of Dan Sill Hill overlooking the site of what's come to be known as the Mountain Meadows Massacre. The monument was etched with the names of 120 children, women and men who had perished in the valley below. The carnage it memorialized was committed on September 11, 1857—precisely 144 years before the Twin Towers fell.

I've read several accounts of the event. Some writers catalogued the grisly details of the slaughter, like the mother and her babe in arms killed by a single bullet through the child's head. Others focused on who issued the kill order and how it was that devoted husbands and fathers—good churchmen—could have carried out the bloody command.

My curiosity has always been more about the aftermath. So I found my eyes riveted on the last section of stone, a list of seventeen survivors, children ranging from nine months to six years old. The final names recorded were Emberson Milum Tackitt, 4 and his younger brother, William Henry, 19 months. Carved in that lower right corner, directly below the Tackitt brothers, was the shrine's concluding sentence:

AT LEAST ONE OTHER SURVIVOR
REMAINED IN UTAH

Those words hit me like a left cross to the jaw. I felt I knew this last orphan and had to tell his story. In my mind's eye, he was a feisty redhead, age three when he was torn from his biological mother's arms. I imagined the confused little boy delivered to the doorstep of a childless couple in nearby Parowan with a command from local church leaders to "Raise him as if he were your blood and tell no one whence he came."

In my mind, Eva and Thomas bonded as mother and son for two years before Major James Carleton and a contingent of US Cavalry arrived in the territory with orders to round up the surviving children and transport them home to Arkansas. Why, I wondered, was Thomas left behind, and what ultimately became of my little friend?

☙❧

While I no longer fully subscribe to the faith tenets of the Church of Jesus Christ of Latter-day Saints, I remain a proud fourth-generation Utah Mormon whose maternal grandmother was the youngest of handcart pioneer John Watkins's thirty-two children (three wives). At the feet of my Granny Lily, I heard first-hand tales of life in a polygamous household.

Growing up a Utah Mormon, I was also steeped in stories of the Brigham Young-led migration and colonization of the mountain west. I know the area where most of this story takes place. My lifelong love affair with southern Utah has included cumulative months hiking and mountain biking between historical sites in the sagebrush desert and red rock country.

The Last Orphan is set in actual places, populated by many real people, and intersects with historical events such as the Civil War. Most major characters are, however, fictional. Some of the imagined people who inhabit the story are the Dunning family, Eva, Bennet, Thomas and Woobydog; Millicent and

Clara Gale; Bishop Warren Dunning; Grandma Ruby and Harold Seddon; the Edward and Naomi Shand family; the Quincy and Jezzie Gale family; Peter Wilton; Charles and Lottie Hopkins; and Niall Gallagher.

I hope readers will find the characters' journeys satisfying, even uplifting. However—spoiler alert—in this story, God does not step in to grant everyone a happily ever after. The book is set in the most troubling period in the history of The Church of Jesus Christ of Latter-day Saints. It was not written to disparage adherents (like my amazing friends and family) or the church. These events were limited to a tiny frontier community at a single point in time. They should not be considered representative of the church, then or now.

Readers familiar with southern Utah geography will note that while all the locations are real, I sometimes changed their proximity to one another for the sake of a more succinct story. Whatever other flaws and errors the book may contain are mine alone. I urge readers to bear in mind that while I've done diligent research, I'm not a historian, just a teller of tales. At its root, the book is fiction. "Historical" is an adjective.

ACKNOWLEDGEMENTS

Many thanks to talented friends and family without whom you, dear reader, would not hold this book in your hand.

First and foremost is my wife. Thank you, Nancy, for tolerating untold hours with your husband sequestered and unavailable.

I'm also deeply indebted to Brenda Lowder, Chris Lowder, Nancy Barker, Harriet Wallis, Morgan Lee, Shaun Lowder, and Karla M. Jay for reading and critiquing various drafts. Their insights were vital to three years of rewrites.

I am fortunate to meet regularly with a critique group of brilliant writers. Thank you, David Tippetts, Ericka Prechtel, Sherri Curtis, Linda Orvis, Richard Casper, and Karla M. Jay for your wisdom and your honesty.

I'm grateful to the following for great ideas—and encouragement—when I needed them most: best-selling author Jamie Ford, Professor Alyson Hagy of the University of Wyoming, Elizabeth Trupin-Pulli, CEO of Jet Literary Associates, and David Nelson, writer/reporter for the San Francisco Chronicle, now retired.